I0663905

BOOK 4
CLANS
OF
MULL

THE
TORMENT OF A
Scottish Warrior

KEIRA
MONTCLAIR

Alex Grant Family Tree

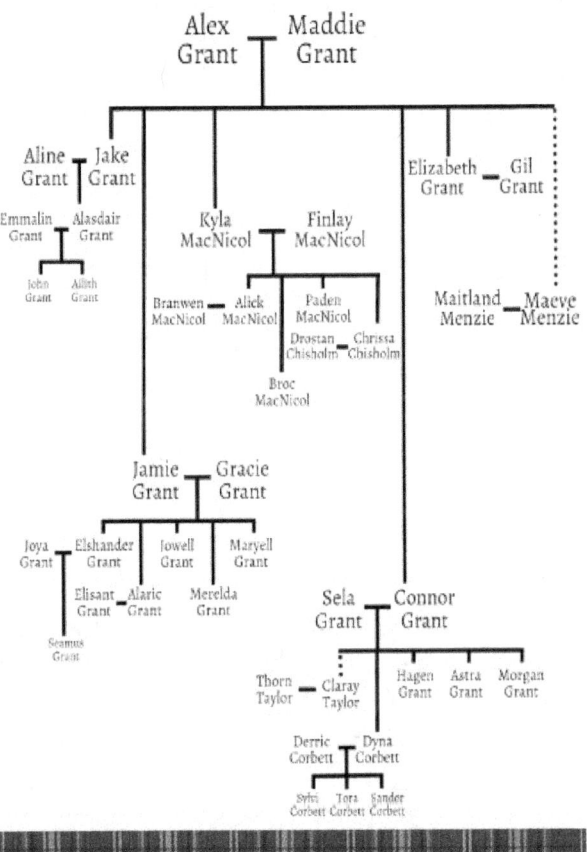

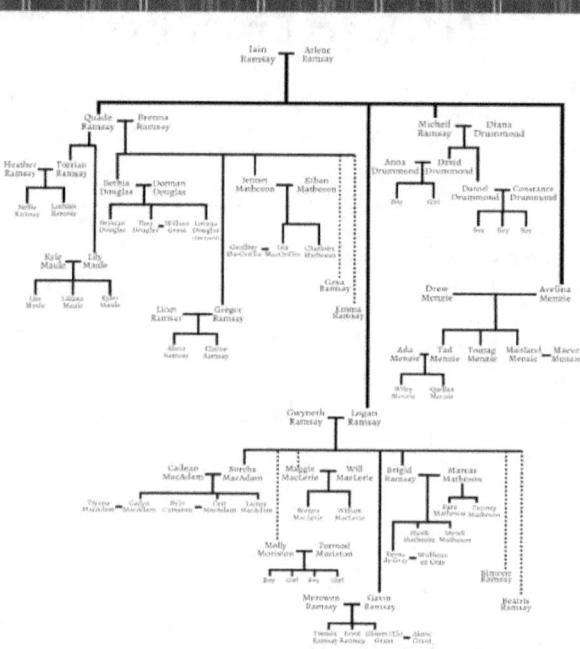

PROLOGUE

*Over a year ago in the Borderlands
between Scotland and England*

"WHAT IS HAPPENING?" Merryn MacClane screamed as the pounding of horses' hooves surrounded their small village. One of five homes in the rural area near the Borderlands of Scotland, their hut housed her parents and her brother Tristan, while her sister Nara lived next door with her husband, Kelvan Mortimer, and their wee daughter, Shealee.

The other three cottages were friendly neighbors, but they were not relatives.

Screams carried to her from the first hut. Cries of pain and clashing of swords echoed across the clearing in the center of the five cottages. Merryn was about to run into the middle of the village, but Nara came in through the back door of the four-room building and thrust her daughter Shealee at her. "Hide her, Merryn. Hide her well and do not allow Kelvan to touch her or to know where she is. Promise me!"

"I promise." Confused, Merryn took Shealee

and held her tight while Nara ran back out the door, yelling for her husband as she went.

Merryn did as her only sister asked and headed into the secret hiding place in the back of a storage chamber, climbing in with the wee bairn, but not before she made the mistake of pulling the fur back far enough from the window to peek outside. Kelvan, the man who'd been married to her sister for three years, dropped from his horse to thrust his sword into her sister's midsection.

Merryn gasped from the shock of seeing Nara grab the sword that had pierced her back and exited through her belly, the tip and blade stained red with her blood. The sharp edges sliced the tender skin of Nara's palms, and she crumpled to the ground, her eyes locked on Merryn's. "Save her."

Merryn dropped the fur before Kelvan's gaze found her, then opened the door to the storage and crept into the hidden section in the back, something her sire had built for his bairns in case of an attack. Shaking with fear, she inhaled the sweet scent of her niece and clutched her tight, rocking her to sleep. If she cried, Kelvan would find them.

George MacClane had often spoken of the possibility of an attack from the English and gave strict instructions to his three bairns to hide when in doubt. They told no one about the hidden spot, not even their closest friends. George had made Nara promise not to tell her husband.

Their sire must have had an inkling about Kelvan.

Merryn pulled the top of the closet tighter over their head, Nara's precious bairn sound asleep in Merryn's arms. At only three moons old, Shealee was oblivious to most everything going on around her. Merryn clutched her tightly to her breast, praying the child wouldn't awaken from all the noise.

She heard nothing more until the door opened to their cottage and her sire's voice rang out. "Get out of here, Kelvan Mortimer. I saw you kill my daughter with your own hands. You are sheer evil!" Her father unsheathed his sword, a sound they were all familiar with. Her mother screamed and the sudden sound of iron blades clashing set Merryn to shaking violently, but the wee lass in her arms slept on. Closing her eyes, Merryn dipped her head to shield the child from the atrocities occurring outside their small hiding place.

She knew exactly when her sire died and then her mother, their shrieks of pain and the odd sound of a dying breath all carried to her through the thin walls, but she held strong in her spot.

Kelvan called out, "Merryn, where are you? And where is my dear daughter? She is mine. I'll let you live if you give her to me." He paced through the house, opening doors and cabinets, even the closet where Merryn was concealed, but he didn't notice the hidden door.

Kelvan cursed several times but finally left as another voice called to him, "Mortimer, we must move on. There are half a score horses headed this way. Grab any valuables and come along."

"God's rotten teeth," Kelvan called out. "I'll find you, Merryn. You can count on it."

Then he left, mumbling and muttering. He called to another, "I wanted my daughter. I have a contract for a wee bairn."

Merryn had no idea what that meant. What kind of contract? She couldn't think on it. Shealee would stay with her. If they were lucky, Tristan would survive also. He'd come back and save the ones who were left. He had to.

She couldn't be alone. Where would she go?

She huddled inside the small cupboard and waited, praying her brother would be part of the horses who were about to arrive. Tristan fought and trained with the men from their uncle's clan, the MacLeans. Their father wished to live on his own, and his foolishness cost him the ultimate price. Mama, Papa, and Nara were now dead.

Where would she and Shealee go? She said a quick prayer that Tristan would survive. If they got away, Merryn would go straight to Clan MacLean and hope her brother was still there. But first, she had to wait for someone she trusted to come along.

Leaning back against the hard wood of the cupboard, she ran her fingernails lightly down the inside of their hiding place. If she had to stay for long, she would surely end up clawing her way out. What if someone locked the cabinet? Or nailed it shut? Or set it ablaze? Her hands shook as her thoughts bounced around in the silence, the smell of the wood reminding her that she couldn't move, couldn't stretch out, couldn't stand. She wiggled her foot to keep the cramp at bay.

Her mind tore through all the things she would need to grab for sweet Shealee before she ran to Uncle Neil's—raggies, fresh gowns, blankets, and milk. Young enough to still be at the breast, Shealee would have to settle for goat's milk. Somehow, she'd find some for the wee lass.

The horses came closer, and shouts of pain and anguish rang out. Merryn nearly opened the door and screamed for Tristan, but she didn't dare, afraid that Kelvan would be nearby.

She waited, the fate of the innocent lass in her arms entirely in her control now.

It was nearly an hour before the door to her hiding spot opened. Merryn's whole body trembled, but she held her breath, letting it out in a loud gush the instant she saw who it was. "Oh, Tristan, it was horrible. Kelvan killed Nara. And Mama and Papa. I heard him."

"Come," Tristan said, tugging her out of the compact closet, easing her to her feet as she held Shealee tightly. "I'm so happy to see you two managed to hide. Praise God for this. We'll go to Uncle Neil's, then he'll find a safe spot for us. Kelvan will be back. He's traveling with a cruel group. I'll go with you to grab a few things for the bairn, then we're leaving immediately. Do not tarry, Merryn. We must hurry."

She stepped out and headed to the front chamber, but Tristan grabbed her, turning her toward the back of the hut. "Nay, you do not wish to see what's in there."

"Mama," she whispered.

"They're both gone. I checked them all. Move quickly. I'll find another gown for you and a tunic for myself while you find things for Shealee, then I'll meet you at the door. I'll get your mantle."

Merryn did as her brother asked, Shealee still sound asleep. How she wished she could stop her hands from shaking, but it was not to be. The shock of losing her parents and her sister all at the same time began to settle in, tears misting her gaze.

But she had a wee lass to save first. She fumbled through the few belongings they kept in their hut and collected enough for now—raggies, gowns, blankets, a tiny bonnet to keep the bairn's head warm. She stuffed them into a small sack and then returned to Tristan, who'd gathered some belongings along with some foodstuffs. "Here, put on your mantle. The wind will be cool. Keep her next to your warmth, lass."

Her brother handed her the bairn after she mounted, climbed up behind her, then headed away from their home, checking the surroundings before venturing farther from the protection of the building and onto the main path. "Don't look, Merryn. Kelvan is mad. Everyone is dead that I saw. I have no idea if anyone survived. All for gold coins. How did you have the sense to grab the bairn and hide?"

"Nara gave her to me. She saw Kelvan coming and told me to hide. She must have seen him attack the others. I peeked out the window before I hid, and I saw him strike her from behind. She

was running and then she was dead. Oh, Tristan.
She looked at me and I could read her lips. *Save
her.*"

"And you did it. That's the sign of a strong
lass. I'm so proud of you, Merryn. You and I and
Shealee, we'll survive. Uncle Neil will help us."

Strong was not the word she would use to
describe herself at the moment. She willed her
trembling to stop, but it would not.

The three arrived at MacLean Castle an hour
later without interruption, their uncle greeting
them at the gates. "I've heard about the attacks.
They are still out there and killing more. He has a
group of English guards with him. I have land on
Mull. I'm going to have a group of guards escort
you there. They can stay and help you finish the
work that needs to be done, Tristan. I'll go with
you, but only to show you my land and then I
must return. Kelvan will kill both of you if you
don't leave. I don't know why he's turned daft,
but I always thought he was not to be trusted."

Merryn couldn't think of anything else but the
wee lass awakening at her breast. "Goat's milk,
Uncle. I need food for Shealee."

Uncle Neil peered at the sweet bairn he hadn't
noticed under her now untied mantle. "Bastard.
Coldhearted bastard. You can feed her in the
kitchens while I arrange your transport, Merryn.
I'll send along some goats and chickens, sacks
of grain and vegetables. You'll need them." He
paused to stare at her. "Truly? Nara is dead? He
killed his own wife?"

"Aye. I saw him. She gave Shealee to me and told me to hide just before …"

He clasped her shoulder. "Then we have no time to waste. He'll kill the rest of us without hesitation." He led Merryn into the keep and called a serving lass over, giving instructions to prepare food for the journey, find the goat's milk, and package some extra plaids and linens to take with them.

Merryn sat in a chair and sobbed.

They were headed to the Isle of Mull, a place she'd never been before. Would they survive?

CHAPTER ONE

Broc

Autumn, 1316, Isle of Mull

BROC MACNICOL MOUNTED one of his favorite stallions, Midnight Majesty, then led the beast out of the gates behind Alasdair, Dyna with Sylvi on her lap, and Dyna's brother, Hagen. The four were headed out to patrol the isle with five other guards.

Ever since Logan had heard that K's wife was Glenna of Buchan, the granddaughter of an old nemesis of Clans Grant and Ramsay, they'd established more frequent patrols to look for new activity on the island. Any threat of invading the isle had to be taken seriously, though with three sound allies on Mull, Connor believed they couldn't be conquered, especially with the extra guards he'd brought over.

Alasdair said, "I am pleased to finally have Emmalin and the bairns here. It's been too long."

Dyna noted how her horse, Midnight Moon, seemed to be enjoying the fine weather as they trotted up next to Alasdair. "I would feel better knowing that the sapphire sword was here. I hope John brought it with him. With Lia and the talk about Grandda and Grandmama, I am relieved to have him here. How old is he now?"

"John is four and ten. The two girls are a year younger. I don't ask him about the sword. He handles it just fine on his own."

Broc added, "It feels more and more like home now with your small family here, Alasdair. I'd love to see my parents, but I know not if they will come."

Alasdair said, "I felt bad for leaving Alick alone as chieftain of Clan Grant, but as Uncle Connor says, half of our guards will be here soon. I told Emmalin we'll stay for another moon or two, then go home."

Hagen, newly arrived, said, "I'm glad Da said for me to come. The isle is beautiful. I hope we get high enough on this journey to look out over the sea. How far to MacLean land?" Hagen was one of five bairns of Connor and Sela Grant. His sister Claray was the eldest, and then Dyna, Astra, and a younger brother, Morgan.

Dyna pointed to Ben Buie. "We'll pass that peak in a bit. The view is lovely from up there. The journey should take about half a day. According to Thane, Tristan MacClane has been here fixing an old cottage and attempting to finish a tower for nearly a year. He has about ten guards with him who are helping to work on the castle in the MacLean name. It's his uncle's land. I thought it only right to bring a few gifts along with us."

Sylvi said, "And I brought two play bunnies in case they have any bairns."

Hagen asked, "Are you expecting any more battles?"

The isle had struggled ever since a man known only as K had started stealing bairns to sell to others off the isle. There had been two kidnappings, but the Mull clans had banded together to retrieve the bairns. Fortunately, both times had been successful, and though K had lost several men, he was still alive and likely to attack again from Mingary Castle on Kilchoan.

Dyna replied, "K will be back in time, but he has to rebuild. Derric and I decided we would never travel with the bairns all together. We didn't think anything would be more difficult than having a child stolen until two were taken. Thank the Lord we still had Sylvi to hug."

Broc said, "Thank God and Eva."

As they climbed the path to higher ground, Broc took the time to admire the scenery. He loved the Isle of Mull for all its opposites. This path along the southeastern side of the isle was completely different than the edge near Duart. Ben Buie was to their right, forestry and deer abounding. But his gaze was drawn to the coastline, something they didn't have on Grant land.

Sylvi shrieked. "Mama, look at those birds with the orange beaks!"

"Those are called puffins. Are they not adorable?"

"I want one. Can we get closer?"

"Not now, but when we get to MacLean land,

we'll be closer to the water, and you may see them there."

"I want to make a puffin to sleep with. Could Grandmama help me make one?"

"I think so. We'll ask her."

Broc smiled, thinking on his fabric puppy who looked like the wolfhounds they often had on Grant and Ramsay land. He peered across the water from their vantage point, the gray sky keeping the sun from reflecting off the ripples of the Firth of Lorn, the jagged coastline beautiful to him. There were spots of silver-white sand that turned into an endless sea of rocks a bit more down the coastline. It struck him that the isle couldn't decide which it wished to be known as—peaceful and serene or rough and difficult. Mountains on one side, sandy beach over the next crest.

Broc understood the contrast. Sometimes his training made him feel highly skilled, other times he couldn't measure up to any of his cousins. What made the difference? He'd yet to figure that out.

Dyna looked over at her brother. "This is the last settlement we're aware of on Mull. It's important we learn as much as we can about the MacClanes. Da knows his uncle who lives in the Borderlands, I believe. We'll spend a night or two, then return home. We should arrive before dark."

"Where are the others?" Hagen asked.

Alasdair said, "Clan Rankin is on the northern tip of Mull, while Clan MacVey, the largest of the three, is between Clan Rankin and Duart Castle."

"Then MacVeys must be just north of Craignure, where we landed? I saw it when we came across."

"Exactly. I think MacVey's wife is making a map of the isle for each of us."

"And the last clan?" Hagen asked.

Alasdair continued, "Clan MacQuarie is on the northwestern part with beautiful beaches and not far from the isles of Ulva, Coll, and Staffa, so I'm told. Iona is just off MacLean land. Some of us have been on Ulva and Coll. There are more in the Hebrides to explore. MacClanes are the only ones on the southwestern part that we know of. Much of it looks uninhabitable."

Hagen asked, "MacClane or MacLean?"

Alasdair said, "Thane said Chief MacLean of the Borderlands owns the land. His brother went by MacClane, and it is his son that is working on the MacLean Castle that is nearly done. It's quite close to the water's edge."

The group reached a crest, so Alasdair, in the lead, held up his hand to stop the group, his gaze scanning the horizon. "Amazing."

Dyna brought her horse up behind Alasdair's mount. "Oh my."

"Mama, it is beautiful. May I go swimming when we get there?"

"Mayhap, Sylvi. We'll see. We have to meet new friends first."

They'd been traveling half the day when the sun finally came out. "I think we're nearly there. We should be. Keep your eye out for any structures," Dyna said.

Broc stared out over the landscape as the group

continued, taking in the beauty of the sea in front of him. Whitecaps dotted the water, and thanks to the sun peeking out, the blue sky turned the sea nearly the same color. Up ahead, two buildings sat not far from the coastline on a knoll—one cottage and a half-finished tower behind it with a low curtain wall being constructed. There were men working, but they hadn't noticed the approaching group until a shrill whistle broke them apart, all reaching for their weapons.

Broc stayed behind his two cousins, his hand going to the wound on his face, something he did without thinking.

Hagen must have noticed, because he mentioned the one thing Broc hated to think about. "Have you seen any boar here?"

"Nay, not yet." If he didn't come across any wild boar here, he might never leave Mull.

Broc had been hunting at around ten summers old when was attacked by a boar in the Highland forest. His horse had been spooked by something and threw Broc straight into the path of three boars. One had assaulted him, piercing his belly with its tusk. He'd also gotten a nasty laceration down his left cheek, one that didn't make him attractive to the lasses. The scar bothered him enough that he'd grown his beard to hide it when he moved to Duart where he was meeting new people, though it didn't hide it completely. He hated it. He understood that he'd been fortunate because the attack had nearly killed him.

But he still hated his scars.

His wounds had mostly healed on his belly and face, leaving visible scars, but the scars inside still held fast. Every time he'd seen a boar outside Grant land, he'd frozen, something that his sire had done his best to help him get past, but he couldn't rid himself of the vision of the boar just before it had pounced on him. He'd dealt with nightmares for years, though they'd lessened here on Mull.

He was eight and twenty, still unwed, but the sad fact was that he hadn't had a girlfriend yet. Oh, he'd had a tussle or two with women when his brothers and cousins had taken him to Edinburgh, but the questions and the look of disgust he'd noticed on their faces when they'd seen the scars on his belly had convinced him to abandon the idea of someday marrying and having a family.

He'd also gained a fear of hunting. He went along, usually in the back of the group and not far from his father and brothers, people he knew would try to protect him if attacked by another boar. He practiced his sword skills so he could protect himself, and his sire had given him a dagger that he could fit in the smallest fold or boot. That dagger went everywhere with him.

He fingered the dagger attached to the belt at his waist, something he did every day of his life. It was as if it were a specter that would protect him at all times.

He hadn't been attacked since then.

As they approached the group, Alasdair held up his hand to let them know he did not bear any weapons. He stayed mounted to make sure they'd be welcomed.

One man led the way with two directly behind him, their hands on the hilts of their weapons.

Alasdair said, "We are the new inhabitants of Duart Castle and as your neighbors, would like to acquaint ourselves with your clan. We bear gifts, if you'll allow us a brief repast. I am Alasdair Grant, and these are my cousins, Dyna, Broc, and Hagen. All from Clan Grant but now at Clan Grantham of Duart Castle."

The man in the front said, "Greetings to you all. Tristan MacClane of Clan MacLean. We are building on my uncle's land. Please bring your cousins inside for a brief repast, and your guards can share an ale with our men, who are about to break from carrying stones for the curtain wall. There's a nice area near the beach they prefer."

"Many thanks to you." Alasdair nodded to the others and moved their horses closer to a line of trees. They dismounted and handed the reins to their guards, knowing they would feed and water the animals while the five went inside to meet with the clan leader. The bubbling sound of a small burn nearby called to their horses after the half-day journey.

The cottage was long, finished with a fine thatch roof and a few chickens running off to the side in a fenced area.

Dyna grabbed a small crate with holes in the side. "We brought two chickens as gifts. Hagen brought a slab of smoked beef we can share this eve, if you like. And we have bread, wine, and mead, along with a sack of vegetables from our garden. Turnips, beans, and some parsnips."

"We are grateful. It's hard to get supplies here, as you know, and the men work hard to finish. We hope to complete the wall before…"

Alasdair tipped his head but said nothing.

"Come inside and we will explain." Tristan gave them a weak smile and led them into the hut. "We have several men who help us build, and my sister is here with two lasses who help with the cooking and cleaning." Tristan was tall with dark curly hair and wary brown eyes, broad-shouldered, but a sadness in his countenance that Broc would ask Dyna and Alasdair about later.

Broc grabbed the bag of vegetables and carried them in while the others took care of the livestock and the beverages. Once inside, Tristan introduced them to the two females they saw first. "This is my sister Merryn and our niece Shealee." The wee one looked to be under two summers old, with red hair and a bright smile, though she hid behind Merryn.

Referring to the lass as "our niece" made Alasdair wonder where Shealee's mother was.

"And the two lasses by the hearth are Olivia and Euna. If you need anything, they can help you."

Sylvi smiled and glanced up at her mother. "May I play with Shealee, Mama?"

Dyna looked at Merryn for guidance. "Absolutely, but she doesn't have much experience with playmates here. We are quite isolated." The lass toddled about but didn't say much, hugging a small piece of plaid to her side as she smiled at the newcomers, her green eyes taking in everything.

Sylvi gave Shealee one of the fabric animals and the lass hugged it with a squeal, smiling. The two headed off toward the hearth to play with blocks while Merryn poured wine into goblets to share. "Welcome to our hut. We have not been here long. I can offer you some cheese and apples."

Broc took one look at Merryn and had to admit he'd never been affected by the appearance of a woman as much as this one. What he couldn't understand was why. He had such a visceral reaction to Merryn, something that coursed through him so quickly he hadn't known how to react to it. At first glance, she appeared to be quite plain, but when she smiled, her face lit up. Her hair was a most unusual shade of red and gold, and she had a smattering of light freckles across her nose and cheeks. Not too tall and not too short, she had curves in just the right places.

He tore his gaze away and looked to the other two by the fire. The one named Olivia was also quite pretty, but she did not affect him in the same way. Euna was quite a bit older with wide hips and graying hair.

Dyna said, "Merryn, we brought bread and smoked beef to share. Our guards have food for themselves, but we would appreciate the cheese and apples."

Merryn made two trays of food and set them down on the table, which had two benches along with several stools scattered around the chamber. There were no tapestries on the wall or dried flowers anywhere. The furniture was sparse, the area clean and sufficient.

Once they were all seated, Tristan said, "Please allow me to explain, then I'll ask you to tell us what you know of the isle. We have reason to know all, but you'll understand soon enough."

The group settled as Merryn, Olivia, and Dyna found beverages for everyone before Tristan took his seat, Merryn sitting on a stool on the other end near the bairns. "Our family lived in a small group of cottages set outside MacLean Castle near the Borderlands. Merryn and I lived with our parents while our sister, Nara, lived in the next cottage with her husband Kelvan and their daughter Shealee.

"Nearly a year ago, I was training in the lists at our uncle's castle when the surrounding villages were attacked by a band of men led by Kelvan Mortimer. Merryn watched the bastard kill his wife—our sister—then kill our parents while she hid with Shealee. When I returned from the castle with ten guards, we found our village massacred, nearly everyone dead. Kelvan committed the evil acts with his band of misfits, though we have no idea where he found the men other than he did spend much of his time in taverns along the border.

"I immediately escorted Merryn and Shealee to the castle, and my uncle insisted on bringing us here. He'd pledged to his brother, our father, that he would always protect us should anything happen. Since Kelvan is still in search of his daughter, our uncle believed this to be the safest place for us. His guards had been here at one time and started building the tower for a castle and had already built this cottage along with the small barmkin for protection, so he brought us here along with several guards, pledging to send more to help us finish the castle.

"The work has been slow, but we have made progress. I wish we had the curtain wall finished so we weren't so open to attack, but our aim now is to finish the tower before winter arrives. It's not as high as my uncle had wanted, but we are ready to put the roof on soon so we can all be protected. We will continue our work." Tristan paused to sip his mead. "I thank you for your gifts. We appreciate your generosity. Please tell us what you know of Kelvan or about the attacks you have seen."

Alasdair spoke first. "We've had two abductions of our bairns by different groups of men, but with one common connection. A man who goes by K is in charge of the group and resides in Mingary Castle near Kilchoan on the mainland. His castle is a gateway for any questionable characters coming from Europe or the north."

"And what was his purpose for stealing the bairns?" Merryn asked, surprising them all by the intensity of her gaze.

Broc explained, "He sells them. He kept a few on Ardnamurchan, but some of his men lost their lives trying to sell our bairns. Fortunately, they weren't sold, but K persists in stealing more. Now he threatens to steal another of our bairns who he believes is a faery. We've hunted many of them

down, and we will get him before we finish.
Know you of a man named K or of a woman
known as Glenna?"

Merryn looked to Tristan, then shook her
head. "Nay to the woman, but K must be Kelvan.
There can't be that many evil men in the world.
He told us once of others who bought and sold
bairns, but I thought he was jesting. And when
he left after killing our parents, I heard him tell
one of his accomplices that he wanted Shealee
because he had a contract. Know you what that
would mean?"

Dyna cleared her throat and whispered, "A
contract to purchase a child of her age would be
my guess. So you think K and Kelvan could be
the same?" She glanced from Merryn to Tristan
who nodded.

"Nara's husband," Tristan whispered. "I never
trusted him. I'm certain we speak of the same
man."

Dyna said, "Kelvan has a new wife. Glenna of
Buchan, so we've heard."

Merryn glanced at her brother and whispered,
"He's going to come for her, Tristan. And he'll
kill both of us."

"I'll send a message to Uncle Neil to see if he'll
send more men." Tristan got up and paced, then
put more wood into the crackling fire in the
stone hearth. "I fear we'll not be safe here until
we have the tower finished and the wall around
it. This cottage won't protect us any more than
the cottages we were in at the Borderlands."

"How can we be of assistance to you?" Alasdair

asked. "We have many Grant guards looking for work to keep them busy until they are needed. After the other trouble we've had, the old chieftain brought another four score guards here in case they are needed. At the moment, they are cutting wood and working in the lists. We'd be happy to help erect a stable or complete the tower roof. We would gladly send two score for a fortnight. We have some skilled in thatch roofing. It could hold you through the winter."

Dyna added, "And as one of the chieftains of Clan Grantham, I offer protection to you, Shealee, and Merryn whenever you need it. Duart Castle is well built with a strong curtain wall. We have plenty of beds and food. We are presently keeping six score guards about."

Merryn gave her brother a beseeching look, nodding. "Mayhap it's time, Tristan…"

Tristan held up his hand to his sister. "If we determine that he is on the isle and searching for Shealee, we may take you up on your offer by sending the lasses your way. I'll stay and fight. I love it here, but we would be grateful for any assistance you can give us. We're hoping to finish the tower. The gables are up, but we need to work on the inside. And a thatch roof for now would be appreciated. We'll do whatever we can to get through the winter. We'd also love to build a stable, so if you could assist us with that, we would forever be in your debt," Tristan said.

"What livestock have you?"

"A few goats and some chickens. We've planted

apple trees, but that will be a while before they grow, as you know."

"Horses?"

"Three. Enough to travel to Craignure for necessities. Our uncle sends a boat occasionally, but we get what we need from the forest or at Craignure. And the fishing is plentiful, of course."

Alasdair said, "We have many guards, so I'd be pleased to send two score to you for a fortnight. Broc," he said, turning to his cousin. "Would you lead that group? Bring them back in two days?"

"Two score would be greatly appreciated," Tristan said.

Broc said, "It would be my honor to return to assist you. At present, we have plenty trained to protect our land. One score is with MacQuaries because he's still building his force. We'd be happy to assist in any way possible. I helped build the new stable on Grant land. We can build the same here. We can bring the axes to chop down the trees we'll need. Have you any archers?"

Tristan shook his head. "I only trained with my sword. The ten guards and the two lasses do plan to stay, so we would train if we had someone to teach us archery. It would help us to hunt, and there are plenty of deer on Ben Buie and around Loch Buie."

Broc said, "I'll bring an archer along to train anyone who is interested. Our archers are mostly female. That will not bother you?"

Tristan grinned. "Our men would love to meet any lasses you wish to bring here. They'll be respectful, I promise. Olivia will have ten proposals before the first snowflake falls, if I were to wager."

Merryn spoke up quickly. "I'd like to learn archery, if you please. I have trained a wee bit with a local lass, but she's not here often. And please tell everyone that Shealee is my daughter. We don't want Kelvan to know she is here."

Dyna perked up. "Who is the local lass? I would love to meet her."

"She lives on Iona. Her name is Simmy, and I met her when she and her husband were hunting deer. She's been a great help to me."

Broc asked, "Would you like a pet for Shealee? We have a new litter of wolfhounds. We'd be happy to bring a couple of pups to you."

Tristan said, "We'd love whatever you don't need. We are just starting here, and while we were grateful to have a place to hide Shealee from Kelvan, we had verra little to begin with. Anything you wish to share with us, we will appreciate. We will repay you when we are able."

Broc glanced over at Merryn, surprised to find her studying him. He said, "I'll be back in two days, and I look forward to it."

He had one goal in mind—to get Merryn to smile again.

CHAPTER TWO

Merryn

TWO DAYS LATER, Merryn wandered over to the sea, one of her favorite spots. She loved to jump from rock to rock, and the sound of the water helped to drown out the pain of her memories. Losing her sister and her parents on the same day to such a violent act gave her nightmares and recurring headaches, but she stumbled forward for the sake of Shealee.

"Merryn, be careful!" Tristan shouted from the castle wall they were building.

She waved back to her dear brother, content that she didn't need to worry about Kelvan reaching her here. The evil man hated swimming, so he'd never approach across the rocks. This was the safest place of all, part of the reason she loved it here.

Euna and Olivia watched over wee Shealee in the morn so Merryn could take a walk. Kelvan hated to get up early, so it was the safest time to be about. Merryn's life had changed so much in less than an hour, yet even a year on, she still had not adjusted to it.

The coast was her favorite place. It was a place where she could cry over her losses and the waves would hide the sound of her sobs, a place where she could feel safe, and a place where the beauty of the isle would pull her from the depression that forced itself into the tiniest parts of her being. Somedays the darkness was too much for her, so she came out here, especially on sunny days where the warmth of the sun would bring a smile out.

Tristan's whole outlook had improved since the Granthams had left. He'd whispered to her, "See. We are not alone, Merryn. We have somewhere to go if we need it this winter. That pleases me."

This was a lonely life on Mull, Olivia and Euna the only other females here to help build the tower they would eventually occupy. Not that they did much with the boulders, but they made sure the men working on the castle were fed. Evening meals were often outside, overlooking the sea unless the weather prohibited it, something she enjoyed. It allowed her to stare off and think about all that had happened.

And what was next?

Tristan had talked with her about marrying someday, but he knew it was too soon. They were both still grieving their losses. "I pray that the day will come when we will both find someone to love. I don't wish for us to be alone forever."

Merryn didn't see it ever happening. Oh, there were times when she would play with Shealee and forget the atrocities she'd witnessed, but the haunting memories always returned. At present, it was more important that they do what they could to protect themselves and Shealee by finishing the tower before winter set in. They were close. With a bit of help, they could finish soon. They were all hopeful, the drops in temperature reminding them that the seasons were indeed changing.

She busied herself by making clothing and warm blankets for the lass and for herself. She wasn't much of a seamstress, but Shealee didn't care how her creations looked. They also had a cold cellar in the tower, so she spent much of her time picking fruit and vegetables to put in storage for winter. How she wished she'd spent more time asking her mother about her tasks. On occasion, she felt useless, but she persisted for the wee lassie she adored and for her brother who worked so hard.

Merryn's plan for the day would be to take care of Shealee, pick apples and pears, help Euna wash clothes in the nearby burn, and then practice her archery with her new friend, Simmy. After that, she hoped to see their new friends return from Clan Grantham.

Today would be a better day. The Grantham's surprise visit had brought a hope to her that she'd not expected. The hope of new friends, ones who would come to their aid if needed, and the oddest hope of a man in her life.

Something she'd never expected, sometimes feared, but ultimately set butterflies deep in her belly. Someone who noticed her. She couldn't wait to see them all again, especially the man named Broc.

To her surprise, Simmy approached the edge of the water. "Can we practice now, lass? I was hunting nearby and decided to stop in."

"Of course. I'll be right there, Simmy. I'm sure Olivia can watch Shealee."

Merryn hurried over to the area in front of the cottage where Olivia watched Shealee, feeding her an apple. Ever since she'd seen Kelvan kill her sister, she'd done everything she could to learn to protect herself and her niece. Archery had been the first defensive skill she'd learned, and she loved it.

She found her gear, spoke to Olivia, then met Simmy out near the practice area they'd made at the edge of the forest. "I'm ready, Simmy."

"Great. See if you can set yourself up and I'll judge how well you do."

Merryn let her first arrow fly, pleased when it hit the target. "I did it! Not in the center, but I hit the target. And my first one too!"

Her trainer said, "Well done, Merryn. You're doing a fine job. Every day you get better."

"I'm pleased. I forgot to tell you that we have more visitors coming later. They promised to return in two days and I'm excited."

Simmy reached for her water skin, taking a deep drink before sitting on a huge boulder nearby. When she finished, she leaned back, setting her hands on the rock so she could tilt her face toward the bright sun. "Tell me about your visitors. They were here already?"

"Aye, from Duart Castle. They were all from Clan Grant but came to the Isle of Mull."

Simmy's eyes narrowed. "I'd heard that King Robert took the castle from the MacDougalls and awarded it to Clan Ramsay."

"They call it Clan Grantham, but the four we met were all Grants. Alasdair, Broc, Dyna, and Hagen. They brought us two chickens and a slab of beef, plus a sackful of vegetables and wine. Shealee loves to munch on carrots, and there were a few in there. Her face was orange when she finished. And the wee lass named Sylvi brought her a fabric bunny. She hasn't set it down yet."

Merryn glanced over at Simmy, wondering if she could ask her a personal question. "Simmy, may I ask you something odd?"

"Sure. I'm here if you need me, lass." She sat up and reached over, tugging Merryn to sit on the rock beside her. "Ask."

Merryn blushed, thoughts of the handsome man fresh in her mind. "How does one find a man to marry?"

"Och, you liked one of the Grants. Better than any of your uncle's guardsmen? Have they not tried to steal a kiss or two?"

"Aye, a couple have tried."

"And?"

"And one did, but I didn't like it. I don't like him either. But one of the Grant swordsmen was quite handsome, and he was verra kind."

"Must be Broc," Simmy said, grinning from ear to ear. "His mother is a Grant. One of Alex Grant's daughters. Broc is noble blood. He'd be a fine match for you."

"How do you know all that?"

"My sire. He used to talk about the wonderful Grants years ago. He was friends with Alex Grant."

"Oh. I'm not noble, so he'd never be interested in me."

"Love doesn't care about blood. If Broc is interested in you, he'll find a way to make you his. Many handfast these days because it's hard to find a priest. Especially on the isles. Did you like him?"

"I did," she admitted, her cheeks flushed. "He's big and strong and has a kind smile, but I don't think I'll ever marry." Merryn stopped to think back on her sister. "Kelvan was so sweet to Nara, and then, after they married, he used to beat her. She was often crying, carrying bruises. My sire spoke to Kelvan about it once, and he stopped for a bit, but then it started again. He was mean to my sister, especially after she had Shealee. Whenever the bairn cried, he would yell at her to make her stop and then slap Nara and run out. I saw him hit her once, and I wished to slap him myself. Are all men like that?"

"Nay. Tanner has never hit me. He'd regret it if he did." Simmy hugged her knees to her chest. "You are doing the right thing learning archery. Every lass should know how to protect herself. Men are bigger than most women, so they can hold you down and do horrible things to you. Knowing how to use a dagger is something else you should learn. I'll bring one along the next time I come. Tristan is busy enough with the tower, so he doesn't have time to show you, but don't give up on men completely. There are many good ones out there."

"How can you tell which ones are good?"

"I look at how they treat their horses and their dogs. It can be telling."

"I need to forget about Broc. It was just a passing thought. For now, all I wish to do is raise Shealee and protect her. She has no one else. She calls me Mama. Is it wrong to allow her?"

"Nay, you will be the only mother she knows. But when she's older, I would tell her the truth. You should tell her all about Nara and what you loved most about your sister. It's important to know where you came from, I think."

"I will when she is older. I just pray we will both still be here." Merryn would make sure that Shealee knew how sweet her mother was. Nara had caught many men's eyes when she grew up, but she'd only been interested in Kelvan. It was her sweetness that always helped her to get an extra piece of fruit at market or an extra ribbon for her hair. Sweet and beautiful. That was her sister Nara. Merryn was not nearly as attractive as her sister was.

But none of that mattered anymore.

Simmy squeezed her hand. "The Grants will protect you. I will if I'm here. Tristan and his men will protect you."

"But you live on the isle." As far as Merryn knew, Simmy lived on Iona, only traveling to Mull to hunt deer once in a while.

"But I can visit more often if Kelvan continues

to bother you. Tell me more of what you learned from the Grants."

"They said that a man known as K was stealing bairns, that he'd done it twice, but they were able to save the bairns before he sold them."

"Sold them to whom?"

"To someone in Europe. I think he said K lived at Mingary Castle. I am certain that K is Kelvan, so I have to be sure to keep Shealee well hidden."

Simmy sat up at the mention of bairns being kidnapped. "Evil bastard. Should have someone cut his tongue out so he can't make any deals."

Merryn said, "To sell bairns would be evil. Who would do such a thing?"

"Oh, I've heard of much worse. I know an archer on the mainland, a woman, who pinned a man to a tree by his bollocks for stealing bairns from their parents and selling them."

Merryn had never heard of such a thing. "By his what?"

Simmy grinned and pointed to the juncture between her thighs. "My, but you are an innocent, Merryn. Have you never changed a lad's raggie?"

Merryn shook her head, blushing a deep shade of red.

"Men have a penis to pish from and two bollocks. One on either side to carry their seed. And it's also the place that can cause the most pain for a man. So hitting him with an arrow there would paralyze a man. He'd not be able to move at all."

"You saw her do it?"

"Nay, but I heard much about it. She's renowned

for it. Makes men cringe whenever they hear her name. Gwyneth Ramsay. I heard she passed recently, a sad event for the Scots if it be true."

"That is sad. I would love to train with someone so skilled."

"Gwyneth trained many female archers. Granddaughters and great-granddaughters. Sons. So many. Probably whomever they bring will have learned from her."

"How do you know all this, Simmy?" Merryn had met Simmy in the forest once when she'd put an arrow in the flank of a deer. Merryn had been picking berries when she heard the sound and jumped as the deer fell not far from her. She hadn't screamed, though the constant fear of running into Kelvan never left her.

Simmy had run over, afraid she'd hit Merryn with a previous arrow, but she'd been gracious enough to bring the deer over to MacLean land, and once they'd skinned it, she'd offered the fur to them and generously left them with a slab of meat. Tristan had been delighted.

Simmy had brought her husband, Tanner, with her, or they never would have been able to carry the big stag to MacLean land. They spent the evening visiting, and upon learning of the issues the brother and sister faced, Simmy had offered to teach Merryn how to use a bow.

"I traveled on the mainland years ago. I know of the Ramsays, the Grants, the Camerons. They are all fine clans. The Grants are returning?"

"Aye, later this eve, I believe. They promised to help us build a stable and finish the roof of the tower. They are bringing two score of men to help cut trees down. Tristan is excited."

The steady drum of horse hooves through the forest caught them, but it wasn't from the path the Grants would be on. Merryn stopped and set her bow and quiver down, hiding them in the bushes.

Simmy sat up, grabbed her bow, and whispered, "Run. I'll take care of whomever it is. Go find Shealee."

Merryn didn't wait. She raced toward the cottage, ignoring the fast beating of her heart and the bushes slapping against the tender skin of her arms. With every step, she prayed this was not Kelvan. As the horses drew near, the one sound she'd dreaded for so long sent her entire being into a fear she hadn't experienced since she'd witnessed her sister's brutal massacre.

"I know you're here, Merryn. I want my daughter!"

Kelvan.

Tears raced down her cheeks as she approached the cottage, yelling as she moved along. "Tristan, he's coming! He's behind me." She had no idea where Shealee was, but she would protect the lass with her life. Under no circumstances would she allow Kelvan to take the bairn, no matter his intentions.

Someday, he'd sell her, but only over Merryn's dead body.

She let out as loud a scream as she could, the hut appearing ahead, while the volume of Kelvan's voice told her he was drawing closer. "Merryn, I want my daughter back. She belongs with her father!"

The chill traveled up her spine and her breath hitched, but Merryn didn't pause. She would not allow him to change her course of action.

And then the Lord brought her exactly what she needed. Down the main path from the opposite direction came an army of horses, their riders wearing the red plaids she recognized as belonging to Clan Grant.

"Help me, please!" Her voice carried to one rider who headed toward her as she broke through the bushes onto the path. He bellowed instructions, sending the other horses in different directions.

"Put your arms up over your head, Merryn. I'll get you!"

Trembling with fear, she did as he asked, immediately recognizing Broc's voice. She needed to get to the cottage before Kelvan reached her. This was the only way, so she closed her eyes and did what he requested.

Broc leaned over and scooped her up easily, lifting her and tossing her with an unladylike plop in front of him, but she did the oddest thing ever. She whirled around and hugged him, grabbing him so tight, never wishing to let go.

This man would protect her.

Broc wrapped an arm around her and said, "I'm taking you to the hut. Do you know who is attacking?"

"Kelvan. I heard his voice."

Broc called over to a lass with a bow, "Shoot to kill, Eli."

One man dared to come closer, and Broc adjusted Merryn to his left side. "Don't move. I have to fight!"

She stayed still, peeking out as he controlled the majestic stallion with his knees, drawing his sword out of its sheath and waiting for the one man who dared to attack him directly. The attacker had a paltry weapon against Broc's giant sword that he held and swung deftly at the last minute, driving it into the man's belly with a grunt, shoving him off his horse.

The power in Broc's thrust was so strong that the vibration shook her to her core, but she had a solid grip on his upper arm, keeping her on the horse. Once they moved past the one attacker, Broc slowed his mount, picking up the reins again while he settled her back in front of him. "You are hale, lass?"

She nodded, a lump in her throat that wouldn't move, the terror raging through her slowing but not stopping. It wouldn't leave her until she was certain Kelvan was gone.

"I saw him. He is here. I left Shealee with Olivia. I must find her."

"I'll get you there. And if she's gone, we'll go after her. Fear not." Broc leaned over and used his thumb to brush dirt from her cheek, Merryn finding the small intimacy both shocking and pleasing. "He'll not touch you, lass. He'd have to kill me first, and I would wager he's a weak man who prefers to have others fight his battles."

Her gaze locked on his blue eyes for a moment and heat flooded her, something she'd never experienced before.

"Merryn, do you see him? Scan the area because if he's still here, I'll find him. I'd wager he's gone already. I can drop you in front of the cottage and go after him. Many of the others have run in the opposite direction. They didn't have enough to fight our two score of guards."

She peered around him, shaking her head, relieved she didn't see Kelvan. They were nearly at the cottage when a voice caught her by surprise.

Kelvan was behind them.

"Merryn. Just give me my daughter and I'll never bother you again." He sat a distance away, alone on his horse. "She belongs with her father, not with you. She's mine."

A fire from deep inside bubbled to the surface. She said, "Never. I saw you plunge your sword into Nara's middle. You'll never touch Shealee again." She was so committed to protecting the innocent lass that she would scratch out his eyes if he came close to either of them. It was the least she could do for her dear sister.

"Be stubborn and suffer the consequences, no matter who you have to fight your battles. I'll leave now, but I will return. And the next time, I'll have the stronger force, and I'll take both you and my daughter. I need a plaything. You'll be my new mistress."

"Like hell. You'll never touch either of them," Broc bellowed. "In fact, once I get her inside, I'm coming back for you, you ugly bastard. You better start that wee pony of yours moving now. My stallion will catch you in no time and trample your mount."

"We'll see. I'll steal her before you know what happened, Grant. Take your red plaids back to the mainland. You're not wanted here."

And Merryn had no idea what propelled her to speak again, but she shouted, "You'll not touch me if I kill you first."

Kelvan turned his mount around and chuckled all the way down the path, three men with him.

An arrow sliced through the air and hit one of his men, who fell off his horse. Kelvan sent his animal into a gallop.

"The next one will come from my bow," Merryn shouted. "And I'll aim it at you!"

CHAPTER THREE

Broc

ONCE THE ATTACKERS had taken off down the beach toward a galley ship, Broc knew they had no chance.

"I should have gone after him," he said, cursing under his breath once they were all joined together outside the cottage.

Tristan said, "You had my sister on your horse. I'm glad you didn't. Kelvan would put a sword in her chest without giving it any thought."

Alaric said, "There was no reason to follow him. The three he had remaining were already retreating. He was the only one left, and he had a clear path to the ship. Eli and I went after the others instead of him. That saved his arse. We'll get him."

Broc said, "But it changes our plans. Someone must return to let Dyna know they're being aggressive. We thought we had a brief respite from their attacks. We were wrong."

The small group stood outside the cottage door discussing the events. Tristan ran his hand down his face and paced, staring at the ground. "I have ten. That's not enough men to protect Merryn and Shealee. And we have Olivia and Euna to protect too."

As if on cue, Merryn came out the door, Shealee on her hip. The wee lass pushed against her and pointed to the sea of horses not far away. "Hosee!" Merryn set her down and Alaric took her hand and led her over to his horse. She giggled, so he lifted her up to the warhorse's face, letting her pet him.

She gave the animal a kiss. "Hosee!" He promptly nickered for her, sending her into a flurry of giggles.

"How old is she?" Eli asked.

"One summer and a few moons." Merryn brushed a tear from her face. "She doesn't remember her mother or what happened, I don't think. She's calling me Mama."

"Did she witness it?" Broc asked.

Merryn shook her head. "Just me."

Eli looked directly at Tristan. "I think Merryn and Shealee would be safer at Duart Castle. We have plenty of room, other bairns to keep her entertained, and nearly a hundred guards to protect her. Think on it. I'll be right back." Eli took off into the bushes.

Tristan glanced over at Merryn, but Merryn's gaze was locked on the tall woman just joining them from the beach. She had a quiver on her back and wore leggings, something they didn't see often unless they were on Ramsay land.

"What do you think, Simmy?" Merryn spoke loudly enough for her friend to hear her.

The woman said, "You need to go to Duart Castle. He will not give up, Merryn. I will find him. I was raised by one of the best trackers in the land of the Scots. I'll go to Kilchoan and search him out. The best place for Shealee is Duart now that he knows you are here."

"Please let us know if you find him," Broc said. "We have many looking for him too. You're always welcome for a repast at Duart Castle. I'm Broc MacNicol, this is Alaric Grant, with his wife Eli Ramsay," he said, looking over his shoulder. "Who just took off to take care of her needs."

Simmy nodded to the three, studying Alaric the most, but then said, "A pleasure to make your acquaintances. Merryn, take the sweet lass to Duart Castle. I'll catch up with you there."

She turned around and headed into the forest, lithe and quick as a deer.

Broc looked at Alaric. "Do you recognize her? She must be related to your wife."

Alaric asked, "Why would you think so?"

Eli rejoined the group. "I caught a glimpse of her, and Broc is right. Grandmama's style leggings and a Ramsay fletching, I think. Trained by one of the best trackers? That would be Grandda, but I have no idea who she is since I didn't see her face. No one I know lives here. She could be one of the adopted ones. They all moved away years ago. She's been working with you, Merryn?"

"Aye, I met her when she dropped a deer near me when I was picking berries one day. She's come back three times to teach me how to handle a bow. She lives mostly on Iona, I believe."

"Do you have an arrow nearby that I could look at?"

"Aye." Merryn stepped back into the hut and returned with one arrow.

Eli and Alaric both smiled. "That's a Ramsay-style fletching. She was trained by Grandmama," Eli said.

"Who is your grandmother?" Merryn asked.

"Gwyneth Ramsay."

"She mentioned that woman but said she had passed on. She's alive?"

"Aye. She's living at Duart Castle, but she nearly died not long ago." Eli asked Merryn, "What think you about going to Duart Castle for a while? Just until we find Kelvan."

Tristan moved over and kissed his sister's cheek. "I think you should go, Merryn. Now. I can't lose you and Shealee, and Kelvan will not give up." He glanced around at the group. "Is there someone who could escort her or should I go?"

Broc said, "We brought two score. I'll escort her to Duart Castle and take six guards with us. The six can return on the morrow. That leaves you with enough men to get a good start on building the stable and to begin the work on the roof. Eli can stay to train two archers. You've got horses and a cart to help bring the trees in. Use them. I'll send the men back as soon as I can."

Tristan gave her a hug. "Until we finish the tower and the wall, you're not safe with him around. I promise to visit often. Pack your things and go before it's too dark."

Eli said, "We have several bairns so we have

extra clothes for Shealee, and I have leggings that will fit you. You'll love them."

The group broke up, and Merryn approached Broc. "I'll pack a few things. How long is the journey?"

"About half the day. We should return before dark or shortly after. I wouldn't spend the night out. We'll travel in the dark for a bit, but I know the path well enough and it's nearly a full moon."

She cleared her throat but then asked the question that was most important to her. "May I ride with you, Broc, if you please? I don't think I could ride a horse and manage Shealee at the same time. Would we both be able to ride with you?"

Merryn's gaze caught his, stirring feelings in him he hadn't experienced before. He had this sudden need to protect her against anything and everything.

"Aye. We'll do fine. It's probably best because we'll travel quickly." Then he nodded to the arrow in her hand. "We have plenty of bows for you. You can continue your training. Dyna and Eli train all the time. No need to bring a book either. We have plenty."

Merryn blushed, and he tipped his head.

"I can't read. I've always wished to learn."

Broc leaned down to whisper in her ear. "No worries. I'll teach you."

For the first time in a long time, Broc wondered if it was possible for a lass to be interested in him, because he was surely interested in Merryn.

CHAPTER FOUR

Kelvan

———❧❧———

LATER THAT DAY, Kelvan jumped off the galley ship, in such a hurry that he shoved at one man's chest hard enough that the brute fell into the rough salt water. The weather rocked the boat enough that two had already heaved their insides out over the bow. "God's rotten teeth, get the hell out of my way."

He glanced up at the woman at the top of the parapets, looking as though she thought she were the queen of the world. Nearly snorting over this ridiculous thought, he held it in because though she wasn't much to look at, she was smarter than any other woman he'd known. And he needed her knowledge of the foolish Clan Grantham to finish what he'd started.

"Did you find her?" Glenna called out.

"Aye, but there were at least a score or more men in red plaids," he muttered as he climbed the stone steps up to the curtain wall around the castle he'd taken over as his own. "We had to get the hell out of there. They took down four of my men."

Glenna stood there with her arms crossed, a sly smirk on her pale face. "You've met the Grants?"

"Aye. One of them picked Merryn up just as I was about to grab the bitch." He cursed, picking up a rock and hoisting it over the edge of the parapets. "Their horses are massive."

"Ow! You hit me." One of his horsemen glared up at him, rubbing his scalp.

"Get the hell out of the way, and I won't hit you," he shouted down at the fool who was dumb enough to stand directly beneath him. Frustrated, Kelvan moved over to a stool at the edge, plopping down and staring up at his new wife, one who would only be around for as long as he needed her. He'd found a man who wore a frock to pretend to be a priest to marry them. Of course, it was all false, so she had no hold on him. He'd never marry another.

"We came up from the beach and Merryn was practicing at the archery field, the wee idiot. As if a female could ever be a good archer."

"Don't be a fool, Kelvan. The Ramsays have some of the finest female archers in all the land. Did you learn naught from the battle on Loch Tuath? Were there not two archers there who took out three of your men?"

Kelvan lifted his face to glare at his wife simply because he hated it when she was right. She shouldn't be right. Women were not better at archery and were put in the world to service men. There was nothing more to it than that. Glenna would service him by teaching him which among Clan Grantham would need to be eliminated first, then he'd take over the rest and control them all.

Including the faery and the wee lad who was too small to fool with yet.

"I can see everything in your face. Stop dreaming so. Take over the Isle of Mull and that's it. I know you have these ridiculous ideas that some faery or sword will make you take over all of the land, but there's no such thing. Focus on Mull. That will be enough."

Kelvan snorted but said nothing. She had no idea how smart he was.

"You will lose if you underestimate anything about Clan Ramsay or Clan Grant. Did you not see Odart's burned palm? Or what about the creature seen by three men?"

"All lies. No power in the lad and no sea creature. There were big waves and—"

"And powerful swimmers? Is that all? So, four bairns, two women, and one man were able to strategize better than all your men combined? Enough to get away before you could transfer them to your ship?"

"That's right. There was no magic, no sea creature. There's only a wee faery who doesn't know what to do with her talents. I'll show her exactly what I want done. My power is stronger than theirs. I'll have to be on the next ship myself instead of leaving it to incompetent men who are useless at following orders."

"So, the next time. Now that you know where your daughter is, what is your plan? Because I'm gathering my men to attack the isle in a fortnight.

That's how long you have to get the special ones away. What are you hoping to accomplish?"

Kelvan thought for a moment, revising his tactics just a bit. If a strong female archer truly existed, perhaps he needed to steal one for himself. But how would he know which one was the correct archer to steal? He'd have to give that careful consideration.

But that didn't change his immediate strategies. "I'm going to give Merryn three days to take her timid arse to Duart Castle. She'll go there, I'm certain of it. I'm seeking my daughter and the faery. And her brother. If I have him, the faery will do whatever I ask." The rest of Kelvan's thoughts stayed within him, unspoken.

Because once he had the faery and her brother, he'd threaten to kill him if she didn't make him the king of the isle.

Glenna could take her fleet of galleys and go after someone else. Once he took over the Isle of Mull, Clan Grant would run tail back to the mainland and he'd control the others.

All of them.

CHAPTER FIVE

Logan

"I GOT YOUR MESSAGE. What are you worried about?" Logan asked as he approached the tall woman.

"Eli is your granddaughter, so she's a bit wiser than most. I could tell things were clicking in her mind when I glanced over my shoulder at her, but she didn't get a good look at me. I don't want anyone to know I'm here. I've told you that we wish to stay hidden. I made enough enemies when I worked with you, but there will be questions when they return. Merryn is coming with Broc. Eli, Broc, and Alaric will ask questions. Put an end to the evil bastard."

"So that's why you stay secluded. I don't know why you worry so. No one will see you here. I might just tell them who you are." He brought his mount closer to hers.

"Nay, you don't understand. We can't be caught yet."

Logan tipped his head. What the hell was she talking about?

"Never mind, Da. It's a long story, but Tanner knows Glenna, and Tanner has done some things he's not proud of. He's gotten away from all that, but he doesn't want anyone to know of his past. Promise not to say anything. He wishes to keep his past a secret."

Tanner had worked with one of the men on Ulva, though he used it to do good things too.

"Fine for now, but if they steal any bairns again, it's all changing. We need you. Then there will be no secrets. That kind of worry is the kind to put me in the grave, lass. If they do, all secrets are out, and I'm coming for you."

"Fine. I'll agree to that. I'm going after the bastard myself. Tanner will stay back. Please don't say anything. I love him. This could become distasteful and nasty."

Logan narrowed his gaze at this woman whom he adored. He'd respect her wishes for now. "I'll agree. But as soon as the bairns are involved again, all secrets are open to discussion."

"My thanks to you. I'll go see what I can learn and let you know what I uncover."

Logan grinned and said, "Wait. What did you think of your niece? You met her but didn't tell her who you were? You have restraint."

"I observed her before I approached. She's feisty like her aunt, and she looks like Gavin. I'll introduce myself when the time is right. I can't risk it now. I have to move on before she gets closer." The woman turned her mount around. "They'll be back shortly."

Logan yelled after her. "I wanted to know the secret myself. You can't go without telling me first."

She waved at him, keeping her face forward.

She knew exactly how to taunt Logan Ramsay.

"God's teeth, lass. You push me too far sometimes."

"But you still love me!" she shouted.

"Blast it all, but I do."

She was one of the few people he let get away with things.

CHAPTER SIX

Merryn

THREE DAYS AFTER she moved into Duart Castle, Merryn sat at a table in the middle of the great hall, watching the bairns play amid the large arrangement of furs near the hearth.

"They're fine," Broc said as he joined her, glancing back over his shoulder at the grouping. Tora and Sylvi were busy playing mother and father to Shealee and Sandor.

"They are. She adjusted quite quickly," Merryn said with a smile before returning her attention to the handsome man in front of her. "I love seeing her playing with the others. She's so happy. Fortunately, I don't think she recalls any of what happened."

Broc said, "That's probably best, don't you think?"

"Aye. Though I wish she would remember Nara. I'll make sure she knows all there is to know about her mother."

"You will be a wonderful aunt to Shealee."

"I hope so. All that I know to do is love her."

"Talk to Dyna. She's raised three."

"I will. She seems so well-adjusted." Merryn's gaze drifted to everyone around her. Living at Duart Castle had turned out to be something entirely different from either of her previous lives. When her parents had been alive, she'd learned to cook and sew, helping her mother with all the household chores. She'd helped Nara with the bairn when Kelvan was gone, which was most of the time.

On Mull, she and Olivia and Euna had worked together to make a life for them, cooking and washing, working in the garden, tending to Shealee's many needs, while the men worked to build the tower and the wall for protection. It was a slow process.

Here at Duart Castle, everything was different. She'd learned that there were two lairds here—Maitland Menzie and Dyna Grant Corbett. Eli and her husband Alaric were in charge of the guards. "Is it usual for a woman to be a chieftain of a clan?" Merryn brought her gaze back to Broc, keeping her voice low so as not to disrupt the bairns and their play. "Are there many others?"

"Diana of Drummond was chieftain of her clan before her sons took over. But most times, they are men."

Merryn thought for a moment, then said, "That surprises me. I couldn't imagine being in charge of so much." She lifted her gaze, while Broc fussed over what he had in front of him. She could stare at Broc all day. His blue eyes mesmerized her, the silver flecks that danced letting her know when he was serious or when he was jesting about something. He loved to jest. He had a small imperfection on his cheek, but she hardly noticed it because his looks were far more appealing than any other man she'd ever met.

He grinned, catching her off guard. "You're staring, lass. I think that's a good thing. Is there a bug crawling across my face that you wish to crush with a slap?"

She laughed, so glad that he hadn't tried to embarrass her but instead resorted to humor. "Nay, no bug. It's just that ... Life is so different here. I've never been around so many people, and mostly, not this close to a man." She had the undeniable urge to touch him, so she reached out. "Do you mind?"

"Nay." Broc's smile disappeared and he had a look of uncertainty about him.

"Your beard. I've never been so close to a man's face, other than my father. Mayhap my brother when we were younger. I just wish to touch it. Is it rough or soft?"

His smile returned and he waggled his brow. "You tell me." He leaned forward for her.

She cupped his cheek and brushed his beard a wee bit. His hair had strands of red in the sun, but inside it was darker. His beard carried more red in it than his long locks. She was fascinated by all the colors. She ran her hand across the rough plane and pulled back quickly.

"Ow! That is quite stiff. More than I expected." She blushed a deep shade of red, the same that she always did when she was close to someone she didn't know well. "Forgive me. That was rude."

He shook his head and said, "Your touch would never be rude, Merryn. Your skin is as soft as a bairn's. Men and women are different. It is the way of it."

"Sylvi, don't be so rough with your brother." Dyna entered the hall, but she barely noticed them, giving them a quick wave.

"Everyone works hard here. You all have your assigned chores," Merryn said.

"We do. Only the elders get to sit, but they create their own chores. Gwyneth loves to sew leggings, and Logan is trying to create his own special brew like Sloan's. I wish my parents were here so you could meet them. Mama loves to watch over the bairns, and Da is always observing the lists or brushing down a horse or two. Mayhap someday soon."

"I would love to meet them."

He changed his position. "As much as I enjoy chatting with you, I must move on because I'm expected in the lists for training later." Broc brought her attention to the parchment in front of him. "So, here is a list of all the letters in the alphabet. Once you learn their names and how you say them, then we can put them together and you can begin to learn words."

"What about writing? I'd like to learn to write too." She'd always had the dream of learning how to read when she'd seen her male cousins learning in the castle. Reading was a skill not offered to most females.

"First you learn how to read, then write." Broc smiled and her belly did this odd flip whenever he looked at her like that. "Though you could certainly try to copy the ones here. I can bring the materials for you the next time."

"Do you all know how to read?"

Broc nodded. "Grandmama insisted on teaching all of us. My mother loves to read and teaches bairns when they turn around six or seven summers. If you were in the clan, you learned to read. My mother took over much of the teaching as Grandmama stepped away. She used picture books to tell stories, but then she progressed to reading and writing."

Broc continued, pronouncing each letter as he pointed to it, waiting for her to repeat him. It was the best activity because it gave her time to study him, this man who brought such strong feelings to the surface. They confused her, but she found them pleasing and, oddly, something to cherish.

Instead of visions of her sister dying, she forced herself to think of Broc.

He had such a strong jawline under the wee beard on his face. His hair waved in different directions all the time. How she wished her own hair could look like that instead of messy on a wind-blown day. But what drew her in were his eyes.

They were the loveliest shade of blue she'd ever seen. She and Nara once found a nest full of birds' eggs, and Broc's eyes were the same color, with flecks of darker blue and silver everywhere. And when he looked at her, she had the urgent need to sigh, but she contained herself.

What was happening to her?

Merryn cautioned herself to stay true to her goals. Since Kelvan's visit, she'd had the incredible drive to end his torture of the people of Mull. She had no idea he had stolen the sweet bairns away, but now that she knew, she was possessed with the need to get rid of him. It didn't matter where or what he did; he just had to leave. To gaol, over the water to the east, or back to England where he came from.

Every night she lay in her bed thinking of all the atrocities he had committed. He didn't deserve to live, to continue his rampage. But what was one lass to do about him? Nothing.

Yet she would someday. She vowed to find a way to rid Shealee of his intrusion into their lives. Nara would want it that way. It was Merryn's charge to see it through. She would learn to read and learn archery. Those were her two immediate objectives.

Her long-term goal? Until Kelvan Mortimer was gone, she didn't have time to devote to any man. Even Broc.

The door opened, pulling her from her thoughts. A group of people entered, all chattering as if they were the best of friends.

Broc set his implements down and said, "Mama? Da?" He broke into a wide grin, then looked at her and said, "My apologies, but my parents have arrived from the mainland. Could we work again on the morrow?"

"Of course," she said, putting everything back into a small crate and setting it on a side table where it had been before. Merryn moved over to the hearth, standing in front to warm herself as she observed the happy group.

A tall woman with hair a shade darker than Broc's stepped inside first, laughing and setting down the sacks in her arms. "Broc, get over here. I've missed you terribly."

The man behind her had hair mostly gray with shocks of red still visible. He was tall and bubbly, his laughter contagious as everyone behind him laughed along. The three bairns ran over to greet the newcomers while Dyna came flying out of the kitchens.

"You're here! And you've brought food! I can smell the boar meat!"

"Greetings, Auntie Kyla," Sylvi said as she hugged her aunt. "And Uncle Finlay too. Did you bring any toys?"

Kyla winked at Sylvi and said, "I might just have a new set of blocks all carved out for you. It's like a puzzle. But you must wait, lassie. It's packed in a bag somewhere. Will you help me carry our things to our chamber?"

Merryn sat in a chair as Maeve and Maitland came in, carrying Grant.

Broc's mother reacted instantly, her voice full of joy. "Give me that sweet bairn. I've missed him. Look how he has grown!"

To Merryn's surprise, after Lady MacNicol picked up Grant, Broc came over, took Merryn's hand, and brought her over to his parents.

"Mama, this is Merryn. She's from the MacLean holding in Mull. We've had some trouble with the bairns of late, as you've probably heard, so we brought Merryn and her daughter Shealee here. Merryn, these are my parents."

"Greetings to you, my lady," Merryn said with a brief curtsy. "Shealee is playing with Sandor and Tora."

Kyla stared at Merryn and handed Grant back to his mother without taking her eyes away from Merryn. "Merryn, is your husband here too?"

"I'm not married yet." She looked at Shealee and blushed. "It's complicated." Afraid of what the woman would think of her, she leaned forward and whispered, "She's actually my niece. We're hiding her from the girl's father."

Kyla took both of Merryn's hands in hers and said, "My, but you are a beauty with that golden-red hair. You remind me of my husband's family."

Merryn blushed and Broc said, "Mama, stop staring at her. You're making her uncomfortable. She just arrived and doesn't know anyone here."

Kyla dropped her hands and stepped back. "Please call me Kyla. No reason for formality here. We aren't like that. There's too many of us. If anyone called out 'my lady,' ten people would answer."

Merryn moved back over to the chair, picked up a toy, and handed it to Shealee, who had grabbed ahold of her skirt, hiding in the fold. "This is Shealee."

"Merryn," Kyla said. "She's lovely. May I ask you an odd question?"

Merryn nodded. What else could she possibly say? Broc was busy speaking with his father and the two were heading up the staircase with the bags behind Dyna.

"What think you of Broc's scar?"

Merryn was totally confused, not knowing how to answer the odd question, so she answered with complete honesty.

"What scar, my lady?"

Kyla grinned and hugged her.

CHAPTER SEVEN

Magni

———— ∿ ————

LIA CAME DOWN the stairs at Castle MacQuarie and waved at Magni. "Come, brother. I'd like you to listen in on this conversation."

Magni glanced around the great hall at Tamsin, then at Thane's parents. Alana was still sound asleep. Early morn by the hearth was his favorite place to be because he could smell the bread baking in the kitchen (his second favorite place to be). He loved a nice line of honey running across the middle of his bread, especially if it dripped over his fingers. And if it was still warm, it was even better.

"Why, Lia? What is it?" He didn't like this. He understood that his sister was different. After all, she wasn't really his sister since he'd found her under a frond and all; she grew into a girl only once he'd turned his head. And he'd learned that Lia had a way of sticking near people who were about to be in trouble.

"Not me, is it?" Magni asked, his heart thumping

in his chest at the memory of those mean men in the kirk who locked them up.

"What do you mean, not you?" Lia stopped, smoothing her green skirt.

"You always pick someone to protect, but that means they'll be in trouble. I don't want to be in trouble again." He stood up, scowling at his sister. "I love you, but you shouldn't have to protect me again."

Lia smiled and tipped her head, then clapped her hands. "Come with me and you'll see."

She knocked on the door to Thane's solar where he often sat to count his coin before they made a trip to Craignure for supplies.

"Come in," he said.

"Master Thane, could we speak for a moment, if you please? I have a pressing matter I must discuss with you."

Mora came flying down the staircase. "Nay, please say you are not leaving again, Lia. Please stay. I like it when you and Magni are here with us, especially now that Tamsin is carrying a bairn. I wish for you to see the bairn and protect it. Naught can happen to a wee bairn. If you …"

Lia reached up to take Mora's hands in hers. "The bairn will not be born for a few moons yet. Do not worry yourself about him."

"Him! Did you hear that, Thane? Lia said *him*. And she was right about Grant. Will the bairn be a laddie? It would be sweet for Thane to have a laddie just like him. But I would love a lad or a lass equally. Is it a laddie? Or a beautiful lass?"

Tamsin moved over to the group gathering near the solar. She rubbed the growing mound of her belly and looked directly at Lia. "Tell us, please. Laddie or lassie, Lia?"

Lia set her hand on Tamsin's belly and uttered a quick chant before nodding subtly at Tamsin, but she didn't dwell on it. "He's fine and happy in your warm belly, Tamsin. It's exactly where he belongs right now. I must speak with Thane."

Thane came out and said, "Come. We'll sit by the fire, Lia. Who is it this time?"

Magni threw his arms up over his head. "I knew there's to be more trouble. Not me. Please, not me."

Lia stopped and looked up at him. "Magni, you are my dearest brother. You know I would not allow anything to happen to you, do you not?"

Magni thought of how he felt before he'd found Lia under the frond. He'd been alone in the forest after running away from the mean men who'd stolen him from his parents on Tiree. And the mean old men had told him that his parents were dead after they threw him in the boat and landed on Mull. If his parents were still alive, he would have tried to return to Tiree, but they'd all laughed about killing them. Fools had laughed so hard that Magni snuck away, telling them he had to whiz in the bushes and they waved him on.

And he ran and ran and ran so far that when he stopped, he couldn't think right, didn't know which way to go until he looked down and noticed the faery under the leaf staring at him.

Tears gathered in the corners of his eyes, and

he nodded. "I know you will always save me, Lia. You love me, do you not?"

"With all my heart, brother. You remember what I told you in the forest?"

Magni had looked behind him to see if he was being followed, and when he turned back, Lia had transformed into a wee lass. And he'd hugged her right away. "Save me, please. They're coming for me."

"I know. That's why I'm here. I promise to protect you until you no longer need me, Magni. Just tell them I'm your sister, and I'll be by your side whenever you feel you are in danger."

Magni nodded to Lia at the fond memory. "You said you'd be by my side whenever I needed you. And you promised to protect me."

"And have I kept my promise?"

Magni swiped the tears away and nodded.

"Then do not worry. But I do have someone new to meet. Thane, will you please arrange for an escort to Duart Castle?"

Magni shouted, "I'm coming too."

Thane arched a brow at him. "Are you sure you wish to go with us?"

Magni didn't tell him what he really thought. He had to stay near his sister because she was his protector. He'd never feel safe if she wasn't nearby. It had been difficult for him when she'd stayed by baby Grant's side. Magni had stayed in the same castle, but he had to know she was not far away.

But he'd never tell Thane so because he'd think he was not strong enough. "I think I told

Grandsire I'd visit soon. As long as you are going, I should go with you. Grandda likes to see me once a moon. Did he not tell you that?"

Thane smiled and nodded. "I think Logan did say something like that. Of course, you may join us, Magni."

"Lia, is it going to be someone you have to stay with all the time like Grant?" He stared at his sister, his face covered with worry.

"Nay, this is someone I will protect, but wee Grant was extra special. He was so tiny, Magni." She smiled and patted his shoulder. "I'll still have time for you."

"Good," he said, wishing he hadn't said it. It was true he liked to see Lia often, but he didn't wish to appear selfish. He loved his sister. That was surely all it was.

Tamsin said, "I'm going to stay here with your parents, Thane. My belly is not up for a long journey."

Thane moved over and wrapped his arms around his wife. "I know. They say the sickness will go away soon. I'll leave Artan and the Grant guards here."

"Nay, you must take some. Please, Thane," Mora said.

"Aye, please take some, Thane," Magni begged, staring up at the man who reminded him of his father. "We should have some to protect us in case …"

"Of course." Thane bent down to look the boy in the eye and whispered, "I won't let anything happen to you either, Magni. You have three protectors—Lia, Grandsire, and me."

Magni threw his arms around the large chieftain and buried his face in Thane's waist.

He wouldn't let anyone see his tears.

CHAPTER EIGHT

Broc

THE NEXT AFTERNOON, Broc grabbed a meat pie from the sideboard and strode over to the group near the hearth. Alasdair and Emmalin stood chatting with Gwyneth who was seated, enjoying a goblet of wine. Dyna came down the stairs carrying Sandor while Tori and Sylvi followed. "All rearranged, Emmalin. We have you set up in the larger chamber. The housemaid moved all your belongings."

Sylvi said, "I helped."

Tora said, "Me too."

Connor and Logan came in from outside, arguing about who was the strongest swordsman in the lists.

A serving lass set a platter of fruit and cheese on the sideboard with a pitcher of wine, and the group grabbed what they wanted and settled around the hearth, some standing, some sitting. It would be a couple of hours yet before the evening meal.

Laughter and boisterous chatter echoed through the hall until Tora ran over to Connor, climbed up on his lap, cupped his cheeks, and said, "Pay 'tention, Gwandda."

Then she hopped off her grandfather's lap and raced over to Alasdair and repeated herself.

Connor paled, and the group quieted as Sandor got up from his spot on the floor with his toys and began to race in circles, Tora doing the same in a different direction.

Alasdair glanced over at Connor, then moved over to Emmalin and gripped her hand. "Come," he whispered. "I'd like your opinion on this. Listen carefully." Then he leaned over to the lad. "Sandor, what are you doing?"

It became so quiet that they could've heard the pitter-patter of a mouse scurrying across the chamber. All eyes were on the two wee ones giggling and running in odd paths around the hall.

Just like before.

Sandor giggled and waved his arms. "Stop, Unca Shakie. Stop ticka me." Sandor would stop and wave his arms, then take off running again, giggling uncontrollably. Every once in a while, he would pause, his wee hands pushing against an invisible force. "Stop, Unca Shakie."

Emmalin whispered to Alasdair, "Unca Shakie? As in Jakie?"

Alasdair nodded. "We think so."

Uncle Connor said one word, "Tora."

"'Tis Gwandda and Uncle Jakie again."

"But I'm here, Tora." Connor's gaze locked on the two bairns in front of him, his elbows resting on his knees.

"Nay, Gwanda Alex ticklin' me." She stopped and pushed both hands against something.

Sandor howled with glee and shouted, "'Top, Unca Shakie."

Connor stood and strode slowly over to Tora, then Alasdair and Emmalin did the same to Sandor.

Connor said, "Tell me what Grandda Alex wants, Tora. Tell me. Why is he here?"

Tora stopped and tipped her head back, looking up in the opposite direction at nothing. "Gwandda says be caweful. Twouble coming."

Alasdair stood still, Emmalin behind him with her chin on his shoulder. She whispered, "Jake, I wish to meet you sometime. I adore your son."

A sudden breeze of mint leaves blew her hair away from her face and she smiled.

"What, Da? Why are you here?" Alasdair asked.

Sandor stopped and made a fist with one hand, shoving it in one direction, then the other. Alasdair whispered, "What does Uncle Jakie say, Sandor?"

"Unca Shakie says keep da bwue sord cwose. Shon need his sord."

Broc moved closer to the group, then looked from one face to the next, not understanding what the entire situation was, but he'd heard that Alasdair believed his deceased father could speak through Sandor. Was it happening in front of him?

Then Sandor stopped and waved at the door. "Bye, Unca Shakie."

Tora said, "Bye, Gwandda."

No one spoke, but the door opened and another five people entered. Connor rattled off a list of names and said, "In the solar now."

Broc was shocked to be called among the others, but he followed the group inside, still wondering what he'd just observed. He couldn't wait to hear everyone's interpretation.

Broc sat in the back of the solar, glancing from one person to the next. Uncle Connor, the two chieftains—Dyna and Maitland—Logan, his parents, and cousins Alasdair, Alaric, and Eli. The gathering alone told him that something big was about to happen.

Once everyone had an ale in hand, Maitland motioned to Dyna, and she shut the door. Then the two stood in front of the group. Maitland started, "Based on what we just saw and heard, we have trouble coming. Broc, I want a full retelling of all that you saw and heard at the MacLean holding. It has to be related."

Broc straightened in his seat. "Kelvan came in a galley ship with six men. Wanted his daughter returned. According to Tristan MacClane, his sister Nara was married to this man Kelvan, who came through and massacred an entire village in the Borderlands, including Nara and the MacClane parents. This was almost a year ago. Kelvan stole anything of value and left. Tristan was at Clan MacLean when it took place. Nara gave her infant daughter to their younger sister Merryn to hide when she saw Kelvan and his men coming. Merryn and Shealee were the only survivors. When we told the story of K and his attack on Mull, Tristan and Merryn both believe Kelvan to be the man we know as K."

Logan asked, "Seven arrived. How many left?"

Broc replied, "Three. Kelvan and two guards. Buried four. Said he would be returning for Shealee, which is why we brought the two here. Kelvan also threatened to take Merryn as a plaything. She's terrified of him. She actually witnessed Kelvan thrust his sword into her sister's back, killing her within moments."

Eli added, "I'll add that Merryn said she'd never let him touch Shealee. She's fiery, but she's not skilled in any combat. She was learning archery from someone known as Simmy, who lives on Iona but comes to Mull for the deer. I've asked Grandmama if she knew her, but she's playing innocent. Says she has no idea who she is. Grandda?"

Logan smirked but shrugged.

"Who is she, Logan?" Connor asked.

He deftly changed the subject. "It's time for a visit to Kilchoan. I'd like to meet Kelvan, or K, myself. I'll ask him directly if he's missing a daughter. Kyla, what do you know of Glenna? Finlay, did you ask Fergus?" Finlay's brother Fergus was married to Davina, Glenn of Buchan's only daughter. The couple had no sons, so Glenna could not belong to them.

"Aye, I spoke with him," Finlay replied. "Apparently, Glenn had a son he kept hidden from all. The youngest son was sent to live with Glenn's brother when the trouble started. He didn't want his bloodline totally lost. Davina said her brother took over the castle a decade later, married, and had three daughters. Two have left and married, but Glenna is the odd one. Tried to convince King Robert that she deserved Ramsay land and the castle, but he sent her away. So now she's angry at our king and all the Ramsays. How she met up with Kelvan, no one knows. Are we sure he's the same man as the one at the MacClanes?"

"We won't know until we ask. I'm going to give Glenna what she wants. Time to meet the bitch. Who wishes to go with me?" Logan stood and moved over to the door.

Connor said, "Logan, you shouldn't go without a force of two score or more."

"Nay. One-to-one this will be. I wish to meet the two without warning, see the true situation there. How many. Their weaponry. Their ships. You'll never know unless you go unannounced."

"You can't go alone, Grandda," Eli said.

"I'll take two. Any volunteers?"

Alasdair said, "I'll go."

"Emmalin will skin me." Logan stopped to shake his head at Alasdair. "Nay. Who else? And I'm not risking my neck being slashed in the middle of the night by a Norse princess, Connor. You're out too." Connor's wife Sela was Norse.

Dyna giggled, but said, "Nay for me. Not with the three bairns."

Broc said, "I'll go."

Alaric said, "Me too."

His mother said, "Broc …"

Logan turned on her before she could finish

her sentence. "He's old enough and one of the best swordsmen here, Kyla. I need him. He and Alaric and Eli are the only ones who saw Kelvan, and I wish to know if K and Kelvan are the same man. I have to bring Alaric or Broc to uncover the truth. Are we fighting one person or two? And Broc is not married either, so no wife will cut my throat in the middle of the night. Broc's coming with me and Alaric, if Eli agrees."

Eli said, "Me too."

"Nay," Logan quickly barked at his granddaughter. "You're staying back. No couples going together. This is a Buchan we're dealing with, and no Buchan is trustworthy. Even Davina tried to bring harm to Torrian."

A knock sounded at the door.

"Enter," Maitland called out.

The door opened and a serving lass said, "There's someone who wishes to see you."

A small golden-haired figure moved the serving girl out of the way. "Pardon me, but I must speak to someone."

Maitland took one look and said, "Shite." He fell into a chair and waved for Dyna to take over.

"Who are you here for, Lia?" Dyna asked, her voice trembling.

"Where's the new lass? I'd like to meet her." Lia smiled and folded her hands in front of her just before someone shoved her to the side and bolted into the solar, throwing himself into Logan's lap.

Dyna whispered, "Shealee. She's here for Shealee. That's a good thing in my eyes."

Magni whimpered, "Protect me, Grandsire?"

Logan wrapped his arms around the lad and whispered, "With my life."

Broc shuddered, an uncontrollable force overtaking him. He had the oddest feeling that no one knew how close to the truth Logan's statement would prove to be.

Logan said, "We leave on the morrow."

CHAPTER NINE

Merryn

———⚬⚬⚬———

WITH SHEALEE FRESHLY awakened from her nap, Merryn came down the stairs carrying her on her hip, uncertain of what exactly was happening. A large group had gathered in the hall, much larger than usual, and before she reached the bottom of the staircase, Merryn could feel the mounting tension.

Sylvi raced over and said, "Shealee, would you like to play with us?"

Of course, Shealee pushed against Merryn with one word. "Down." She followed Sylvi over to the area where they played not far from the hearth, her fabric bunny still in her grasp.

Dyna and Broc joined her, along with a new young lass who began speaking immediately. "Greetings to you. My name is Lia, and I plan to stay here at Duart Castle. I'd love to play with your niece."

Dyna said, "Lia, give us a chance to speak with Merryn. You go introduce yourself to Shealee by the hearth."

More confused than ever that a strange lass

would know she was Shealee's aunt instead of her daughter, Merryn didn't know what to do. "She talks as though she is much older, does she not?"

"Aye, she does. Would you like to go for a stroll outside? I'll explain more about Lia. We consider her a blessing, but she is unusual," Broc said.

"Great idea," Dyna said. "I'll watch over Shealee."

Broc led Merryn out the door, ignoring the few who asked her to join them for a chat. The two elder gentlemen called her over, but Broc just said, "Later."

He guided her out the front door and through the gates to an area not far from where the guards practiced, somewhere that seemed safe, yet away from anyone who wished to interrupt them. He found an apple tree and grabbed two ripe pieces, handing one to her before he pointed to a nice spot to sit under the tree.

"Broc, I don't understand what that lass was trying to tell me." She took a bite of the apple and glanced over at him to see if he would tell her more about the girl who spoke like an adult. There were so many people at Duart Castle that she was more confused than ever.

He said, "You know that we explained how we have had some bairns kidnapped by K, but we've brought them back. Well, Lia is one of them. And …" He paused for a moment and stared up at the fluffy clouds overhead.

"What is it, Broc? I can handle anything, but I need to know what is happening. No surprises, no secrets. Please."

"Do you believe in faeries or seers or witches? Any of that? Many do, many don't."

"Witches? Nay. I don't believe in witches. What do you mean by seers?"

"Someone who can see things that the rest of us can't. Dyna is a seer and so are her bairns."

"I don't understand. What can she see that I can't?"

"Things a distance away. Things that will be happening before they do. Sandor can see his deceased great-grandparents and his dead uncle. And so can Tora. They say they come and chase them. You heard of the trouble in the water, right?"

"You mean the battle with the three ships? Aye. We heard about it."

"Tora said her great-grandfather swam with Eva and helped her support Sandor and Tora in the water. And Dyna was able to see what was about to happen. From a distance too far to be visible to our eyes, she knew which boats the bairns were in, and … Let me change everything. Let's try this."

"Good, because I'm verra confused."

"Lia is a faery. She will tell you that she is a type of angel, a guardian angel, sent here to protect certain people. She protected all the bairns and helped to get them home again. I know I sound a wee bit daft when I tell you these things, but Lia says she has the power to protect whomever she is assigned to. On the last jaunt, she was assigned to protect Grant."

"The wee bairn?"

"Aye. And so once she learned Grant was her target, she never left his side. And when the men came and gave us all the sleeping potion, K's men stole Grant, but Lia went along with them to control what happened. She got him home safely."

"But I thought she had a brother named Magni."

"She says so. Magni explains it better than anyone, but he met her in the forest when he'd been kidnapped. He managed to run away and ran into Lia. He came with her today." Then he stared at Merryn.

"What are you trying to tell me, Broc?"

Broc cleared his throat and said, "Lia is here for Shealee."

"What? She's going to kidnap her?" Merryn pushed away from Broc after tossing her apple core over his head.

"Nay. Nay, wait, please."

She settled back down next to Broc, trusting him more than anyone, but what was he talking about? Faeries and seers and invisible dead people? "Go ahead. I'll listen."

"Lia is here to protect Shealee. It means she believes trouble is coming, and she was given instructions by someone in the universe, the heavens, whatever you wish to think of it, to protect Shealee."

"I don't doubt that. Kelvan is coming for her. He said he would, and he won't stop until he gets her. Tristan and I have to stop that from happening."

"We will all help to prevent that from taking place, but basically, you have a helper who will never leave Shealee's side. Lia says that someone in the heavens sends her to protect certain people, mostly bairns. I know it requires you to suspend your beliefs, but after watching all that has happened over the past few moons, I unequivocally believe that Lia is an angel sent to protect bairns."

"Nara." She stopped to stare at him, her eyes misting. "Nara sent her." Merryn stood, brushing her hands down her gown, her thoughts bouncing from one place to another. "Or Mama or Papa. That I would believe. I know Nara is watching her."

"I don't know. She may not tell you, but we have to accept the fact that Kelvan is coming for Shealee. As soon as he discovers she is here, he will come for her. It's what we all believe. We already discussed everything."

"And so do you want us to leave?" She panicked, wondering where they could go. "But where? I don't know anyone else …"

"Nay, no one wishes for you to leave. You belong here for now." Broc took her hand. "Nay. We will protect you. I will protect you, Merryn. We won't let him hurt either of you. Just know that Lia is here to protect you as well."

"So, do we just sit and wait? What do we do? Should we go somewhere else? Back to the mainland? I don't know what to do."

Broc cupped her cheeks, brushing his thumb across her tears of fright. "Nay. You are inside one of the thickest curtain walls on the isle. I will be going with Logan and Alaric to Mingary Castle to confront K and the woman named Glenna. Alaric and I go because we've seen Kelvan, so this is how we will know for sure if Kelvan and K are the same man. What I would like you to do is tell me everything you can about Kelvan. Does he have any weaknesses? Any other bairns? Anything at all?"

Merryn fell against him, and he wrapped his arms around her. She gave in to all her worries and doubts. "I don't know anything. Do you wish for me to go?"

"Nay, you stay here with Shealee. You are all she has now. I would not split you two apart, and I know what I've told you is confusing, but please allow Shealee to get to know Lia. Ask Lia anything you like. She'll answer all your questions, though evasively at times. But she will answer."

"Broc, I'm so scared for you now. You have to be careful. You saw how he can be. He could kill all three of you. Please take more men."

"Logan and Uncle Connor decide on the important tasks. They are the strategists because they have more experience at it than any of us. I trust their judgment. I'll return to you, I promise."

Merryn glanced up at him. "I will hold you to that promise."

"I have to come back. What I want more than anything is to get to know you better, Merryn MacClane. We just don't get enough time to talk." He reached up to tuck a lock of hair that had escaped her plait behind her ear. "I see a lovely lass who I'm drawn to, yet so much is happening, I feel I'm ignoring you. Please don't think it is intentional."

"I don't. And everything you said pleases me. I feel the same."

"Tell me one special thing you'd like me to know about you. Just one." He grinned and held her hand, brushing his thumb across the inside of her wrist.

She thought for a moment, then said, "I love the sea. I love to swim, and I hope someday that when Kelvan is gone, I can spend more time with Shealee on the beach. It's so wondrous. I learned to swim in the loch near my uncle's castle, but my first experience with the sea was when we came to Mull."

Broc smiled. "I have to agree. I am surprised at how much more scenic Mull is than our land in the middle of the Highlands. And the sea is lovely, but not near as lovely as you."

Broc surprised her by leaning down and brushing his lips against hers, a brief kiss, but a kiss nonetheless.

A gaggle of hoots and whistles sounded from behind them from the lists, causing Broc to roll his eyes. "Ignore them."

She grinned. "Then next time, please find a more private spot."

CHAPTER TEN

Broc

———∽∽———

THEY LEFT EARLY the next day. The group headed to Clan Rankin and borrowed one of Sloan's boats. They were about to get in, Ingelram shoving them off, when Sloan came flying down the hill. "Greetings, Granthams."

Logan said, "I see you have eyes only for your new wife, Rankin. Go be with her. We'll update you when we return." He held up his hand for Ingelram to pause so they could speak with Sloan.

"But is it true that K was married to MacClane's sister? And he killed her? His own wife?"

"Aye. He's a wily bastard and I'm about to meet him. Keep an eye out for our return and I'll fill you in."

Sloan waved them off, shoving the boat with Ingelram. Broc began to row alongside Alaric, something he loved to do. He'd never done it before moving to Mull, but he loved the feel of his rippling muscles as he pulled against the water in the sound. Once he and Alaric established their rhythm, the boat sliced through the water with such grace that it made for a magnificent journey. The sky was blue, the water calm, and it was a warm, sunny day.

Logan said, "You finally found the one, Broc. Good choice."

"What?" He checked his belt to be sure that his favorite dagger was still there.

Alaric chuckled. "Everyone spread the word about you and Merryn under the apple tree. You know how tongues like to wag about that. All the guards were cursing because a few of them had their eye on her, but you stepped in first. She's a pretty one."

Broc couldn't help but smile, as he'd been even more pleased when she hadn't pushed him away, even suggesting they find a more private place. That was exactly his plan after they finished this task. "One kiss does not make her the one."

Alaric said, "It's time. You're old enough. You're eight and twenty. Get married."

"Make sure she's the right one. You'll know when she is," Logan said.

Broc wished to ask how he'd know for sure, but instead, the warmth of the sun settled on all three of them. His mind wandered back to his time with Merryn, thinking about spending time on the beach with her. Could there be bairns of their own in the future? That picture warmed his heart even more than the heat of the sun. He was loving this new life near the water. If only they could get rid of the ugly troll sitting in Mingary, life would greatly improve for everyone on Mull.

As they drew closer to Bloody Bay, Logan said, "I think I'll go alone." Logan was bull-headed and stubborn, they all knew it. But this would not happen. Broc glanced over at Alaric, who gave him a subtle shake of his head.

As if he had eyes in the back of his head, he declared, "Don't tell me what to do, lads. I know my way around. I've got a bit more experience than you two together."

Broc couldn't argue that. The man had to be nearly in his seventh decade, yet he was still built like a bull. True, his long hair had turned gray, but the eyes still saw all. He had the mind of a twenty-summer-old and an uncanny sense of the world that no one else had. And his shoulders were still massive.

Logan Ramsay had been known as the beast for years. He still was a beast in Broc's eyes. But he was not invincible. He couldn't go alone for good reason. Now Broc had to convince him.

Broc said, "Nay, Logan. One of us must go with you. We're the ones who saw Kelvan, not you."

Logan side-eyed him with a smirk. "Fine. You two decide."

Logan turned around once the group approached Mingary Castle. "Who's joining me?"

Broc said, "I'll come with you."

Alaric said, "I'll stay with the boat. I didn't get a clear look at Kelvan at MacLean's. But if I don't see either one of you within half the hour, I'll be coming inside."

Logan snorted. "This will take less than that. I just need to find out who the hell is running this operation."

"Who would be running it besides K?" Alaric asked.

"I need to know exactly who his wife is. I have to look the bitch in the eye. If she's a Buchan, I'll know it. She'll look daft, trust me. Those Buchans are not the brightest in the land. They have those wild eyes, the kind you don't wish to meet in battle because you can never guess their next move."

Broc looked over at Alaric before questioning the elder who used to be a spy for Scotland's king. "But we know who she is. Didn't he tell you his wife was Glenna of Buchan?"

"He did." Logan climbed out of the boat with Broc, the two pulling the hull up onto the beach. "But until I see the woman for myself, I won't believe she's here. I need to look her in the eye. I was there when your grandsire put his sword in Glenn's belly. That bastard deserved what he got and more."

"Uncle," Broc said, using the term they all did on occasion. "Will you ask who she's after most?"

Alaric added, "Aye, I'd like to know that too. It could be Uncle Connor, or Alasdair, or Jamie."

Broc said, "Or my parents."

Logan stopped and stared at Broc. "You are correct, I'm afraid. Finlay saved Kyla and killed Simon de La Porte. Your grandsire put the sword in Glenn's belly, so it could be any Grant."

"But Davina married my uncle Fergus."

"And they have bairns, from what I heard, but all girls. Glenn also had a son who never fought. One he kept hidden with his brother. I just learned of him, so this must be his youngest daughter. She would be Glenn's granddaughter, if I'm correct. I'm going in."

Logan led the way around the castle to the front gate where the drawbridge was down, Broc alongside him, his hand resting on the hilt of his sword. They approached the keep, and the door opened as soon as they came near. The man motioned for them to enter the chamber at the end of the hall.

Logan strode inside the nearly empty building, his eyes straight ahead, while Broc took in everything about the castle—the layout, the number of servants, any stray weaponry. He didn't see any guards beyond the front gate. The place look deserted.

Once inside the chamber, Broc recognized the man seated as the one they'd seen at MacClane's. This was definitely Shealee's sire.

The man smirked but said nothing, tipping his head to the woman who stood over his shoulder. "My wife, Glenna. And who is the man you have with you? Grant or Ramsay?"

"Doesn't matter," Logan snapped back. "What the hell do you want? Don't you know enough to quit yet? Now that we are on the Isle of Mull, you have no chance of overtaking the entire isle. We can have a thousand soldiers within a sennight, and you know it."

"Who says we want anything?" Glenna asked, a sly grin covering her face. Her brown hair was pulled back into a tight plait, and she wore gems around her neck and on nearly every finger. Her gown was well made with intricate lace and a tight bosom, showing off her assets.

Logan was totally disinterested.

Broc's mother and father had fought hard against Simon de la Porte and Glenn of Buchan, who had terrorized their clan and Clan Ramsay for many moons.

The two had captured and beaten Kyla until she was near death, but she was strong like her father and fought to survive. Alex had been the one to end Buchan's reign of terror by thrusting his sword into the bastard's belly, Finlay there as witness along with Logan. Kyla had married Finlay shortly after being given their freedom.

"If you are related to Glenn of Buchan, you'll want something. He was always wanting what wasn't his. Had he not, he may have lived a bit longer."

"You remember my grandfather, Ramsay?"

"I was there the day Alex Grant put his sword in your grandsire's belly for beating his daughter. Your sire was stupid enough to think he could just take Clan Grant and the castle. Have you learned nothing?"

"I learned who killed him and who was there. I know Alex Grant's weapon killed him, but I know his daughter and others will be on the isle soon. I want Kyla and Finlay, one of their sons, and Jake's son, Alasdair. Give them to me, and we'll leave the island alone."

Logan snorted, so entertained by the foolish woman. "And why would I be ignorant enough to do that?"

"Because we'll keep coming after your bairns if you don't."

"So, you think you'll be as successful as the last time you tried it? How did Garvie and Odart and Egan and Dante and all their men work out? Have you any of them left?"

Kelvan held up his hand. "Enough of this. Glenna, keep your tongue in your mouth. I'm tired of the arguing. Here's what we want, Ramsay. I want the faery and the lad with the sword. Just those two. I saw the faery's powers myself and heard about the boy. Give them to me, or I'll steal her along with any bairn near her. And Glenna wants three. You choose, Glenna. Who do you want?"

"My first choice? Hmmm …" She paused to fold her hands across her wide waist. Pretty at one time, she showed the signs of a woman who spent her time angry with life. Pale faced, thin lipped, and a double chin were a testament to what she spent her time doing. "I want Kyla and you, Logan. That should suffice. One Ramsay, one Grant. And one more."

She ticked her finger against her chin as though she were counting.

"Kyla's son. I hear you have one of their bairns. I want that one so I can slice his throat while she watches."

Logan didn't look at Broc, but he prayed he would hold strong and not reveal his identity.

"Bring those two, the faery, and the lad with the sword to us, and we'll leave the isle alone. Otherwise, expect an attack in a sennight."

Logan smirked.

"What's so amusing, Ramsay?" K asked.

"Are you not forgetting someone on that list?" He glanced over at Broc who gave him a subtle nod. He knew Logan was asking if K was Kelvan.

Glenna said, "Nay, those are my demands."

Logan stared at K. "And yours?"

"I told you. I want the faery and the lad with the sword."

"Is that all?"

Broc guessed that Logan was trying to let K know that he knew his identity. He prayed he wouldn't give away Merryn and Shealee's location.

"I don't know what you speak of," K said.

"Kelvan." Logan paused while Kelvan registered the shock of his true name being used. "That is your name, is it not?"

"How the hell?"

"And haven't you massacred a clan on the mainland? The sheriff of the Borderlands has not caught up with you yet?"

"I've done naught. Keep your mouth closed, Ramsay, or I'll have my men slay you now." Kelvan became so red in the face that Broc guessed he didn't think anyone here knew what had happened in the Borderlands.

Logan smiled and said, "I'll keep your secret. But don't worry. I will be back."

The two left through the front door, no one following them. They had to walk across the drawbridge and around the back to get to the coastline where Alaric waited with their boat.

They'd almost made it when something came flying out of an alcove of the curtain wall straight at them, and a sword caught Logan in the flank as he turned to confront the unknown assailant.

Broc unsheathed his weapon and swung at the attacker, his strike so powerful and fast that it separated the hand from the arm that bore the weapon.

Glenna screamed, grabbing her arm. "I hate you, Logan Ramsay. I'll kill you and all of your clan. All of them! The war is on!"

Logan dropped to the ground, his hand gripping his side where the blood poured out, so Broc did the only thing he could think to do. He sheathed his weapon and lifted Logan into his arms, running to their vessel as quickly as he could.

Glenna had acted alone, so no one chased them. There were very few men around the castle, so he had only one priority—saving the man they all loved and looked up to. "Alaric! Get the extra plaid!" He hoped Alaric could hear him. They didn't have much time.

Broc came around the corner of the curtain wall, finally spying their boat and Alaric.

Logan mumbled, and Broc leaned his head down to listen. "Just get me to Rankin land. Dinnae let me die here, Broc." Logan's voice weakened, but he fought, his grip strong on Broc's arm. "The bitch took me by surprise. And if I do die here, take me off this land and back to Gwynie."

Alaric yelled, "What the hell happened?"

"After we left, Glenna came out of a hiding spot and struck him in the side."

"She won't be doing that again, will she, lad?" Logan drawled.

Broc ignored him, focusing on what they needed to do to get away quickly and save Logan. "Get the plaid, and we have to tie it tight around his middle to stop the bleeding." He glanced back over his shoulder, but no one came their way. He set Logan down on the grassy slope not far from the boat, putting pressure on the gaping wound, blood everywhere, on his hands, his clothing, all over the grass. "If we can stem the bleeding, we can get him to Rankin land. The MacVeys have a healer."

"I'd go for Eli if we can keep him alive that far." Alaric brought the fabric out and tied it around Logan's torso, pulling it tight. "Shite, Logan. Sorry."

Logan groaned, but said, "Pull it taut. You cannot hurt me."

A few moments later, Broc thought the bleeding had slowed a bit, so he peeked at it. "It's not as big a wound as I thought. We'll get you home, Logan."

"You can't row and hang on. I'll have to put pressure on it. Get me in the boat."

"Nay, not until it slows a bit more. Mama always said stop the bleeding first, then get help."

"I need Brenna."

"Brenna trained Eli. She'll sew you up nicely."

"She better. Because I'm going to come back and kill that bitch."

A voice carried over the edge of the curtain wall.

"We're coming for all of you, Ramsay. Every one of you will be dead!"

Kelvan.

"Get him in the boat, Alaric. We don't have time to waste. Help me pick him up."

The two men lifted Logan and set the old warrior in the vessel, then climbed in to start rowing. Broc said, "Just keep pressure on the wound, Logan. We'll be there soon enough."

They left the coast, going with the wind fortunately, but they had a problem.

"Logan?"

No answer.

"Shite," Alaric said. "He passed out."

CHAPTER ELEVEN

Kelvan

"WHAT THE HELL were you thinking, Glenna? You can't fight two Highlanders that size," Kelvan bellowed while two men carried her back into the castle.

"My hand," she mumbled. "Get the gems from it, Kelvan. They're worth a fortune."

The men got her into her bedchamber, one of them tying a tight band around her arm to stop the blood flow. "Get the healer here to sew her up." Kelvan paced back and forth, not knowing what to do next. "You're a volatile fool, Glenna. Not meant for battle. You're too emotional."

"Well, I got what I wanted. It happened exactly as I wanted it to." Her head fell back, her eyes closing, but then she jerked back up again. "It would have been perfect if his friend hadn't caught my hand. That could still prove to be a death blow to Ramsay."

"Too late now, you fool." Hell, but the woman was too emotional. Women were only good for one thing, and she was proving no different. "Now you've thrown everything off."

"Nay, I set it up perfectly. You don't understand strategy, Kelvan."

"What the hell are you talking about?"

"Their entire clan will be so busy trying to save him that they'll be ripe for an attack. Now's the perfect time to come in from the back, climb over the wall, and get the bairns. They won't be paying them any mind. I set this up for you, my love, so you can get your daughter. We can get the bairns first, then negotiate for Kyla and her son."

Kelvan fell into the closest chair. "You're right. They'll have healers flying around and never notice anyone in the cellars."

She was smarter than he thought. This was his chance to retrieve his daughter. Sweet Shealee was the best thing that ever happened to him. The wee lass looked at him as if he were the best person in the world, which, of course, he was. Smarter than anyone else. Shealee would probably follow him wherever he went, kiss his cheek whenever he asked her to, and she always smiled at him, even as an infant. Then when she was a bit older, he'd sell her like the others. What good were lasses, anyway?

Word had reached him that his daughter and Merryn had left MacLean land. If he had to guess, he would wager they were at Duart Castle, whose occupants took in everyone who needed protection. He had to go and see if his daughter was there. Then he'd steal her away and keep her until she became like all the other needy females of the world, so annoying that he'd sell her to someone in Europe.

Glenna had passed out, his men busy getting the healer, but Kelvan didn't have the forces he needed to follow Logan and his men. He couldn't gather a large enough number for what he needed for another two or three days, but by that time, Logan would be suffering from the fever and probably near death. That would still mean the entire group would be unsuspecting, so upset that they would not be as aware as they should be.

He went over and kissed Glenna's cheek. "Many thanks to you, my love. You are right. Instead of waiting a fortnight, we'll attack in three days."

Then he grabbed a drink, sat down, and set his feet up on a nearby stool. "I'm coming for you, Shealee. Soon you'll be where you belong."

CHAPTER TWELVE

Broc

A LARIC PULLED THE boat up near Rankin land and asked, "So now that you have seen him, is K the same as Kelvan?"

"Aye, he is the same. Bastard was surprised when Logan called him Kelvan. I thought he was about to pass out from shock."

Sloan hurried toward them down the hill. "What the hell happened? Is he dead?"

"Nay, he's alive, but we have to get him to Eli quickly. Can you have the lads ready our horses?"

"Who did it?"

"Glenna of Buchan."

Sloan whistled and headed back up the hill. "I'll see the horses are ready for you. Tell me what happened later."

Broc couldn't stop the roiling deep in his belly. He'd failed the man who was as close to everyone as any Grant in the family. He should have made sure to walk behind him to protect him from such an attack.

He would probably become a pariah to the Granthams. The Ramsays would surely hate him for bringing Logan back in such a condition … *if* they made it back.

Hellfire, what the hell would happen to Broc if Logan died on the way? Broc had to keep Logan alive. He adored him, always admiring his brusque ways, his ability to track in the woods, to know what was going on everywhere. How did he know everything?

Lennox had told everyone Logan knew more about his sister than he did, knowing that she was on MacQuarie land when he thought Eva was sitting quietly in the castle with their mother.

"Logan, wake up," he said as he lifted him out of the boat.

Logan opened his eyes and whispered, "Gwynie. Get me to Gwynie."

"Nay, don't talk like that," Alaric yelled. "We're not taking you to Gwyneth until you wake up, Ramsay. You aren't going anywhere yet."

"We need you to stay on the horse, Logan. Eli first, then Gwyneth."

"Can't …"

Alaric saw something behind a tree and moved over to grab it. "Put him in this cart. We'll get him up the hill."

They managed to get him to the stable without much trouble, the horses there as Sloan had promised.

Broc said, "I'm getting on Midnight Moon. Hand him up to me and I'll carry him back in front of me. We have to move fast."

Sloan said, "Are you daft, Broc? You cannot carry a man of his bulk all the way back to Duart.

You'll never make it. The horse will never make it. That's too large a load."

Alaric said, "Midnight Moon carried my grandfather, and he's carried Uncle Connor many times. He can handle it."

"Bring me two apples," Sloan called to his stable lads, then handed the animal one while Broc mounted.

"What's K planning?" Sloan asked as he fed the two horses.

"An attack on Duart if we don't give him what he wants."

"And what exactly does he want?"

Broc said, "Glenna wants three people. Logan and my mother. And if she doesn't get them, he's coming for the bairns. He wants his daughter, though he didn't say it, and Lia and John."

Broc mounted and Alaric handed Logan up to him, arranging the old warrior the best they could in front of him.

"That's only two. Who is the third that she wants?"

"Me," Broc said.

Alaric said, "I'm guessing they want Kyla's son. Didn't know you were hers, right?"

"Aye. And we didn't tell Kelvan that we have his daughter either."

Sloan jumped on his horse and shouted, "Ingelram, I'm going with them. Tell Eva I'll be back before the evening meal."

Alaric mounted, and the three headed down the path toward Duart Castle.

"We're keeping him alive, Grant," Broc yelled to his cousin.

"The bleeding has definitely slowed."

"But that's only the first hurdle. Get him sewn, then see if he can beat the fever. You both know how that goes."

Broc had so many terrifying thoughts, but he kept coming back to one.

As long as he's alive when we go inside the castle gates. I can't have it be all my fault. Please, God, keep him alive.

Midnight Moon led the way, galloping as if he knew his task.

Halfway there and Broc thought his arms were about to fall off. Logan was all muscle and dead weight against him, something far more difficult to hold on to than he would have guessed.

Sloan hollered, "We can switch him over to Alaric. He's not moving. That weight is tough to carry."

"Nay, he's fine, Rankin. I'll get him there." He had to. It was on his shoulders to get Logan to Eli. Then he'd probably be sent back to Grant land. There were worse things, though he'd been excited at the prospect of a possible relationship with Merryn.

But Broc couldn't let that affect him. Merryn would leave soon enough, and he'd be left alone again. If he had to return to the clan's main holding rather than slander his family's name, he would do it. He'd explain to his parents how

Glenna had been hiding in an alcove, how he hadn't seen the weapon until it was too late. How …

"Stop blaming yourself, cousin. You didn't hold the blade, and you've done more than anyone could do to get him home."

They were nearing the castle, thankfully, because Broc could barely hold the man upright. He felt for the beat of his heart at a spot on his arm, pleased to feel it still there, though weaker than usual. "He's still alive. For that much, I'm grateful."

Sloan said, "You think one wound is going to take out a man like Logan Ramsay? You don't know him well enough. He'll be bellowing from his bed on the morrow. Men like that don't go down easy."

They approached the gates, and something sent a chill down his spine.

Eli stood on the parapets and let out a scream unlike any he'd ever heard.

CHAPTER THIRTEEN

Eli

E LI HAD BEEN pacing at the top of the parapets for the longest time. She was never away from Alaric for long, but it was important that he completed this task on his own, much as she hated not to be there to protect him. That made her smile because Alaric always viewed it the other way around—he always protected her.

She let him think that, though she knew better.

Pausing to listen, she thought the sound of horses' hooves were a distance away. She leaned over the parapets, staring at the three horses coming up the path. She saw her husband first and waved, a sigh of relief coursing through her. How she adored the man.

Then she looked at her grandfather in the back, but he didn't ride like her grandsire. He rode more like Sloan Rankin.

Confused, her gaze went to the third horse, noticed it was Broc, but someone was in front of him.

Grandsire. She let out a wail when she saw the blood and noticed he wasn't moving.

"Is he dead?" she screamed as loud as she could, knowing everyone would hear her but she didn't care. "Is Grandda dead, Alaric?"

Her husband shook his head, so she raced down the stairs to the gates that had just been lifted, the three horses going straight to the keep steps.

She ran behind the animals shouting, "What happened?" It was time to get her emotions under control. Aunt Brenna had warned her many times that when it came to the worst injuries, she would have to throw her emotions aside and act like her patient was not someone she knew.

But Grandsire? Could she do it?

The courtyard filled as Alaric dismounted and shouted to Eli. "Get your needle ready. You have to sew him up. Go ahead of us, Eli. He needs you. We'll bring him in."

Maitland was out the door next, cursing. "Shite. Who did this?"

"Glenna," was all Broc could get out. He was exhausted but so wound with fear that he kept going.

Maitland said, "I'm taking him, Broc."

"Nay, I have him."

Uncle Connor came up behind Maitland. "Let him go, Broc. You're about to drop from exhaustion. We'll get him inside. You got him here and that's what counts. We'll take him. Follow us in, and you and Alaric will tell Eli what she needs to know, then you'll leave him be."

Broc said, "Nay, I can't leave him."

Uncle Connor came behind Broc, stopped him

by grabbing his shoulders, and said, "Hand him to Maitland. We've got him."

He handed Logan over to Maitland and said, "His side. His sword side took the slice."

Maitland took Logan from him while Uncle Connor took Broc's shoulders and led him inside the keep. "You'll sit in the chamber and drink. Alaric will talk. You did well getting him back here. I can see that it was a struggle. And Sloan wouldn't have escorted you back for no reason."

Eli motioned them to the healing chamber, looking at her husband first, then Broc. They were both ready to drop, if she were to guess. Alaric kissed her cheek and said, "You can do this. Love you, El."

"You are hale, husband?"

"Broc and I are fine. Fix Logan. He's lost a lot of blood."

Eli nodded, then pointed to the bed, and Maitland settled him on it the best he could.

Aunt Kyla appeared in the doorway. "Broc! What happened? You look awful. And Logan?"

Uncle Finlay said, "I'll get Gwyneth."

"I'm fine, Ma. A drink, if you please."

Maitland let out a whistle and said, "All quiet. Whoever was with him when it happened, tell Eli the exact details, then we are all stepping out. Kyla and Dyna will help you, Eli."

Broc took a quick swig of a goblet that was handed to him, then swiped his hand across his mouth before he spoke. "Logan went inside and met with Glenna and Kelvan. K and Kelvan are the same. When we left, we walked out the front of the keep and across the drawbridge to go around the curtain wall to the back. Glenna was hiding in a hidden section in the wall. Came out before I could stop her, sliced Logan's side before he could draw his weapon. Alaric and I stemmed the bleeding enough before we got him in the boat. That's all I can tell you."

"Alaric, anything you wish to add?"

"Just that I can't believe Broc was able to keep him on the galloping horse for so long."

The door opened and Finlay held Gwyneth in his arms. "Oh, Logan. Glenna?"

Broc replied, "Aye. My apologies, Gwyneth."

Maitland said, "Everyone out. Get Alaric and Broc something to eat, Kyla. Then we'll meet in my solar. Many thanks for escorting them back, Sloan. Get yourself a drink too."

The group exited and left Gwyneth with Kyla and Eli. Dyna came in and said, "I brought a basin of water to clean the wound, Eli."

Gwyneth tugged on Dyna's hand and said, "He doesn't look good. Send a messenger for his brother and Brenna too."

Dyna nodded and left. "I'll tell Avelina."

Eli set to her task, removing Logan's tunic and cleaning the wound with Gwyneth's help. When she was ready to sew him up, Logan's eyes opened and he said, "Don't give up on me yet, wife. Eli, don't be timid. Just sew it."

Aunt Kyla said, "You are drinking this, Logan."

Aunt Brenna had always insisted on giving her patients water that had been boiled, something her father had taught her. Everyone told her it was foolish, but she insisted.

Gwyneth, being very familiar with Brenna's practices, asked, "Boiled earlier?"

"Aye," Aunt Kyla said. Logan drank it before Eli set to her task.

"I love you, Grandda." She pierced his skin and began sewing.

He never made a sound.

CHAPTER FOURTEEN

Merryn

MERRYN HAD BEEN practicing at the small archery target inside the castle walls when the chaos began. Eli screamed just before Broc came inside the gates on his horse, carrying one of the elders of the clan in front of him.

Broc looked so strong on the massive warhorse, like a fierce warrior, his sword bloody from something. He never noticed her standing next to a tree in the outskirts of the courtyard. He didn't appear to be wounded, but the man next to him looked nearly dead. Merryn would have loved to go to Broc, but he was too busy to bother with her.

Shealee was playing with an imaginary friend, but then Lia came out of the hall. "Oh, there she is. I was looking for her inside."

Lia approached Merryn and said, "It would be best if she didn't move far from me."

Merryn, confused, asked, "Why do you say that, Lia?"

Lia sat down on a tree stump and smoothed

her skirt. "Has anyone told you that I'm a faery, Merryn?"

Merryn nodded, thinking on all that Broc had told her. Broc and the others had all moved inside, so she sat down to chat with the wee lass who spoke like an elder. "He did mention it, but I'm not sure if I believe him. Exactly what is your job as a faery, Lia?"

"I am sent by the universe to protect certain people to help make things happen. I have been sent to protect Shealee from her father. I'm sure you understand why better than I do. He is on a mission that will not end well. If you just allow me to stay close by, I can protect her from the terrible man."

"How do I know you are telling me the truth?"

Lia leaned over and whispered, "Nara said to tell you that you should listen to me. The same way you listened to her and hid in the secret box Da built for you."

Merryn gasped. "You can talk with her?" She hadn't told anyone here about the box; only Tristan knew of it.

"She's listening to you now."

Tears fell down Merryn's cheeks. "Please tell her I miss her, and I'm sorry Tristan and I didn't stay to bury her and Mama and Papa."

Lia tipped her head for a moment, then said, "She said Uncle Neil buried them. Do not worry. And she doesn't mind if Shealee calls you Mama because the two of you were so close."

Merryn didn't know what to think of this odd

conversation. How she wished her sister were standing in front of her so she could ask her about Broc. Was he a good man? Should she pursue a relationship with him?

Was kissing him the right thing to do?

Lia got up to chase Shealee as she ran after a squirrel, but she turned back to say, "Your sister says aye, aye, and aye."

Merryn let a few tears fall and said, "I miss you so, Nara. And Mama and Da too."

A loud cry rent the air, and Magni came flying out toward Lia. Merryn picked up Shealee to bring her back because Magni was sobbing.

Merryn asked, "What is it, Magni?"

"Grandsire. My grandsire is terribly hurt. Someone struck him with their sword and he's sleeping. I heard them say that he wasn't moving when they stitched him. Lia, is he dead? Is he going to die?"

"That was your grandsire, Magni? There are so many people here I cannot recall them all." Merryn could see how terribly upset the wee lad was over the sight of his grandfather.

Lia patted her hand and said, "It's complicated. Magni, please calm down. Logan is not dead, and he's not ready to die yet. But he will not be riding a horse for a bit. You may have to sit by his side to keep him company for a few days, but you can do that."

Magni scowled and rubbed the tears from his eyes. "But now I only have two protectors."

"You will always have me."

"And Thane, but he's going to have a new bairn

soon. He'll have to go back to protect Tamsin and Mora."

"Not soon. But he will go home, and I'm staying. Would you like to remain here to help your grandsire get better? I'm sure Thane would understand."

Broc came out of the keep and headed straight for Merryn.

Lia said, "Come with me, Magni. We will watch Shealee so Broc can speak with Merryn. He needs her right now."

Magni spun around to face Broc. "Is he dead? Is he going to die?" He rubbed at his tears again. "I'm not crying either. Warriors don't cry."

Broc said, "Aye, warriors cry sometimes, Magni. Logan is not dead, and I think Eli has stitched him up. He woke up to speak with Gwyneth, so that's a good sign. But he needs rest now. He may not awaken until the morrow. Do not worry overmuch."

Lia said, "Come with me, Magni."

Once the wee ones had gone in the opposite direction, Broc wrapped his arms around Merryn.

Merryn asked, "You are not hurt, Broc?"

He pulled back and looked at his tunic, noticing all the dried blood on it. "I'm fine. I just needed a hug. My thanks for allowing it."

"Of course. I was worried about you because you look exhausted."

He took Merryn's hand and led her over to a bench near the small orchards inside the wall. "Alaric and I went with Logan so we could verify if K was indeed Kelvan. He is. I will tell you that first. He didn't say anything about Shealee, but I don't think he knows you are here with us. He has a new wife named Glenna who bears a grudge against both Clan Ramsay and Clan Grant for something that happened years ago. It involved my parents."

"Both of your parents?"

"Aye, they were kept in a dungeon and eventually escaped. Glenna's grandfather nearly killed my mother, and my grandfather killed him for it. It was more complicated than that, but Glenna wants my mother, Logan, and me. If we go to her, probably so she can kill us, then they won't come after the bairns."

Merryn gasped again. "Which bairns?"

"K says he wants the faery."

"Lia?"

"Aye."

"Then he'll come for Shealee. You won't go, will you? You can't. Please say you won't go, Broc."

He lifted her hand and kissed her knuckles, one at a time. "I don't know what's going to happen. We're meeting in the chieftains' solar in a few moments. I wished to chat with you first, let you know what I could."

"Promise me you'll stay away, Broc. Please? I couldn't bear to lose you after losing my sister and my parents."

"I can only promise I won't go alone. I honestly don't know what will be decided. It could be a full-blown battle. That's how Clan Grant handles those who try to destroy us. And that's Glenna's goal. She ultimately wants to destroy both clans."

Merryn's heart nearly broke in two. She was just developing feelings for this man, and he could die soon.

Broc's father came outside. "Broc. We're meeting and we need you. Sorry, Merryn."

Broc nodded and stood, pulling Merryn to her feet while his sire returned to the keep. "I'll look for you at the evening meal."

She nodded. What else could she do?

CHAPTER FIFTEEN

Broc

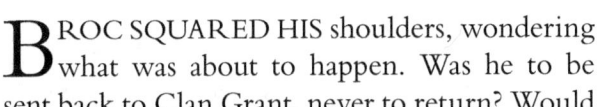

BROC SQUARED HIS shoulders, wondering what was about to happen. Was he to be sent back to Clan Grant, never to return? Would they send him off to fight Kelvan alone?

Finlay MacNicol clasped his son's shoulder and said, "You did a fine job getting Logan back here. That wasn't an easy task. But I recognize that expression on your face. It is not your fault."

"Da, if I'd been standing on the other side of him or if I'd been behind him, I mayhap could have stopped it. I had no idea she would attack. There'd been no threats, no weapons drawn. We'd seen no guards but the few on the wall. Naught."

"I believe you. It's exactly why Glenn was such an evil bastard. It's in their blood to be underhanded, to kill for no reason. Do not take this on your shoulders. Please."

"I'll do my best," he answered, knowing that it was nearly impossible. They made their way into the keep, passing Avelina as she hurried down the stairs, heading toward the healing chamber.

Would she ever speak to him again once she learned the truth?

His sire opened the door to the solar, so Broc took a deep breath and crossed the threshold into the den of inquisition. He nodded to Maitland who stood at the front beside Dyna. Also in attendance were his mother seated next to Uncle Connor, Alasdair, and Alaric. Maitland pointed to a chair near the front, and Broc took it.

Maitland said, "Tell us exactly what happened. Alaric told us what he knew, but he didn't go inside with you."

Broc took a deep breath and repeated everything he remembered about the situation, glossing over one part. But Maitland caught him and held up his hand to stop him.

Maitland said, "Who do they want? You said that if they didn't get the three they wanted, they'd steal the bairns. Who exactly do they want? And which bairns?"

Poor Maitland paled, probably for fear that his son would be stolen again.

"I'll tell you exactly what they said. Glenna wants Kyla, Logan, and me. We didn't let on that I was Kyla's son. Kelvan wants the faery and the lad with the sword, though I'll add that I don't think he's aware that we have his daughter."

Maitland clarified, "So there was no mention of Grant or any of Dyna's bairns? No seers, no wee bairns? Naught like that?"

"Nay. They said if they turned us over, they would not kidnap any more bairns."

"And how long do you have to do that before they attack?"

"A sennight."

His father spoke up immediately. "Neither one of you are going. Don't even think on it."

His mother said, "Finlay, Broc and I could go. I know it's not ideal, but I do not wish to hear of any more bairns taken. That's simple cruelty. If Broc and I go along in a sennight, it would give you the time to gather forces to attack on the mainland. Do you not agree? That would give plenty of time to ready your warriors."

Uncle Connor said, "I agree with gathering forces, but nay, sister. You are not going. That clan has tortured you enough. I'll not allow it."

His mother stood and said, "You don't control me, Connor. I'll do what I need to do."

"Kyla, don't be foolish. She nearly killed Logan. What the hell do you think she's got planned for you two? Vengeance. Plain and simple. Neither of you are going. We'll come up with something."

Broc's father paced in the back of the solar, tugging on his beard. "Nay, nay, nay. Do not even think it, Kyla. I agree with Connor."

Eli stepped inside quietly, making her way over to Alaric.

Dyna stopped and asked, "How is he, Eli?"

"He's holding up. I sewed him, but he didn't flinch. Whether he was passed out or withstanding the pain, I couldn't tell. But we have another problem."

"What?" Alasdair asked.

"I don't have enough of the poultice that keeps

the fever at bay. I'm nearly out. I was going to send a messenger to Aunt Jennie or Aunt Brenna, but now we will need it soon. Verra soon."

Dyna said, "We already sent a messenger to Clan Ramsay and to Clan Drummond. I suspect Micheil will be here soon. Mayhap Aunt Brenna will be here too. But I'll send another message to Clan Ramsay."

"We can only hope," Maitland said. "I'm sure Uncle Micheil will get here as soon as he can. Aunt Brenna? I'm not so sure."

Uncle Connor said, "I think I speak for all of us, Broc, that we are grateful that you were able to get Uncle Logan back here in time. It could have been much worse. Alaric told us how Logan wished to go in on his own, but the two of you argued with him. I'm glad to hear you will stand up to him. Logan can be a bit stubborn, as you know. We thank both you and Alaric for your quick thinking and action."

His back was thumped a few times, but Broc said, "I should have been able …"

Uncle Connor stood and said, "I'm going to stop you right there, Broc. There is no one I know who is more clever, more astute, wiser, or better to have with you going in to battle than Logan Ramsay. If he didn't see it coming, no one would. None of what happened is your fault, yours or Alaric's."

"I should have gone with them," Alaric said, his arms crossed.

"Nay, no more of that. If Logan couldn't stop it, no one could."

Broc couldn't help but think how he wished people would be able to say the same about him someday.

Maitland said, "We'll meet in two days to decide our plan of action. I don't wish to wait a whole sennight. If we're going to attack, there is no reason to wait. Discuss it and come up with ideas. Hopefully, Lennox or Tristan will visit so we can determine what is happening elsewhere."

Dyna added, "And we're all praying that Logan heals so he can tell us his own version. He knows more about the Buchans than anyone but Torrian, probably." Logan's nephew Torrian had almost been forced into a marriage with Buchan's daughter. They attempted trickery, but an astute Jennet had saved Torrian from a lifetime stuck in an unwanted union.

Broc was pleased they weren't blaming him for the attack, but he did resolve to train harder. He'd already trained as hard as he could with his sword; perhaps it was time for him to take up archery. He needed to be skilled at both, so he could do better next time.

Perhaps he could train with Merryn on the morrow.

They made their way into the great hall just as the evening meal was brought out. Sloan clasped his shoulder and said, "I'm grabbing a meat pie and going home. Thane is staying until the morrow. I'll return to see what you've decided to do."

"Many thanks, Sloan, for all your assistance."

"I couldn't have done what you did, Broc. Logan is a beast."

Broc's fears lightened a bit. He wasn't going to be sent away. He scanned the hall and saw Merryn sitting at a table with the bairns. Dyna made her way to join her, so Broc did too, both taking a seat.

Merryn arched a brow at him, and he nodded to let her know that he felt better.

But then Dyna added, "He's not going to be asked to return to Clan Grant as he feared. It was unanimously decided that if Logan couldn't see it coming, then no one could. Do you not agree, Broc?"

He nodded, giving Dyna a small smile of gratitude. "It was totally unexpected."

He'd only feel better if Logan survived. Time would tell.

"Dyna, may I train with you on the morrow? I'm taking up archery."

Dyna smiled. "Can't wait for it."

"Truly," Merryn asked, her green eyes locked on his. Hell, but every single time he looked at the lass, she grew more appealing. Her skin was flawless, her lips as rosy as they came, but it was her eyes.

Broc could always see it in a lass's eyes when their gaze fell upon his scar. They would stare at the large imperfection, then look away, their expression changing to one of disgust or revulsion. Their gaze would then return again before they would look across the hall and escape.

Every time. He was used to it. Only his close

family members were accustomed to the scar and no longer stared, but the young lasses always noticed.

Merryn hadn't stared at it yet. It freed his mind from worry. Even though he'd grown his beard to cover it, he knew the scar was still visible, especially up close. Sometimes, if he met someone new, he would count to see how long before they noticed.

He gave up counting with Merryn.

"You wish to be an archer, Broc? I find it challenging. For you, it will probably come easily."

"I need to make myself a stronger fighter. I was always in awe of the Ramsay guards who were good at both. Logan is a powerful swordsman and an amazing archer. I don't know how he is so skilled. His son Gavin, Eli's sire, was also excellent at both. I need more skills. I've tried archery before, but not seriously. I must work harder at this. Do you mind if I join you?" He arched a brow at her.

"I would love it." Merryn smiled.

He could never allow such a situation again. Dagger, sword, bow—all of them had to come easily. Switching from one to the other would be a challenge. But he was up to it. He had to make his elders proud of him. He reached down to make sure his father's dagger was still attached to his belt. It was.

Somehow, he had to make up for the travesty he'd just been involved in. He glanced around the hall, pleased to see no one paid him any mind.

Well, no one but his mother, who would glance

over at him with Merryn and grin, then she'd whisper to his father. They'd pushed for him to find someone, but it had never happened. He'd blamed his scarring, but was it more than that?

He'd not think on it and instead focused on the lass next to him.

At the end of the meal, Sandor jumped up from his spot and began to run circles around all the tables. In and out he traveled, giggling and pushing against something imaginary.

Alasdair got up quickly and went to Sandor's side, stopping him. "Is it Uncle Jake again?"

Broc was close enough to hear everything, the shivers traveling up his neck whenever Sandor spoke.

"Aye, Unca Shakie chaseen me aden." The lad pointed at an empty spot behind him. "Wight dare. Unca Shakie wight dare."

Alasdair whispered, "Why, Da? Why are you here?"

"Unca Shakie say be weddy. Twouble comeen."

"How? When?" Alasdair asked.

"Bye, Unca Shakie!" Sandor waved and returned to the table.

What the hell was going to happen?

CHAPTER SIXTEEN

Kelvan

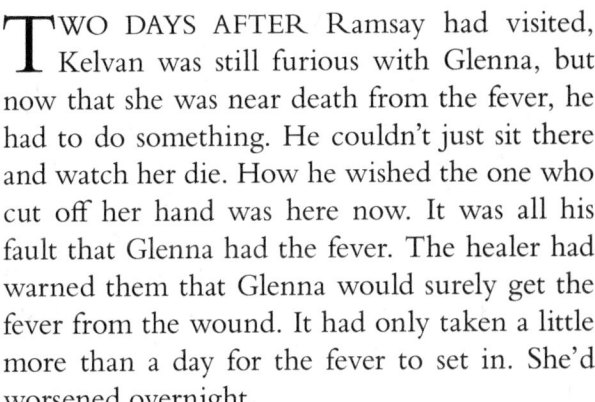

TWO DAYS AFTER Ramsay had visited, Kelvan was still furious with Glenna, but now that she was near death from the fever, he had to do something. He couldn't just sit there and watch her die. How he wished the one who cut off her hand was here now. It was all his fault that Glenna had the fever. The healer had warned them that Glenna would surely get the fever from the wound. It had only taken a little more than a day for the fever to set in. She'd worsened overnight.

He gathered two of his guards and made a decision. "We're going to take three ships and wait a distance down from Craignure. I hear there will be many coming to aid the Granthams, so we shall wait until a ship arrives. Then we'll come in from shore and wait until the chaos begins, and we'll go over the wall and grab bairns."

Samuel, his best fighter at present, asked, "But you said a sennight."

"God's rotten teeth, I changed my mind. Do you have a problem with that?"

"Nay. Go on. Tell me the plan so I can see it done."

"I'd prefer to find Merryn and Shealee eventually, or Kyla and Finlay, but right now all we need is bait. If we have bairns, they'll negotiate. We'll grab whomever we can and wait for them to come and beg for the return of their precious babes."

"Where?" asked Samuel. "Where are you going to stash them all? Not in Mingary Castle. Glenna will never be able to handle bairns crying. You know she hates them."

"I have other places to hide them. I'll send the captives to Tiree or Morvern because the Granthams know we're here, and we can't let them reclaim them. If Clan Grant sends their forces to Mingary, we cannot battle them yet, even with Glenna's men arriving soon. If we have the bairns hidden, they'll not kill us all. Do not worry. But I'm not sitting still any longer. After what that fool did to my beloved Glenna, a one-handed idiot now, there is retribution to be paid. Gather the men and ready them to row shortly. Ready the ships too."

Samuel did as he was instructed, so Kelvan made his way down to the best ship, waiting for the men to come along and row. He knew Duart Castle well by now. From the right spot, one could climb up the bank to a side of the wall where a perfect set of trees grew. He could sit in one and wait. He supposed Samuel could do it, but no one was as smart as Kelvan. All the past blunders were glaring evidence of this truth.

He'd lie in wait at Duart Castle, see what the bastards thought of him then. When the time was right, he'd have twenty men climb over the walls and bring chaos to the courtyard. It was a fine day, so some bairns would be outside playing.

Kelvan considered his plan again, certain it would work. Why, it was a brilliant plan that no one else could have thought of. And sitting here watching Glenna fail more and more each day was proving too difficult for him. The dumb healer he'd found to treat her put a salve on her stub after he sewed what he could, then said there was naught more he could do. Kelvan had to do something. She had the coin to pay all the men they'd hired, and he didn't know exactly where she kept it all.

It was time to make his move.

A short time later, they manned three galley ships after giving orders to the captain of each boat. They were to sit outside the castle and wait for his instructions. He would climb the tree and give the whistle when he wished for them to advance.

They headed down the Sound of Mull toward Craignure, slowing because the afternoon boat was approaching. He smiled after it landed, men leading horses from the lower level while others carried multiple crates and set them aside.

One haughty woman, white-haired and graceful, left the boat, hanging on to a huge man's arm. Kelvan had no idea who either one was, but he'd wager they were headed to Duart

Castle. If he was correct, this would give him the exact circumstances he needed.

Some of the men were guards, and they fussed over the crates, settling them in rented carts to take to their destination. The bear of a man with long dark hair and a full beard lifted the woman onto a mare as if she were but a feather. Then he strode over to his own stallion and fed the animal a treat, patting its flank. Kelvan snorted, wondering why he would waste the treat on an animal, though he had to admit that the chestnut-colored beast was a beauty if Kelvan had ever seen one.

Where the hell did these Highlanders find such magnificent stallions? One snort from the animal would scare a woman into pishing in the path, he swore.

The man barked orders, then mounted his horse, leading the woman up the incline and heading toward Duart. Just as Kelvan had thought.

Perhaps the woman was Logan Ramsay's sister. If so, he'd put a dagger in her throat if he got the chance. Then he decided she was too fine and fair to be a Ramsay.

He didn't care who she was. Once the ship unloaded, took on its new passengers, and headed back to Oban, Kelvan whistled and motioned for their three vessels to head toward Duart. They already knew where to go, knew they were to wait for him to move up the hill to the castle to assess the situation before he would give the sign to attack.

Retribution would be his soon. *Start the war, bastards.* It was all their fault that Glenna was half daft in bed.

CHAPTER SEVENTEEN

Merryn

TWO DAYS AFTER the attack, Merryn sat at the table, working on her letters, when Broc came in from the lists, working hard on his sword skills. She'd never known anyone who worked as hard as he did. He grabbed an ale and moved over to take a seat next to her.

Kyla and Dyna were by the hearth watching the bairns: Sandor, Tora, Sylvi, Lia, Shealee, and Magni. Shealee's giggles were like music to Merryn's ears. Every once in a while, the lass would run over and set her head in Merryn's lap, but then she would run back to her new friends.

It was almost as if the lass recalled losing her mother and feared losing Merryn too.

Logan hung on, fever raging through him so badly that some thought the worst. Gwyneth hadn't left his side, and Eli only came out when she needed to eat or get a hug from Alaric. Eli carried their first bairn, a wee mound to her belly, and Alaric protected her as if she were a bairn herself.

"How are your letters coming? We can work on it again later, if you like."

Merryn glanced up at Broc, the man who was causing all the oddest feelings inside her that she didn't know what to think of.

Except that he surely grew more handsome every day. Was that possible?

"Just a moment, Merryn. I have to tell Dyna something." Broc turned around and strode over to the hearth.

Merryn's gaze locked on his swagger as he made his way across the hall. "Mama, Dyna, I noticed a line of horses headed in this direction. It could be Aunt Brenna."

Dyna jumped up and clapped her hands. "Oh, thank the Lord above. We need her poultices and potions."

The door flew open and everyone jumped. A large man filled the doorway. Tall with massive shoulders, he had dark hair nearly to his shoulders and a full beard. "Where's my brother?"

"Uncle Micheil!" Eli flew across the hall into his arms just as a tall, thin woman stepped in behind him. Micheil moved back and took her bags and her arm to support her.

"Aunt Brenna! We're so glad to see you!"

Avelina flew down the stairs and people popped in and out to greet the two. Broc had explained the elders in the Ramsay family to Merryn. Quade had married Brenna Grant and, as eldest, was the clan chieftain. Logan was next, then Micheil. Avelina, or Lina, was the baby of the family.

It was a joyous reunion except for Logan not being there. Avelina hugged the large man and said, "I'm so glad you came quickly, brother dearest."

Broc greeted the newcomers, introduced Merryn, then said, "Mama, we're going out to practice our archery. We'll stay away until everyone is settled."

Kyla greeted the newcomers, then turned back to her son. "That's a great idea, Broc. Dyna, I'll take the bairns to the courtyard and under the apple trees, let them run about a bit. It is busy, and the talk is going to be quite serious with Micheil and Aunt Brenna here."

Astra chimed in, "I'm coming too!"

Magni and Lia followed.

Broc took Merryn's hand after Shealee ran over to grab her. "Ou'side?"

Dyna shouted, "Kyla, inside the wall only. They cannot even peek through the gate. I don't care how many horsies Sandor sees."

The group headed out while others fussed over Brenna and Micheil, both anxious to see Logan.

Once in the lovely autumn sunshine, Broc said, "Mama, do you mind watching the bairns so Merryn and I can practice our archery a wee bit?"

"Aye, enjoy yourselves, Broc. Astra and Magni are here. They will help."

"Many thanks, we won't be long."

"Go ahead," Kyla replied. "We'll be right here under the apple trees. I can sit on the bench, and they can play catch or pick the apples. Go have some time together."

Merryn gave Shealee a kiss and said, "Go play with Lia and Sylvi."

Sylvi rushed over and took Shealee's hand. "Come, we'll play save the castle."

Then he turned to Merryn. "It is a beautiful day. A perfect day to shoot a few arrows." Broc squeezed Merryn's hand and led her over to the small archery target. "It's not the best, but there's too much going on outside the walls. Uncle Connor's next group of guards arrived with supplies. Aunt Brenna has tons of crates too. She is the healer we all look up to. She's the best in all the land, she and my aunt Jennie."

"And she is a Ramsay?"

"Aye, and a Grant," he said, setting his sword down in the grass while he reached for a supply of arrows. "It's a great story. Logan kidnapped Brenna to heal his eldest brother, Quade. Stole her away in the middle of the night because Quade was nearly dead. She saved Quade and healed both of his bairns from an odd sickness. She married him shortly after her clan forgave the kidnapping. She'd spent a considerable amount of time healing the two bairns, and they fell in love. Once Grandda forgave Logan, they married shortly after."

"Wasn't he married if he had two bairns?"

"His first wife had already died. So, Brenna Grant married Quade Ramsay, and that was the beginning of the alliance between the two clans. Grandsire Alex loved Quade and Micheil … he got used to Logan after a while. Micheil is next in age, married Diana of Drummond, and Avelina was the baby. She has seer powers too, much like Dyna. You've met her."

"Is Diana the chieftain you told me about?"

"Aye, she is. We all love Micheil. He is the nicest and most helpful, always laughing. Unlike Logan. But Logan has special skills. Logan and Gwyneth were spies for the king for years. They are both amazing but verra different."

A scream ripped through the air, and Merryn spun around to see strange men dropping ropes over the curtain wall, climbing down, and running straight for the bairns, weapons drawn and clashing with anyone they ran into.

"Shealee!"

Broc pushed her and said, "Get her. I'll protect you." He picked up his sword, swinging it at the first attacker, sending the brute's weapon flying through the air and over the wall.

Merryn ran for Shealee but couldn't reach her in time. Someone grabbed the wee lass, and Lia followed. Sandor ran toward Merryn, so she caught him and held on tight. Sylvi ran screaming, so Merryn snatched the young lass just as a man reached for her, and Merryn kicked him in his bollocks. He froze, the fury on his face there momentarily before he lifted his sword, but Broc approached, killing the man before he could use his sword or seize Merryn or either of the bairns.

Merryn watched as a man climbed the wall, Shealee held tightly in his grip. She wished to grab a bow, but to do so, she would have to let

Sandor and Sylvi down. And what if she hit her niece by mistake?

As quickly as they came, the ones who were still standing took off.

But she got a look at the attacker who held Shealee.

Kelvan.

One look at the evil man sent so many emotions through her that she could only cling to the two bairns she had in her arms. The moment reminiscent of the time when Kelvan had killed her sister, shock and fear shot through her from the tips of her toes to the hair on her head. Nausea, fear, anger, all fighting to be the strongest.

Yet she couldn't move, paralyzed with fear.

The fear of the same sword piercing her own belly, of dying in an instant, of never seeing her family or her loved ones again. Of losing Broc or what could have been.

She should have been able to go after Kelvan, but she was frozen with shards of fear.

Fear of dying.

CHAPTER EIGHTEEN

Broc

B ROC GOT THE one fool who Merryn kicked in the bollocks, but there were two men to replace him, both reaching for the bairns she held. He battled the two, spearing one with his weapon, pulling it out, and lifting his sword over his head to come down hard on the next man's arm, knocking his small sword from his hands.

That attacker ran to the wall. Broc spun to follow him, but his gut dropped to his toes.

One burly man punched his mother in the face, knocking her out, then he tossed her over his shoulder and retraced his steps.

Broc wanted to vomit. Merryn was behind him, his mother in front of him, but he made a quick assessment, heard a whistle that called all the attackers back to the boat and chased after the men going over the wall—one with his mother, one with Shealee, and two others with Magni and Tora. Lia suddenly appeared next to the two bairns and jumped down, presumably to stay with the kidnappers.

Here we go again.

Kelvan stopped at the highest point of the stone border and waved to Merryn who promptly screamed. Broc went after him, grabbing the rope before he could pull it back up, and scaled the wall. He landed hard on the other side and raced down the hill in time to see the men leap into three different boats and take off faster than he could reach the coastline. There were Grant warriors everywhere behind him, but none could reach the boats before they got away.

His mother was on the boat along with four others.

Shealee, with Lia right behind her.

Magni.

Tora.

Who else did they have?

He scanned the boats, looking for other captives, but didn't see any. Then he made his way back to the front gates. "Open up. They're gone."

Trudging back inside, he wiped the sweat from his brow. He'd failed again. When was he going to be strong enough to protect someone? Visions of a boar racing at him, its tusk coming at his face overpowered his mind. He shoved it back into the recesses of his brain, wishing the awful memories would leave him be.

Merryn came flying toward him, launching herself at him, still holding both bairns.

His father came out of the keep. "Kyla? Where the hell is Kyla?"

Broc closed his eyes and took Sylvi from Merryn while she kept hold of Sandor. Then he strode toward his sire, who took one look at his face and roared. Derric was behind him, Dyna next, and they tore over to grab their two bairns.

Dyna asked, "Tora again?"

Broc nodded.

Derric said, "I was coming from the other side, but I couldn't get to her fast enough. I saw Merryn grab Sandor and Sylvi, and Broc protected them."

His father said, "What about your mother? Did you try to protect her?"

Derric said, "Finlay, Broc was protecting a woman holding two bairns. He couldn't leave them to go after Kyla. There were men everywhere."

Merryn said, "But he did. Once he took care of the three men after us, he went after the man who had his mother. There were so many of them."

Finlay hugged his son. "Forgive me. I know you fought hard. I can see the blood on you and the bodies of the men you stopped. Your mother is strong. She'll survive. Is Lia with them?"

"Aye, and Magni. Shealee, Tora, Lia, Magni, and Mama are all on the ships."

"Ships?" Derric asked.

"Aye. Three of them."

Dyna said, "And they must have been lying in wait. As soon as the guards arrived with the horses who were unsettled from the ship, plus Micheil and Aunt Brenna, everyone was distracted from all the new arrivals. Many came outside with the bairns. We made it perfect for them. We weren't thinking."

"But he said a sennight. It's only been two days."

Broc shook his head. "Never believe anything he says."

Finlay clasped his son's shoulder and said, "Let's go into the hall. Plan our next steps."

Merryn looked up at Broc. How she prayed he wouldn't consider going after them. But if she were to guess, he was already plotting. "Broc, it was Kelvan. I saw him with Shealee. He's the one who stole her in front of me."

Dyna, Derric, and Finlay all stared at them. Derric mumbled, "Damn. Diamond, we have to stop them. He won't quit."

Then Merryn made a quick decision.

When Broc left, she was going with him.

Fire raged through her at all the travesties one man had committed. He'd killed her sister, his own wife, the mother of his wee bairn.

Then he'd killed both her parents and all their neighbors.

His new wife had attempted to kill Logan.

And now they'd kidnapped four bairns and Kyla Grant.

"I'm going with you when you go after them, Broc. I don't care who goes."

Broc said, "I'm not sure if you are ready yet, Merryn."

Dyna said, "She's ready. She had the sense to grab my two bairns and kick one attacker in the bollocks, did she not? She saved Sandor and Sylvi."

Broc tipped his head and said, "So true. I'll take you along if the others agree."

"Good. Because I'm going to kill that bastard.

I've seen enough of his sick, twisted deeds. If I have to put a dagger in his eye, I'll do it."

He had Shealee, and she'd vowed to protect the wee lass.

She owed it to her sister.

CHAPTER NINETEEN

Brenna

———

BRENNA TURNED IN time to see her nephew coming toward her. Connor was the one who reminded her of her dearest brother Alex more than any other. Alasdair was growing more and more like him, but Connor *was* Alex on some days.

"Connor, what has happened? I was afraid to go back outside from the sounds of the clashing swords."

"Another kidnapping, Aunt Brenna. Fear not, we'll handle it. We need your help with Logan. I'm sure you've heard. How may I be of use to you?"

"Micheil is already in with him, but I need my bag of poultices. I had the best of the bunch in one of the crates, with my name written clearly on the top. If you could find it, open it, and bring the sack on the top to me, I would appreciate it. It's wrapped in a Grant plaid."

"I'll take care of it. Go help him. He has the fever so badly that he doesn't even awaken. Gwyneth is losing her will."

"I will do what I can, Connor. I see you have much more important things to focus on right now. Bairns come first." She patted his shoulder as he turned to leave.

Connor retrieved her sack while Brenna took in all the tears and sobbing within the hall, something she should concern herself with, but she couldn't. She was here for Logan, so in to Logan she would go.

She pivoted, holding in her groan from being on horseback for so long, something she wasn't used to anymore, and her sore bottom reminded her. She opened the door to the healing chamber, pleased to see that Eli kept it clean, well lit, and well stocked, just as she'd taught her.

Gwyneth sat on the bed with her husband, almost lying next to him, her stump clearly in view. Avelina and Micheil each sat on nearby stools, which Micheil promptly vacated to offer to her. "My thanks, Micheil." He found another one and brought it close.

She leaned over to give Gwyneth a hug. "I'm pleased to see you, Gwyn. We all needed you to stay with us a bit longer. It was a tough decision for you, and I'm sure it was difficult, but I'm glad you are here. He will need you."

"Will he, Brenna? I don't know if he's going to make it. Please help him. Eli ran out of the fever potion, and she needs more poultice for his wound. It's oozing terribly and I can't stop it." Gwyneth had been around Brenna enough times to know what to do for most any injury or sickness.

Brenna waved her hand, her eyes going to the man who had brought her to the love of her life, Quade Ramsay. Logan had been a thorn in her side many times, his gruff exterior often too much, but she still loved him with all her heart.

She took in the pallor of his skin, set her hand to his wound to check for warmth, and peeked under the bandage, assessing the fine stitches Eli had placed. Then she felt his life's force pulsing through him, set her ear to his chest to listen to his heart and his lungs. She poked at his belly, checked his arms and legs for any other wounds, then cupped his cheek and said, "Logan, wake up."

No reaction.

Her assessment finished, she said to Micheil. "Be prepared. You may have to hold him down."

Micheil grinned, picking up quickly on her meaning, and said, "I'm ready." But Micheil also knew his brother well. He leaned forward onto the end of the bed.

Brenna moved closer to his ear. "Logan Ramsay, I've come a long way, and I have a sore arse from riding a horse so far, so you better wake up to acknowledge me."

Naught. Just a wee twitch of his jaw.

Brenna pulled the linen coverlet back and promptly pinched Logan's nipple as hard as she could.

Logan sat up with a bark. "God's bones, woman! What the hell are you trying to do to me? Some healer you are. That hurts like hell."

"More than your wound? Because I hoped it would." Brenna winked at him.

"You are mean for a healer. Aye. It hurts more than my wound right now. Where did you learn that cruel trick?" He gave her his worst frown.

"Good, I'm glad it hurts."

He fell back, rubbing his sore spot before closing his eyes, and waved at her in dismissal.

Brenna decided to try a different tactic. She knew exactly how to infuriate her brother-in-law. "I came for my book. The one you stole from me so long ago. Get your arse up out of that bed, Logan Ramsay, and return my dear mother's book now. You hid it again."

Logan shot up and glared at her. "I gave you that book long ago, and you know it. I set it at your feet, or have you forgotten already, you old bat?"

Brenna smiled and said, "Greetings, Logan."

He smirked and said, "Greetings, Brenna. What the hell are you doing here? And can't you just leave me be? I was sleeping."

"Nay, no more sleeping. I have your brother here, and he'll hold you down if I ask him to. You know I will."

"Shite, Micheil. Why are you here?"

"To help Brenna. Are you faking it, dear brother?"

"Did you see my wound? I'm not pretending."

Micheil snorted. "Please. Are you trying to convince me that it's the first wound you've ever had? Are you a wee bairn in your old age? Quade gave you far worse wounds before you bedded your first lass." Micheil let out a roar at his own jest, and Logan chuckled with him, gripping his side in pain.

Gwyneth slapped Logan's arm. "Sit up or I'll grab the other nipple, Logan."

Brenna said, "Here's how this is going to go, Logan. And you know better than to argue with me. You're going to sit up and drink this potion. Then I'm sending Lina out to get you some oatmeal, and if we have to feed you with a bairn's utensil, we will. You know better. Micheil will hold you down, and Gwyneth will have the pleasure of shoving it down your throat."

Gwyneth looked at Brenna and said, "I'll share the joy with you, Brenna. You and I have had to put up with the Ramsay men for a long time. We'll take turns."

Lina giggled.

Logan looked at his sister and said, "I don't find their humor the least bit funny, Lina. Have you no sympathy for your favorite brother?"

She snorted and said, "Nay! Not under the circumstances, Logan. And I never said you were my favorite. Sit up and get better."

"Fine. Go get the oats, Lina. Then mayhap this woman of torture will leave me be."

"Aye, you were injured. Aye, you still have a bit of the fever. But if you wish to lie there and give up, it will kill you. I'm not going to allow that to happen."

"You always were a surly witch."

Brenna leaned over and kissed his cheek. "Now that's better. You have everyone upset enough, and they can't worry about you anymore. Understood?"

"You always were overbearing. How did Quade stand you?"

She got up to get his potion, but suddenly Logan called out, "You aren't leaving me already, are you, woman?"

Brenna said, "I love you too. I'm staying."

CHAPTER TWENTY

Kyla

KYLA SLOWLY OPENED her eyes, scanning the area, trying to understand where she was and what was happening.

Magni stood at the end of the bed. "Is she dead?" Tears covered his cheeks, but Lia held firm.

"Nay, she's not dead, Magni. She's just sleeping. They hit her on the head. See that bump on the side of her scalp? That's why she's sleeping."

Kyla rolled onto her back and held out her arms. "Come here, Magni. I'm fine."

Magni rushed over, climbed in next to Kyla, and lay his head on her chest. "You are better? You have to help us."

"I am better, but I think Lia and Tora can help us as much as anyone." When Magni finally stepped away, giving her a little smile as he wiped his tears, she checked the bump on her head and shrugged. "Not as bad as the first Buchan." She'd never forget the horrific treatment she'd received decades ago, but she also didn't wish to experience it ever again.

She pushed herself to a sitting position, assessing their situation.

They were in a bedchamber with one large bed, big enough for all of them to sleep in. From that, she guessed they'd be here a few days. There was only one small window to the passageway covered with a fur, up too high to reach but enough to offer some light.

The chamber had two chairs near a hearth in the corner, though the hearth wasn't lit. The bairns played with some wooden toys, Tora keeping Shealee busy. "What do you know, Magni? Have you seen anyone?"

"Nay. They gave us a basket of apples and a loaf of bread. There's water and we had some goat's milk. No one said anything."

"Well, that's not so bad. I'm certain there will be quite a few people looking for us soon. Have you any idea where we are?"

Magni shook his head, but Tora ran over, leaned her elbows onto Kyla's lap, and whispered, "Tiree, Auntie. The Isle of Tiree." Tora spun around and returned to Shealee's side.

"Tiree. Lia, where is Tiree?"

Lia said, "Next to Coll."

"Close to Mull? I'm not familiar with all these isles here."

Lia explained, "The Isle of Mull is the largest, but there are several small islands not far from Mull. Ulva is the closest. Then there is Iona, Staffa, Coll, and Tiree. We're close to Mull, but we are far enough to require one of the larger ships to cross the often-rough waves of the sea. It will not be safe to use a small boat like they use to row to Ulva."

"Do we have larger boats, Magni?"

"Aye, Thane has three of them. One was a Norse boat. That's where he found the odd-looking piece he uses to peer in the distance."

"So they can come for us?"

"Aye," Lia explained. "If they know we are on Tiree."

"How will they know we are here?"

Tora ran over and leaned on Kyla's knees again. "I aweady told Mama. She wasn't listening yet, but she will. And Aunt Lina knows." Then she took off again.

"That's one way."

"And the other?"

"They'll probably travel back to Mingary with a number of guards and force someone to reveal our location." Lia clasped her hands and said, "See, Magni? We have little to worry about."

Magni climbed on the bed and hugged Kyla.

Somehow, they'd get away.

Now if Kyla could just convince herself of it.

CHAPTER TWENTY-ONE

Logan

WORD TRAVELED ABOUT the attack and before nightfall, the great hall was full. The food was plentiful, but the overall aura was one of sadness and defeat.

Thane had returned when he heard that Magni and Lia were taken again. Tristan had arrived to see how Merryn was doing, surprised to find their niece missing. He'd decided to stay and see what the plan was to rescue the victims. Lennox had come with Meg, and Sloan had arrived with Eva. Alasdair and Emmalin, Derric and Dyna, Alaric and Eli, Avelina and Drew, Broc and Merryn, Maitland, and Finlay were all waiting to see how this problem was to be solved.

Micheil and Connor came out of the healing chamber, Micheil taking the floor next to Maitland, raising his arms to quiet everyone. "With our deepest gratitude to Eli and Brenna, we will welcome Logan for a few moments to give his side of the story, and he will share what he thinks our best approach will be. Before he comes out, as his brother, I'm going to warn you all. He is *not* ready to leave this keep yet. He still has much healing to do, but he's alive, improving, and always ready to share his wisdom."

The door opened and Logan entered the hall, his steps careful, Brenna at his side as he crossed the hall to a round of applause and whistles. Micheil centered a chair not far from the hearth for him, one with enough cushions to keep him comfortable with his wounds. Sloan set a wee dram of his best amber liquid by Logan's chair, with promises of more to come.

The first person he saw was Gwynie, tears in her eyes as she sat in her favorite spot by the fire. That was like a punch in the gut for him. After all she'd been through, he hated to see her go through this, but he'd been bested. There was naught else he could say.

He waved to everyone and said, "Sit your arses down. I have a few words to offer, and while I'm glad to be up and moving, I will not last long."

The group sat down, and Logan stopped by Broc's chair. He looked over the group and said, "I've heard you all thank Brenna and Eli, and I owe them both. But I didn't hear anyone thank Broc and Alaric for getting me back here. And Sloan." He sat carefully into the chair Micheil held for him.

"Glenna is a Buchan to the core, thinks like her grandsire, and she bested me. I did not suspect any direct attack from anyone there. They were not expecting us." He paused to take a swallow of his drink before he continued. The hall was silent, waiting on his next words. "There were less than a handful in attendance, none with weapons visible. When she jumped out of her hiding spot, she came at me from behind and struck me, totally unexpected, thus I dropped immediately." Another pause and he took a deep breath.

"I would not be here speaking if not for Broc. His reaction was as swift as any I've seen, his sword thrust so powerful that he amputated her hand, ending her attack with one move."

Gasps and surprise spread through the hall.

A warm smile creased his face. "Did Broc fail to mention that? I saw it with my own eyes. He cut off the hand that held the weapon that was poised to come at me a second time. Had she succeeded, I wouldn't be here. Had he missed, I wouldn't be here. Her goal was to kill me, and after the first blow, I could not have retaliated. She failed only because of Broc's quick actions, and I thank him for that. And how Alaric and Broc got me back into the boat, rowed me across and back here in time to survive, I'll never know. I don't recall much of it. Broc, Alaric, come here."

Everyone applauded while the two made their way up to his side. Logan pushed himself to his feet and gave each of them as much of a hug as he could tolerate with the wound still paining him. "I'll take you two to fight with me any time."

The men sat back down, and Logan said, "Kelvan and Glenna are going to be tough to beat. They have forces of an unknown number, drawing from multiple places. Lina tells me we have determined through our dearest Tora that the captives are on Tiree. Thane, do you know the island well?"

Thane said, "It's much more fertile than the other isles, less mountainous, and it lies west of Coll. More cottages, so they will be harder to find there. I don't know it well. Sloan?"

Sloan shook his head. "I don't either."

Logan said, "Well, I know someone who does, and she's not far away. And she can also get us to someone who knows Glenna better than we do." He stopped for another sip of his favorite brew.

Connor asked, "Who? You've been hiding this person from us?"

"Nay, I promised not to consult her unless it was an emergency. And this is urgent. If you tell her I was cut down, she'll be here for us in half the day, and we need her. She's one of the finest archers on the mainland, trained by the best, my wife. Better than Gwynie because her sight is so strong. Eli is carrying, so she shouldn't go to Tiree, and Dyna needs to stay here. We need strong archers. Merryn, I'm asking you and Broc to go with Thane and mayhap two others. And I know you know her, Merryn. Go find Simmy for us."

"Simmy? Who the hell is Simmy?" Connor asked.

Logan ignored Connor. "You should leave at first light. She's married to Thane's second, Artan. They spend their time on Iona and Staffa, beautiful islands."

Tristan looked at Merryn. "But Simmy is married to a man named Tanner."

Thane smiled. "Tanner is what Artan uses when he's not on our land. They've been married for a few years. She's one of the finest archers, but she stays hidden."

"Who the hell is she, Logan?"

Logan did his usual teasing, a big smile on his face, then shrugged.

Gwynie shouted, "Logan!"

"Fine. For you only, Gwynie. Simmy is our daughter, Simone."

Avelina sighed, and Micheil broke into a broad grin, shaking his head. "Simone is a hell of an archer. She'll get the bastards. I had no idea she was hiding here."

"Bring Simone to me, Merryn. You and Broc go find her. Thane will help you."

CHAPTER TWENTY-TWO

Merryn

———∾∾∾———

MERRYN MET BROC at the stables at first light. She'd prepared a sack full of dried meat and apples for the trip. The half loaf of bread she grabbed would feed them along the way.

Her brother Tristan came in ahead of Broc, sneaking over to chat with her. "I see he is fond of you, lass. Are you as fond of him?"

Merryn blushed and nodded to her brother. "I'm confused by so much activity. Our place was so quiet, but he's always there for me. He helps me with everything, teaching me how to read, working with the archers. He's wonderful."

Tristan leaned over and kissed her forehead. "I'm happy for you, Merryn. You deserve some happiness in your life."

"And so do you, brother. You work so hard."

"My turn will come."

"But we must stop him, Tristan. I watched Kelvan grab Shealee and carry her over the wall, and I froze. He stopped at the top to look back at me." She closed her eyes to stop the impending tears. "I hate him."

"We will find her, Merryn. We have many on our side now."

Broc entered with Thane behind him, talking about stallions. They both stopped, surprised that Merryn was already up and ready to go.

"Godspeed with you both," Tristan said. "I'm going inside to chat with Alaric." Tristan left at the same time Connor came through the door.

Broc asked, "Did we forget something, Uncle Connor?"

"Nay, I'm coming with you."

"Oh, I wasn't expecting anyone else."

"Kyla is my sister. I know I'm getting older, but I was there when she came back from the beating Buchan gave her. I've never seen anyone so bruised. I can't sit here and do naught. I need to speak with Simone and see her suggestions. I may not be the strongest in battle, but I can strategize with the best."

"Glad to have you along, Uncle."

Connor told the stable lads which horse to ready, then went back outside, Thane joining him. As soon as they stepped out, Broc moved to Merryn and wrapped his arms around her.

She sighed, taking in his warmth, his strength. She whispered, "Did you recall cutting off her hand?"

"Oddly, not right away. I remembered after Logan mentioned it. I was so focused on getting him out of there that I forgot about her. I think once I woke up in the middle of the night with visions of her screaming at me, but I wasn't sure why. That was it. Thought mayhap I imagined it."

"I'm honored to have such a fierce fighter with me." She tipped her head back and kissed the stubble on his chin.

He grinned, "Sorry, I didn't wish to take the time for a trim."

"I don't mind."

He kissed her, and she leaned into him, sighing, parting her lips so his tongue could duel with hers, something she loved. Every time this man kissed her, sensations traveled through her that were so foreign, yet so delicious, that she never wanted the kiss to end.

They were interrupted by a cough and then Alaric, chuckling, came toward them as they separated. He clasped Broc's shoulder and said, "I had no idea you cut off her hand, but the bitch will never forget you, will she?"

"I'm just grateful to see Logan on his feet again," Broc said. "He's even been cursing out Aunt Brenna. Now I know he feels better."

"Maitland and Dyna will strategize here while you're gone. We'll all try to decide the best way to attack these fools. It's good to have Micheil of Drummond here. He will offer a different point of view, I believe. But Godspeed and take care of the pretty lass on the horse next to you." Alaric smiled at Merryn.

"She's riding with me. Thane insisted. If we need another horse, we can use one of his."

Alaric left with a wave and Broc spun around to Merryn. "You don't mind, do you? Thane suggested we need to make as small an imprint as possible. He wasn't certain how skilled you were at guiding horses in the forest. How do you feel about it?"

"I think I would be wiser to ride with you. I didn't ride often, and I rode ponies many times. Not big stallions like this one."

Broc laughed, giving his horse a squeeze. "Midnight Majesty is a fine beast. We'll do well. Come, let's ready ourselves." He took the reins and led the horse out of the stable.

Merryn was even more excited now. She feared riding her own horse, so riding with Broc was perfect. They'd be able to chat more, for certain.

Broc attached two bows and quivers, just in case they needed them. "Will you be comfortable shooting? You may have to."

Merryn's smile left her face, thoughts of Kelvan and wee Shealee dominating her mind instead of the man next to her. Images of Nara's face when the sword went through her belly would never leave her.

Ever.

"Just give me the chance, and I'll put an arrow in his heart. Shealee needs to come home."

She had to pray they would get the opportunity to do just that.

CHAPTER TWENTY-THREE

Simone

SIMONE LAY ON the white sands of the northern side of Iona when she heard the sound that was as sweet as a full colony of puffins in spring.

"Greetings, husband dearest," she called out to him, donning her tunic and running over to where he'd come across the isle. "I was not expecting you. Is something wrong?"

Artan grabbed Simone by the waist and tugged her close, kissing her soundly, something she needed as assurance that he was all right. But then he set her aside and took a step back.

Something she didn't like.

"What is it?"

"Your sire was struck down by …"

"What? You should have told me that first!"

"Now hold on, love of mine. He's hale. Brenna and Michcil are also here. He's holding up so far. But two days after his attack, another group was taken captive, and I thought you should know. Shealee is one of them."

"And Merryn too?"

"Nay, Merryn is fine. Tristan is at Duart Castle. And by the way, Merryn has met someone. Broc MacNicol? Know you of him?"

"Aye. He would be Kyla's son. He'll protect her, fear not. And he'll go after the bastards who kidnapped the wee ones." Simone gathered her things as quickly as she could, leading the way back to their small hut on the other end of the isle. "Keep talking. I'm listening. How did you hear of this?"

"Thane sent one of the guards back as soon as Logan was injured, so I was on my way, but then a second messenger came along to let us know that the bairns were kidnapped again."

"I've got to find this bastard myself. Artan, I'm going after them. I will not allow the man who killed his own wife to kill their daughter."

They arrived at the small hut the two of them built with their own hands, a two-chamber cottage with a thatched roof. Simone loved to decorate their home with the dried flowers she picked all over the isle. She also enjoyed traveling to Staffa to explore the rock formations and caves, one of their favorite places to swim in the summer.

But she had to focus. She grabbed a sack and threw in an extra tunic and leggings, the ones made by her beloved mother. "I need lots of arrows." Then she tossed in a few other small items, finally pulling the ties closed.

"How can I help? Anything I can do for you?"

"Nay. Just tell me everything. Where are the bairns? Do they know yet?"

"Tiree, according to your aunt Lina."

"She would know more than anyone. Hellfire, how can I get to Tiree from here?"

"I made arrangements for one of our ships on Ulva to come for you, then you can meet the group at MacQuarie land. They're sure to send a group there soon. I would guess they will also send another group to Rankin land because Kelvan is at Kilchoan."

"What the hell is wrong with all these men who continue to steal bairns away?"

"Coin, my sweet. Greed, plain and simple. You know it. Are you packed?"

"Aye. Let me stand under the waterfall, then I'll dress and be ready. I need to get the sand out of my hair." She tossed her clothing in a basket, then grabbed a towel and a sliver of soap.

He followed her out to the waterfall, watching the curves of her bare body wiggle across the landscape. "You're giving me my favorite view, lass of mine." He smiled. "You have the finest arse I've ever seen. If not for all that is happening, you would not be getting under the water now."

That was one of the things she loved about Artan. True, their love was very passionate, but he knew when to tone it down. He knew what was most important, which was a wonder, considering his background and where he came from. Working with the Garvies still gave him nightmares. She quickly rinsed the sand off her body because it had the worst way of chafing when she traveled by foot.

Once dressed, she asked, "What is it?"

"Sit for a minute, love. There's more."

She sat down and Artan crossed his arms. "They stole Tora, Dyna's daughter. And Magni and Lia along with Shealee."

"Lia would go, anyway. I do absolutely believe that lass is a faery and a guardian angel of those bairns, especially Magni. Who is she protecting now? I don't believe it's Grant anymore."

"She went to Duart Castle for Shealee. We knew trouble was coming. But …"

"There's more?" What the hell else could be happening? The Granthams had dealt with so much of late. Someone needed to put a stop to this evil bastard. It was time for her to act. She recalled exactly how cruel the evil souls could be, especially to children.

"They stole an adult away too."

"Who?"

"Kyla."

"Kyla? Oh my, Connor will be wild. And so will Finlay. It's a good thing you came for me." Simone got up to head back to the cottage, but Artan didn't move. "What?"

He just stared at her.

"What is it? What the hell could be worse? Is my mother still alive? Please tell me she hasn't been hurt."

"Your mother is fine. It's the partner. Kelvan has remarried."

"To whom?"

Artan paled, tears misting his gaze.

"Artan?" She took a step forward, her fingers brushing his cheek.

"My sister. My brother's evil wife. Glenna of Buchan. And she's plotted revenge against your father, Kyla, and Finlay for a long time. This is going to be bad, Simmy."

"Don't say that!" Simone wished to pull her hair out of her head and then sew them back in. "Why would you say such a thing, Artan?"

He closed his eyes and then stared up at the clouds overhead. "Because Glenna is the reason I left the mainland."

Confused, Simone waited for more. She knew his heritage, but he rarely spoke about his family, claiming he left because he didn't like their way of life. What exactly were they capable of?

"Glenna is the evilest soul I've ever met. She'll be hard to stop."

Simone narrowed her gaze because she had a sudden understanding why this man who she adored was acting so strangely. "Glenna is the one who hurt my father, isn't she?"

"Aye. If not for Broc, Logan would be dead. It was a goal of hers. She swore that before she died, she would see Logan and Kyla dead."

Simone set her hands on her hips and said, "Artan, I love you dearly, but your sister is a dead woman. I will kill her with my bare hands if I must." She had a fury inside her that would not be quenched until there was an arrow that pierced both sides of the bitch's body and a dagger in each eye. "Do you wish to go with me or stay here? I'll not tell you if you don't wish to know."

"I'll go with you. If I must, I'll put the sword in

her chest myself. I know how she is. I'll not hold it against you, Simone."

She stepped closer and kissed a tear from his cheek. "I'm sorry, but I will do what I must."

Artan sighed and said, "We must move. You cannot waste time when it comes to Glenna."

"I'm ready."

She was more than ready. A rage drove her forward unlike any she'd ever experienced before.

Glenna was about to meet her brother's wife.

At the opposite end of her deadliest arrow.

CHAPTER TWENTY-FOUR

Broc

B ROC STOOD WITH Thane on the beach closest to MacQuarie land, watching the approach of a ship coming from Ulva. "Friendly, are they? Do you recognize them, Thane?"

"I believe it's Artan and Simone. Simmy and Tanner. That looks like one of his ships that he keeps on Ulva."

Merryn was inside bathing, something that calmed her, so Broc had promised to watch for Simmy. He'd hoped standing on the beach and taking in the sea air would give him the clarity and calm he needed.

Unfortunately, it didn't give him anything but more worry, more concern, more fear.

What if he couldn't help his mother? What if they couldn't find the group anywhere?

Or what if they found everyone but Shealee? Kelvan was her sire, so could he keep her if he wished to? Would King Robert side with him?

Broc had fought with all the strength he had, had searched all the areas for hidden threats when they'd gone to Mingary, yet still he'd failed. Logan

Ramsay had nearly died in his arms, and it would be a long time before Broc would get over that experience.

The pale skin, the ashen lips, the blood. So much blood dripping from his hands, on his tunic.

Thane said, "I'm going inside for a bit. I'll return shortly."

Merryn came out at the same time as Thane disappeared. "Is it Simmy?"

"I believe so." He wrapped his arm around her, tugging her close. There was definitely a chill in the air, though it didn't bother him a bit.

"What are you thinking about? You look verra serious, Broc."

Should he tell her the truth? He decided it was time to open up a wee bit. "I'll be honest with you. I'm unsettled about going to Tiree. After my experience at Mingary and what happened to me when I was young, I worry whether I'll be able to hold up under the pressure of a sword swinging over my head."

She peered up at him, looking surprised. "But you saved Logan. Why would you worry? And what happened when you were young?"

He sighed and turned his head so she could see the wound on his cheek. "This. You've seen it multiple times. I have this scar and a much larger one on my belly."

"What scar?"

He chuckled. "You're being kind. You know. This one."

Her fingers reached up to his cheek and

touched the scar he'd carried for so long, the one that caused some lasses to look the other way.

"That's not much of a scar. Besides, I thought warriors consider scars a testament to their skill in battle."

"Some do, but this was not gained in battle. A boar got me. My horse threw me into the path of three wild boars. I was gored. Nearly killed me. Not a fond memory. In fact, I still have nightmares. And Logan? Aye, I'm glad he's still with us, but seeing that woman strike Logan down? I'll never get past that. I had this ridiculous hesitation because she was a female. I was raised never to strike a woman, so I hesitated. If I hadn't, could I have prevented his wound? Questions, so many doubts."

Merryn moved to his other side, stood on her tiptoes, and kissed his wound. "Any lass who sees that wee thing as detracting from you doesn't know what is most important in a relationship."

"And what do you see as most important?"

"Honor. Loyalty. Compassion. A warm heart. All things you have." Her eyes misted, and he wished to explore that but decided she would tell him if she wished to. "Those are the important things. My sister …" She stopped, tearing up, and he squeezed her hand.

"Take your time."

"My sister thought Kelvan was the most handsome man she'd ever met. He was loud-mouthed but sweet-talking. The kind of talk that I didn't trust, but she believed all those things he said. I knew better. Mama knew better and tried to warn her away from Kelvan, but she wouldn't be persuaded to give up on him." She stared at the ground. "Mama was right. The evil man stuck a blade in her back. Her back!"

"We'll get Shealee. And the others."

"I fear I'll fail Shealee. Do you feel the same about your mother?"

He nearly shed a few tears of his own thinking on her question. "Aye. I fear it so much. Da wished to come, but Uncle Connor refused. Said he was too emotional, that his emotions got in the way with Glenn, and they might do the same with Glenna."

"Truly? I'd love to hear all about it sometime."

"It's a long story, but Da agreed. Then he came over and put his hands on my shoulders and told Uncle Connor that he trusted me to save Mama. That made me even more worried. So much on my aptitude. My sword skills, ability to fight, to sense out danger. Do I have enough?"

"It's much to put on your shoulders. But I think you are strong enough to handle it, Broc. You are a fierce swordsman. I am honored to have you near, even if for a short time."

He leaned down, kissed her cheek, and whispered, "I don't think it will be for a short time, lass. I'm growing quite fond of you."

She blushed as Uncle Connor and Thane joined them. Thane pointed into the water. "It is Artan and Simone. I've seen that look on her face before."

Broc asked, "What look? What does it mean?"

"It means you better be able to run fast. She's

quite an archer. I've witnessed her hitting targets that I couldn't even see. She was trained by Gwyneth, Molly, and Maggie."

The ship arrived and Broc met them, helping to pull the vessel onshore. Simone was tall, willowy, and beautiful. She wore her dark hair much like her mother and Sela, tied back at the crown, the length swinging behind her head and out of her face.

Her eyes fell on Broc, and she clasped his shoulder, "Well, you surely are a Grant, and one of Kyla's, if I were to guess."

"Broc MacNicol. You know the others, aye?"

"Connor, it's so nice to see you again, though I'm sorry to hear of the circumstances. Know that I'm here to help. Merryn," she said as she took the younger woman's hands in hers. "We will get Shealee away from that bastard. I won't stop until she's back in your arms where she belongs. Thane, do you have plans yet?"

"Nay, come inside for a brief repast, Simmy. I would suggest waiting about two more hours before we head in that direction."

"Have you any more archers? Any of Mama's granddaughters here?"

"Nay. Eli is here, and she's one of the finest, but she's expecting, and Gwyneth would have none of her coming along."

"And how is my sire?"

"He's better." They moved inside and the group settled in the hall, Thane stepping out to speak with his cook.

Uncle Connor said, "I wish you had been there

to see Aunt Brenna call your father out, Simone. Micheil loves to retell the story. Apparently, he was pretending a bit. She played the healer, then she made a move that made him bolt right out of bed, cursing at her. But then he fell back asleep until she accused him of stealing her mother's dear journal again."

Simone broke into a laugh. "Oh my, that would have been fun to watch."

"Micheil said it was the best show he'd seen in a long time. He cursed at her, and she cursed back at him, swearing she'd have Micheil hold him down if she had to."

Then Simone teared up. "Da would have a hard time accepting that a woman bested him, Connor. I'm sure his self-image is tainted, especially by Glenna. You know that to be true."

"Aye, I agree."

Broc didn't say a word. Did they blame him for part of the travesty?

Simone said, "Sit down, all. You need to know that Artan knows Glenna verra well and could provide us some insight into her thinking."

Connor looked at her in surprise. "He does? Glenna of Buchan?"

Artan nodded. "Glenna was married to my brother."

CHAPTER TWENTY-FIVE

Kelvan

K ELVAN CLIMBED OUT of the boat on the far coastline of Tiree, anxious to see his wee daughter. Shealee was a beautiful lass, and when he'd held her before, she'd always smiled at him, and he told Nara that she even tried to kiss him once. She'd been about three full moons by then.

Samuel strode next to him. "I'm sure she'll be pleased to see you now, Chief. She was upset over the chaos of the kidnapping, of being moved to a new place. That's all it was. She'll be fine now."

"I hope so. I plan to bring her back to Mingary so I can see her first thing every morn. She was brightest and sweetest after Nara fed her and changed her raggies. It was the best part of the day."

Samuel smiled and trudged ahead, scanning the area as they moved closer to the cottage where the bairns were held. There were two older men watching over the five people, keeping the wee ones and the Grant woman locked inside and feeding them.

Kelvan nearly walked up to the door, but then Samuel held up his hand. "Our men should have just left. Allow me to enter first. One never knows who might be inside."

"Of course. I admire your wisdom and your loyalty, Samuel, which is why I keep you around. The others are daft losers." Kelvan was the most important of all. Why didn't everyone understand that basic truth? He was the wisest by far. Everyone had to see that.

Samuel used the key hung on a nail and opened the door to the hut, then stepped inside and went down the passageway to the locked chamber, opening it finally before he called to Kelvan. He was not surprised to see the four bairns huddled around the one adult, Glenna's arch nemesis, the woman named Kyla.

Kyla spoke quickly, "Let us go now."

Kelvan chuckled. "You are not in a position to give orders. I am, and now you will keep your mouth closed."

"I'll speak if I like," she said, setting the child who was on her lap behind her. She pushed herself to a standing position. "Leave the bairns alone. I'll stay willingly if you set them free."

He settled his hands on his hips to stare at her. Aye, she had that foolish look he'd seen in some females, but ones who didn't live long. He did his best to intimidate her, stepping closer and narrowing his eyes, but she didn't budge.

So he promptly slapped her.

Twice.

And the bitch stood and glared at him. "You're an evil man who has a foolish belief that he has the right to take whatever he wants."

"And I do," he proudly announced.

"Not for long. The Grants know who you are, and once they find you, it won't be pretty."

He laughed, tipping his head back.

"And what happened to Glenna's sire, Glenn?"

Kelvan slapped her again. "Close your mouth. You're naught but a worthless female."

Lucky for her that wee Shealee began to cry.

He spun around and reached for his daughter. "Oh, my sweet. I would never hurt you." He picked her up and kissed her cheek, waiting for the girl to realize who held her so she would stop her crying. "You are my sweet lass. I'd never hurt you. I'm Papa. Say it. Papa."

The bairn screamed louder and shoved against his chest. "Mama. Wan' Mama."

"Mama is dead. You'll never see the bitch again," he said through gritted teeth. How he hated that woman.

Shealee began to kick and fight against him, so he raised his hand up to her, but Kyla grabbed it, stopping him. "How dare you hit a child, you cruel, weak bastard."

He hesitated, realizing that he did not wish to hit such a wee one, but he'd hoped that striking her would put an end to her tirade.

Samuel must have been able to see in his mind. "Chief, bairns cry louder if you hit them."

He tossed the screaming lass onto the bed and the three others cuddled her, the wee faery wrapping her arms around the child until she quieted.

He grabbed the faery's arm, but it felt like it was full of nettles. He let go and nearly hit her, but the look on the faery's face stopped him. She whispered, "You don't recall the battle in the sea? The lightning, the creature?"

Turning to Samuel, he shouted, "What the hell is wrong with my daughter? Last I saw her, she adored me."

Kyla said, "If it was more than a moon, she won't remember you. Bairns don't recall things for long. She's already forgotten you."

"She remembers her mother, and she died a year ago."

"Nay, she remembers Merryn, not your wife. Merryn is Mama now."

Tora said, "You killed hew mama a yeaw ago."

"You shut your mouth too unless you wish for a slap." He grabbed Tora by her tunic and lifted her into the air. Kyla tried to stop him, but Samuel held her back.

"You are the witchy one. Send me the coins that I deserve." He twisted the tunic and Tora stared at his shoulder, her gaze locking on the fabric, and then she blew on it.

The arm of his tunic erupted into a blaze of fire.

"Och!" He dropped Tora onto the bed, and he and Samuel grabbed a fur and smothered the flames.

He backed up and said, "Samuel, send them a message. I'll do a trade because I don't want those two wee ones. I want the one with the special sword."

Samuel opened the door, and Kelvan couldn't get out of there fast enough. He nearly ran to the ship because he had a sudden fear of the witchy one and the other one with the golden hair. What the hell were they? Seers, witches, faeries? He didn't know how to deal with any of them.

But he'd heard about the lad with the sword. "What about the sword? What did you call it, Samuel?"

"They call it the sapphire sword. It is said that it holds the power to bring the gates of hell up to thrash the wicked. And that whoever holds it is protected and directs the powers."

"What powers exactly?"

"Of that, I'm not certain. It's said it will protect the holder from any harm. So, the one who carries the sword into battle will be protected. But I also heard it will go against any evil forces in the land of the Scots."

"Then why does a lad hold it? That doesn't make sense."

"It was held by a lass long ago, one who brought fields of men to battle over her heart, so they say. One man was about to gain it from her, but she raised it to the sky and the rains came down from heaven and gave the power to her allies."

"Who the hell were her allies? Do you know?"

"Aye. The Grants, Ramsays, and the Menzies."

Kelvan stopped before he was about to jump onto the ship. He spun around and bellowed, "Why did you not tell me this before?"

"I didn't think it mattered. Glenna is fighting with the Ramsays. Is that not who she struck down?"

"Aye, she struck down Logan Ramsay. But the woman inside with the bairns? Do you know what clan she's from?"

Samuel shrugged. "I thought Clan Ramsay."

"Nay, fool. She's from Clan Grant. Her sire is Alexander Grant."

Samuel whistled. "Och. That's the one who helped the lass win the sapphire sword. And Alex Grant gave it to the lad."

"Who is the lad who has it now?"

Samuel sighed and took a step back before he replied. "Alex Grant's great-grandson."

"Shite."

CHAPTER TWENTY-SIX

Merryn

MERRYN LEANED AGAINST Broc, snuggling into his body heat that warmed her through his tunic. The ship they were on was sizable, a number of rowers beneath the deck because the waters were a bit rough.

They rocked along, the gray clouds casting an angry shadow over the sea, reflective of what their mission entailed.

Connor said, "It looks like there are indeed quite a few cottages together. Is there a town or a tavern where we can ask questions? Someone may have a suggestion of where the crude group might be."

Thane stepped to the bow, pointing ahead toward the land. "There are cottages on each part, so probably best if we separate. I would suggest Merryn and Broc go together, one archer, one swordsman, to the north side. Connor and I will take the south end because you young ones will travel faster than we will. Simmy and Artan, you take the eastern end. Meet back here in three hours, and if we've had no luck, we'll all go through the western end, which is the most populated. I do think Kelvan is likely to be on the eastern part. He'll stay away from the populated areas and stick to somewhere with a nearby escape route. Close to the sea, I would wager. Be alert, Simmy."

Once on the southern shore, the three groups separated, and Merryn didn't mind one bit that Broc took her hand as they headed out. Thane had explained the best route to take as they moved toward the only path heading straight across to the northern shore. He was certain there would be a line of cottages along the way.

"Are you unsettled, lass?"

"A wee bit. I'll admit it. If I see Kelvan, I fear I won't be wise about it, and I'll react with emotion. Will you help me?"

He kissed her cheek. "I will gladly help you with that. I'm going to remain as calm as I can because I will constantly remind myself that my mother's life is at stake, along with the lives of four innocent bairns. I pray they have not been hurt."

"Everyone now believes that Lia is a faery, so will she not protect the others?"

"I believe she will. She's promised to protect Magni forever, and now she has dedicated herself to protecting Shealee, so I believe she'll save her from harm too. The bairns have been taken twice, and none were hurt yet. I believe Lia has protected them thus far, and I hope it continues. Tora is mysterious in her own way. Magni says that she scares the others because she knows things she shouldn't. They think of her as a witch, not a seer."

They moved along, coming to a group of cottages.

"How do we do this, Broc?" She had no idea how to approach. One did not just walk into a stranger's cottage, but she also did not wish to warn them by knocking on the doors.

"Let's ask. Uncle Connor said that was how they learned of their location on Coll. The local villagers told them where the villains were."

As they approached the hamlet, two men sat on a log near the local well, chatting and chuckling. "May we have a drink?" Broc asked.

"Aye. Where are you headed?" One man was clearly much older than the other, gray-haired with the thick, weathered skin of a fisherman. He let the younger man speak while his eyes assessed the situation.

"We're looking for four bairns. Know you where a new group of visitors might be held?"

The two men glanced at each other, then peered over their shoulders, as if making sure they were not being watched. Merryn squeezed Broc's hand with excitement. Perhaps they were about to find the group.

The younger man looked to the elder, who nodded. "Farther ahead and closer to the coast, there's a cottage where there have been some strange circumstances as of late. My brother said he heard crying coming from it when he returned from fishing, as if there were bairns inside. It was previously unoccupied. It stands alone, so no one would know who it belonged to. You could try there."

"Which way?" There was a fork in the path ahead of them, so the younger man pointed.

"Take the path on the right straight to the shore. You'll be there in half the hour."

Broc said, "We have friends who might follow us in a while. Please point them in this direction if we don't return."

"Sure will."

The older man, who'd mostly remained silent, cleared his throat before he spoke. "Godspeed with you. I don't like men who bother bairns and lasses. They have no honor. Remember that, lad, when you stare the evil ones in the eye."

A chill ran down Merryn's spine at the look on the man's face, his words worse than his expression. What were they going to find ahead? She'd known Kelvan for three years. He'd not been terribly kind to Nara, spending more time away from her than with her, but he'd appeared to love Shealee.

When he was around.

What kind of operation was he running? How had he become involved with the others? And what were his plans with the bairns? Selling them to anyone struck her as one of the cruelest choices possible.

But Kelvan had always put his needs ahead of others. Even at meals, he filled his plate first. Now that Merryn knew his true character, she recalled different moments that should have warned them all of what was coming.

How Nara kept her head bowed whenever he was around.

How she had to remove Shealee from the chamber if she cried around Kelvan.

How she had to change her raggies outside.

How Kelvan only spoke to other men. That was part of the reason that she'd never formed much of an opinion of him. He was rarely around, and if he was, he never spoke to Merryn or her mother.

Only their father.

"Broc, do you think a woman is as wise as a man?"

He arched a brow at her. "That would depend on which woman and which man. I've known many women who were wiser than most men. And some who are more intelligent than nearly all men."

"Who do you consider the wisest?"

He shrugged. "I can think of a few, but the one you are most familiar with would be Dyna. She could outsmart all her cousins when she was three summers old. Our grandfather always came to her when the lads were in trouble. She could always outthink them."

"Because she was a seer?"

"Nay. Being a seer helped in many cases, but she was smarter than all of them."

"Which three?"

"Alasdair, Elshander, and Alick. Alasdair became much wiser as he grew, but Dyna was given the lairdship of Clan Grantham for a reason. She's a verra wise woman."

"Any others I know?"

"Logan would tell you that Gwyneth was the smartest of all. They were spies and she could always outthink the enemy. And my father always said Mama was the smartest in our small family."

Merryn peered up at Broc, at his chiseled jawline, and he smiled at her, his blue eyes the finest shade she'd ever seen. They sparkled when she was close, something she preferred to believe happened just for her. His answer was perfect, and her father had thought the same about her mother. It was a matter of effort, skill, and hard work.

Not like Kelvan who believed all men were superior to any woman.

As they came around a bend of trees, a cottage came into view. Broc stopped to listen, scanned the area, then whispered, "This is an isolated cottage. It could be the right one. It's still a distance from the shore."

They checked the area, not seeing anything but a path that continued toward the shoreline. Since they were on land that sat much higher than the coast, they could look clearly down the path to the sea. Multiple boats sat tied up, but Broc had no way of knowing who they belonged to.

Merryn glanced around, checking off a list in her mind: no other cottages, no men about, and no horses. There was a small forest behind the cottage that could hide a few men, but she wasn't about to go search the wooded area.

Broc nodded to her, handing her a dagger while he unsheathed his sword. He tried the door, but it was locked. Pointing over his head, a key rested on a nail right next to them. He grabbed it and forced the key into the lock, wiggling it a bit to get it to fit, but then stood back, standing off to the side and throwing the door open in case anyone was ready to come at them.

Inside was the main part of the hut with a hearth at the far end and a door in the back, but no one was there. A sound carried to them from down a short passageway. "There, Broc," she whispered. They headed that way, found another key, and unlocked the door.

Merryn peered inside, shocked to see the bairns huddled around Kyla on a bed in the farthest corner.

"Mama?"

"Broc? Is that you?"

Shealee came across the chamber, her wee legs struggling to stay steady. "Mama!"

Merryn nearly sobbed at the sight of the lass. She stepped inside and picked her up as Broc came along behind her.

"Hurry, get them out of there," he whispered. "I hear men." He headed back to the main chamber.

She rushed toward the door, the other four behind her while Broc drew his weapon. They made it to the middle of the main chamber when the worst happened.

The back door opened, and three men came in. And they were fighting mad.

CHAPTER TWENTY-SEVEN

Broc

BROC PICKED UP Tora and handed her to Merryn who already held Shealee. "Run. Just run back to the hamlet with these two and I'll find you." His mother hadn't come out yet with Magni and Lia. He couldn't protect six people.

So, Merryn raced out the door with the two bairns in her arms.

Broc asked, "Mama, you are hale?"

The men blocked both doors, arranging themselves in a way they thought to achieve an advantage, but they were wrong. Broc reminded himself that these were men, not boars. He could predict how they would move, and if he did it wisely, he could beat them. He was taught how to do so by men wiser than him.

"Aye, we are all fine. Worry about the two other bairns. I can handle this. Come back for me with more guards, Broc."

"I'm not leaving you, Mama." He swung his sword at the man closest to the front door, knocking it out of his hands. That left two in the back of the chamber. "Magni, run!"

"Lia, come!" Magni shouted, grabbing her hand, but she shook her head.

"Nay, I must stay, Magni. You go."

"Not without you, sister!"

The two men came at Broc, one with a sword and the other with a small dagger. His insides dropped to his toes, the fear of being impaled on a sword slowing his reaction for a moment, but then he swung his weapon in a wide arc. He caught one of the men in the flank with the side of his sword and knocked him over. Broc struck the second man's arm, and he bellowed, grabbing his bleeding extremity and running out the door.

Kyla grabbed the first one by the hair and spun him around to kick him between his legs, dropping him to the floor instantly. Broc manipulated his sword toward the one whom he'd knocked down, now back on his feet and coming at him. He waited until he was nearly upon him, then thrust his weapon into the man's middle. Broc pulled his sword out and stared at the man, knowing he was dead.

There was so much yelling and screaming that Broc wasn't sure what was happening, but he had to save his mother. Someone banged on the back door, yanking on it. He prayed Merryn got away. He turned as the one who took the hit to his bollocks stood up, grabbing his paltry sword, a foolish mistake.

Merryn opened the front door and said, "Hurry, Broc. More are coming down the path."

"Go, Merryn! Run." He impaled the third man on his blade and that fool fell to the floor. The back door opened, and Kelvan stood there.

Shocked to see his face again, Broc turned back to fight him, but three men all pushed around him, bellowing.

Kelvan shouted, "Get the woman and the faery. Let the wee ones go." Then he yanked on Broc's mother's hair and dragged her out while two others came at him. "Kill him!"

"Broc, leave! I'll be fine!"

One man grabbed Lia, and the other one took Magni, pulling him back while he screamed.

Three left and Broc faced one man, taking him down quickly. He headed out the front door because he had to see where Merryn was. She was running in the opposite direction, away from the shoreline, while Kelvan and his group headed toward the shore and the ships.

Broc stood in the path, having to make the decision of which way to go. "Merryn, run for Connor. Don't wait for me!"

Kelvan said, "I'm coming for you, Merryn!" Then he whirled and raced straight for them while he shoved Kyla and the bairns toward the boat, the two men grabbing and tugging the group behind them.

But Kelvan didn't stop.

Merryn set the bairns down and pulled out her bow and one arrow, nocking fast, but Broc went after him, staying off to the side to give her free range to take the shot. She fired and caught Kelvan in the leg.

"You bitch!" Kelvan dropped his weapon and grabbed his leg, trying to yank the arrow out of his bleeding flesh. "I'll kill you, Merryn! Just like I did to your sister."

Broc was nearly upon him, but the bastard spun around and headed in the other direction. Broc followed, but then two arrows came at him from someone at the perimeter.

"Broc, go!" His mother's voice carried to him. "Too many archers. Save those bairns!"

"Broc!" Merryn's voice caught him, so he turned around. He couldn't fight five men by himself. They had two bairns to save. He raced after Merryn who had set Tora down. "I can't carry Tora. Help me, please!"

So, he did what he thought was best and sheathed his weapon, grabbing the crying bairn up into his arms. "I've got you, Tora. Grandda is not far."

"Gwandda coming. I saw him. I want Gwandda."

"We'll find him."

Broc glanced over his shoulder to make sure they were not being followed. His heart sank watching his mother, Lia, and Magni leaving the coast on Kelvan's ship. He couldn't catch them if he wished. He had no boat.

Broc and Merryn ran for a short while until they were at the well, the two villagers still there, one filling a cup with water and holding it out. Merryn said, "Broc, I have to stop."

He nodded. "They're gone."

They stopped and Merryn hugged Shealee so

tight she squirmed against her, but the wee lass cupped her cheeks and kissed her. "Mama."

"Tora, you are hale?" Broc asked, setting her down for a moment.

"Aye, but I want Mama."

A whistle rent the air, and Broc turned to see Connor coming toward them. "I had this feeling." He raced down the path, stopping to hold out his arms to Tora.

"Gwanda!" She launched herself into his arms and rested her head on his shoulder.

"The other three? Where are they? Kyla?"

Broc shook his head. "I couldn't fight them all. Eight total. Two archers. They ran to a ship. We're too late."

Tora said, "They on the boat now. Going to the castle."

Broc took the refilled cup after the others had finished and drank it down. "Hellfire, I failed my own mother." He closed his eyes, handed the cup back, and bent over, his hands on his knees, wondering what the hell he would tell his father.

Connor nodded. "You saved two. You brought the most vulnerable out of their clutches. Great job, both of you. Let's get them home. Lia and Kyla will keep the three of them safe until we get there."

Broc tugged at his hair, groaning because he wished to scream over his failure.

"Broc, I know my sister. If you had her here and any of the bairns were still in Kelvan's clutches, she'd be chastising you for the rest of the day.

Think you she would want to be saved ahead of the bairns? Truly?"

Broc had to chuckle at that image. "Nay, you are correct, Uncle. My thanks for that picture of my mother yelling at me."

The older man spoke, his voice cracking, "How many did you kill, lad? By the look of your sword, you took care of more than one." He clasped Broc's arm and said, "Give me your weapon. I'll clean it for you."

Broc took it out and handed it to the man, appreciating his kind gesture.

Merryn rubbed his back. "He killed three, but then four came in behind us. He took care of one of them, but the other three forced the captives out the door. We had to go. Kyla told us to leave and return with more forces."

Connor sighed. "My sister is a wise one. Always thinking of others first. You did the right thing. Did you recognize any?"

Merryn said, "Aye. Kelvan said he was going to kill me, so I hit him in the leg with my arrow. I was hoping for his black heart, but I missed."

"You hit him, Merryn, and stopped him in his tracks. That was a fabulous shot under the conditions," Broc said.

He retrieved his weapon, thanking the thoughtful man who said, "Nay, we owe you, young man. Our thanks for ridding us of the scum. May they never return to Tiree."

They met up with the other three and climbed back into the boat before Broc collapsed. Thane came over and handed him a hunk of dried meat.

"Eat. You'll feel better. You did a fine job. Two of you saved two. Those numbers are great. Be proud of yourselves."

Broc had to admit he didn't feel like he should be proud of himself, though the look on Merryn's face convinced him they did the right thing. Shealee was back in her arms again, exactly where she belonged.

That and the scream that carried to them from the shore in front of MacQuarie Castle also convinced him they'd done something right.

Dyna stood on the shore and caught sight of Tora, her wail filling the air. Once they climbed off the ship, Dyna grabbed her daughter and asked, "Who do I thank?"

Simone said, "Broc and Merryn. They saved two. The others got away and are headed to Mingary. We split up, so those two fought against eight. If we had stayed together, we might have been able to save them all, but we separated, hoping to cover more ground."

Dyna hugged Broc and sobbed.

Tora patted his shoulder while she held on to her mother.

The pat on his shoulder was worth everything.

CHAPTER TWENTY-EIGHT

Glenna

KELVAN STRODE INSIDE the castle and went up the stairs to his wife's chamber.

"How did it go? Did you bring Shealee back with you?"

"Nay," he barked, hating to admit the truth to anyone, but she deserved to know what had happened. "That Merryn turned her against me. Shealee used to love me, but she pushed me away. Started crying. Saying, 'Mama, Mama.' I don't want anything to do with her. I want Merryn. I need to teach her a lesson. How dare she turn my own daughter away from me."

Glenna's head fell back against the pillow.

"You don't feel any better? What did the healer do?"

"Changed the bandage. Gave me a potion so I can't feel the pain. I'm sleepy."

"We were attacked. Merryn was there with the fool who was here with Logan, the one who cut off your hand. They stole two of the bairns away."

"Why didn't your men kill them? Or bring him back to me? Leave Merryn alone."

"Because there were only three watching them, and he killed two before I got there. And the third one was nearly dead. I didn't care. They stole Shealee and the one who is the witch. I don't want her around, anyway. She knows too much." He leaned toward Glenna. "Do you know what that one wee witch did? She started my tunic on fire. I have a burn on my shoulder. I sent her back. We still have Kyla and the faery and the one lad."

"So that's enough to do what you want. Have you decided exactly what your new plans are?"

"Aye. I'll trade the lad for the one with the sapphire sword. I want that sword. I want to be the most powerful in all the land." If what Samuel said was true, then no one could hurt him if he had the sapphire sword. He'd surely conquer all if the legend proved to be true.

Kelvan paced back and forth, and Glenna could see how upset he was. He was so stupid and vain sometimes. He didn't care at all about what happened to her.

"Kelvan, you need to find out if Logan Ramsay lived or died. I will only be happy when I know I've hurt them the way they hurt my clan. My grandfather and my two uncles died because of Clan Ramsay, and that bitch Kyla caused the worst of it. Have you found out who did this to me?"

He stopped to stare at her. "What? I know you hate the Ramsays, but you already paid them back. You struck down their elder. I'm sure he's dead by now. What else do you expect me to do?"

"I want you to bring me the guard who cut off my hand. I want to cut off his arm. It's only fair. Did you find out his name? Is he a Ramsay?"

"I don't know his name. But I know how I can find out."

"Then do it. If you want my jewels, you better do this for me. Then you can get your ridiculous blue sword."

She fell back on the bed and rolled away from him. He was nearly as foolish as her first husband.

If Kelvan wasn't careful, if he wasn't smart enough to do what she asked, then he'd find out what could happen if he made her angry.

Just as her dead husband had.

CHAPTER TWENTY-NINE

Logan

L OGAN WAS SITTING by the hearth when the group arrived back from Tiree. They'd all been on edge waiting for word on the five missing people. Finlay spent his time fishing, and he managed to get enough of a haul for a fine fish stew.

The others had various ways to pass the time and ease their worry—sewing, archery, working in the lists.

His granddaughter Eli, now carrying her first child, spent most of her time eating. "Eli, if you eat any more fruit tarts, you may turn into one."

She stopped what she was doing, got up from the table, and strode over to stand in front of him. Logan had to control the smile that threatened to break out on his face. Gwynie must have noticed because she whispered, "Logan!"

Then his wife said, "Now, Eli. He's not feeling well. His wound still pains him."

But then Eli spun around to cast a glare at Gwynie. Logan nearly split a gut. It was a good thing he had to keep it inside, or he surely would rip his stitches all out at once.

His beloved granddaughter turned back to him and said, "I should feel bad for you because you had your belly sliced, but right now, I don't. Because you show no sympathy for someone who is about to have her belly swell to five times its size, then will have to carry it around without breaking her back and finally will have to have her female parts split in two just to let the wee creature out. I'm also told I'll bleed half of my life's blood all over and that I'll have to bear more pain than anything else but death could do to me." Then she put her face down even to his and said, "Have you something else to say to me, Grandfather?"

He arched a brow and said, "Not a word. Have another fruit tart, my sweet. If I could get up easily to find one for you, I surely would."

Brenna came along and put her arm around Eli and said, "Do not listen to all the horror stories, lass. And when you hold your wee daughter in your arms, you'll forget about that pain."

"Until I have to do it again. I told Alaric he better do all the coupling with me he wants because he'll never plant his seed inside me again after I deliver this bairn."

Logan choked on the ale he'd just sipped. When he got his breath back, he looked at his wife and said, "She takes after you, Gwynie."

Fortunately, the door opened, and a large group spilled inside, bringing everyone into the hall with them. Tora ran over to her sire, who'd just come down the stairs. "Papa, I'm back."

Sylvi and Sandor ran toward her, Sandor shouting, "Dora, Dora!"

Tristan followed them in from the lists where he'd been working, his eyes lighting up when he saw Merryn and Shealee. "Oh, thank the Lord above."

"There's two," Gwynie whispered. "Kyla? Lia? Magni? Logan, do you see the other three?"

Logan searched for the three but shook his head. "Nay, they're quiet, Gwynie. They look like they've been through hell. Broc is covered in blood and Connor is a mess."

Connor stepped inside, Broc behind him, and both faces told him all he needed to know. Kyla wasn't with them. Finlay had his arm across Broc's shoulders, clasping it as he spoke quietly to his son. "Your mother is strong. Fear not. And Lia will take care of Magni. We'll get her, Broc. Sit. You look like hell. I'll find you something to eat."

Connor came over and took the chair next to Logan while Simone took one opposite her father. Hugging him lightly, then her mother, she whispered, "You should have called me sooner, Da."

"I'm glad you came, Simone. We do need you, but you must not have been with Broc and Merryn."

"Nay, I wasn't," she said. "We split up on Tiree. Merryn and Broc found Kyla and the bairns in a hut together. Broc sent Merryn out with the two youngest, then took on three men before another handful arrived. While Broc fought, the others took the three to the ship. Merryn managed to hit Kelvan in the leg with an arrow, but otherwise, they got away. Four of his men dead, not sure how many survived. Tora said they're going to Mingary. But they said all three were hale. Kyla told him to take the bairns and leave her behind."

"Aye, 'tis true." Connor sighed. "But that would be my sister. Worrying about the bairns before herself. Broc had a hell of a fight. I wish we had been with them, but Tiree is larger than we thought." Connor took out a linen square and wiped the sweat from his face. "So we have to decide our next step. Think on it, Logan, while we eat. We need a brief respite. Dyna's had enough to deal with. I'm glad Dyna came to MacQuarie Castle. Tora never let go of me until she caught sight of her mother."

Logan said, "She has."

Simone said, "Look, Da, Artan and I have plenty of fight left in us. We're going to eat, then plan our next attack. We can go tonight if you wish. I'm not waiting long to get those bastards."

Logan said, "I knew we could count on you, Simone. We have four things we need to accomplish."

Simone said, "I know three of them. Kill Glenna, torture Kelvan, and save the three they still hold. What's the fourth?"

Logan said, "Find Magni's parents. I think Kelvan is holding them somewhere."

Connor let out a low whistle. "We promised the lad we would find out what happened to them."

"Are you sure they are alive?" Simone asked.

"Nay, but my gut says they are. Find them, Simone. A lad is counting on us." Logan got up and said, "I'm going to take a short rest. You all eat your meal. The mean one only gives me broth with vegetables, so I'll eat inside. I'll be out later to see what you've decided, Connor. Daughter, make me happy after this is all done."

Simone caught up with him and kissed his cheek. "You can count on it, Da."

CHAPTER THIRTY

Merryn

A FTER THEY ATE a hearty meal, Merryn set her niece down near the other bairns playing in front of the hearth. Sylvi reached her quickly, and Merryn was pleased. After all the wee lass had been through, she was glad to see she could step away and play with the others.

"Come play with us, Shealee." Sylvi took her by the hand and led her over to the spot where the wee ones played pretend. Sylvi was like a mother to Shealee.

Merryn smiled at their creativity. Sandor had a small wooden sword he could swing nearly in the same rhythm as a warrior. Tora had pretend fabric animals and was playing healer with all of them, setting them on beds before she fixed them.

Gwyneth noticed her husband returning to the hall. "Logan, I think your face should be on all the animals. They're fixing you like Brenna did."

Logan drawled, "If any of them try to pinch a nipple on the animals, I'll know they were peeking in the door."

Merryn's eyes widened, but she said nothing.

Brenna was crossing the hall, so she made a quick adjustment and swerved in next to Logan, swatting his shoulder playfully. She leaned down and whispered, "I'll do it again if you don't behave around the bairns."

Logan scowled and crossed his arms, hiding his chest. "Nay, you will not. That hurt like hell, though I'm certain you knew it would. You have a mean streak in you, Brenna Grant."

"I heard you call me mean before. The truth of it is you are glad to have some peace to consume your broth slowly. You cannot fool me, Logan."

Logan snorted, giving her a side-eye. "You are a bit witchy sometimes, Brenna."

"It's My Lady Ramsay to you." She chuckled and headed into the healer's chamber.

Logan called out, "Is it not time for you to go home, Brenna?"

"Not until this issue is settled! I'm here to help Eli when the wounded come in."

He grumbled a bit, but then Gwyneth said, "She needs to stay, and you know it."

He sighed. "She does, I fear."

"In the solar, group," Connor said, nodding to Logan. "Sela and Astra will watch the bairns."

Broc took Merryn's hand and led her into the chamber off the hall.

She whispered, "Are you sure I should be here?"

"Aye, because I know you," he whispered back, kissing her cheek. "You'll follow me. You need to know exactly what we're fighting."

She couldn't argue that fact. If she had to sneak

out on her own, she'd go to Mingary Castle with Simmy to help her kill that evil man. Seeing him had set the fire in her veins into a rage unlike previous. They had to put an end to him. Poor Magni had the most fearful look on his face. Even Kyla had been upset.

Only Lia had acted like nothing unusual was taking place.

But Merryn would prefer to go with Broc, so she was anxious to see what they'd decided their next step would be.

Broc found her a seat toward the back of the solar, then leaned against the wall next to her while the others entered. Simone, Artan, Thane, Logan, and Alaric, who carried Gwyneth in and set her on a chair near Merryn, Alasdair, John, Maitland, Dyna, and Derric all squeezed into the chamber. Tristan stuck his head in, and they waved him inside, so he stood against the wall.

Dyna moved to the back of the chamber. "Maitland, you can run this with my sire. I'm too emotional." She leaned into Derric, who wrapped his arms around her and held her close.

Maitland agreed. "You need to stay back with Eli and Maeve. We need archers on the wall."

Once they were settled, Connor stood in front. "I sent a messenger back to tell Alick to send two hundred warriors to wait for us outside of Ardnamurchan. We will end up there, of that much I'm certain. Broc and Merryn both saw the group get into a large galley ship, one that could travel the distance to Mingary Castle. They were not heading to Coll in a ship that size. So we will assume that the group is holding the captives in the castle. Agreed?"

Alasdair said, "I don't think you should make an assumption like that. I suggest a patrol to determine exactly where they are. Also to see if they have another holding close to the castle. You cannot assume they are there."

"We can consider that. Anyone else have a suggestion?"

Simone looked at Artan, and he gave her a subtle nod. "Glenna was married to Artan's brother. She had him killed, but we have not spoken to her since. She has no knowledge of me, and we were not seen on Tiree, so I suggest we go inside the castle, greet Glenna, and see what we can learn."

Merryn watched as that suggestion set everyone's minds churning. She glanced up at Broc, wondering what he thought of it, but he smiled and winked at her.

Logan said, "Crafty, Simone. I think you can do it. How will you approach her?"

"I have a couple of thoughts, but what if we promise to find the one who cut off her hand?"

That created a buzz in the room, and Broc turned his attention to the group. "You want to take me to her?"

Merryn watched this man who had stolen her heart so quickly, the suggestion at first not something he was interested in doing. She could see the fear cross him, even watched as his hand reached up to rub his scar, but then he smiled. "I like the idea. Bring me right to her, and I'll cut off the other hand."

Logan snorted. "The bitch stabbed me. She's going to get more than that, Broc. The question is who will exact the revenge. I need to know it's done right."

"I'll do it," Simone offered.

Logan scratched his beard, then said, "I trust you'll do it right, daughter. It has to be either you or Kyla."

Connor added, "I want Kelvan."

Tristan said, "He killed our sister and our parents. I'd like rights too."

Dyna said, "If I were going, I'd demand rights."

Connor finally nodded and said, "Tristan, I'll honor your rights if you are there. We'll see who gets to him first."

"Fair enough."

Connor thought for a moment, then said, "Alasdair, take a patrol of ten from MacVey's land to the mainland at dawn. See what you can uncover. Simone, you and Artan go to the castle from Rankin's and spy on the fools. I don't care when you go, just be quick about it. I'll have our guards in place in case of an attack."

Dyna stood up and said, "Please find Kelvan and end this. I cannot handle my bairns being stolen again. Fortunately, Tora is strong because of her seer's ability. Who knows how many nightmares all the bairns will have for many moons to come. Get the bastard!"

Logan said, "And Glenna too."

"Leave on the morrow. First light," Connor announced.

Sela knocked on the door and stuck her head

inside. "Meat pies, fruit tarts, and baked apples are ready. Let's relax for a wee bit. Have some wine. Rejoice in the two we have back with us."

The group made their way out, settling at the tables while the serving lasses brought out the platters for everyone.

Merryn sat with Tristan and Broc, her gaze locking on Shealee as the lass laughed with Tora and Sandor. "They're so happy."

Maeve joined them and the group chattered all through the meal. The bairns ate quickly, but then they became restless.

Brenna whispered, "Signs of all they've been through. I'll get them playing a game of hide in the corner. John, will you and Ailith help me?"

Coira jumped up. "Me too!"

Merryn leaned over to whisper to Broc. "Who does that lass belong to? Her golden hair is so pretty, and she is a bit reserved compared to the others."

Broc explained, "Coira was adopted by Alasdair and Emmalin when she was just a toddler. John is four and ten while the lasses are three and ten. She and John have been as close as any two young ones could be ever since. Emmalin thinks they'll marry someday. They look like opposites. John looks like Alasdair and Uncle Connor, while Coira is looking more and more like my grandmama. Her hair turns more golden each year."

The bairns all gathered in the center while Brenna explained the rules. Maitland held Grant on his lap, but he wiggled and giggled, wanting to participate. Maeve said, "I'll hold him so he can watch, Maitland. He's restless too."

The game went on for a bit, the wee ones hiding in the easy spots. The night nearly finished, John said to the bairns, "I'm hiding, and it will be a difficult place, one you'll never think of. You have to close your eyes."

John climbed the stairs to one of the chambers, though Merryn had no idea where.

As soon as John disappeared, Grant stirred, kicking and whining. "What's wrong, Grant?" Maeve readjusted his outfit that had nearly become undone. But that didn't appease him.

Merryn said, "He wants John."

Maitland said, "What?"

"He has watched John's every move. He adores him, and John went abovestairs."

Maitland said, "I'll take him, Maeve. We'll test this idea of yours, Merryn."

"He watched him climb the staircase. He'll wish to do the same." Merryn looked to Broc, who nodded in agreement.

"I think she's right. Walk away from the stairs, then walk toward them, Maitland."

Maitland did as Broc suggested and walked away from the steps, but Grant fussed, his hand reaching for the banister. When Maitland turned around, Grant kicked and giggled. "Wia."

Wia was the only word he'd voiced yet, and they all thought it meant Lia, but did it?

Broc got up and said to the wee ones, "We're going to let Grant find John. Would you all please sit for a minute?"

Brenna came out of the kitchens and called to the bairns, "Come finish your baked apples with honey."

The bairns all ran to her side, but Grant was not interested in that at all.

He wanted to go up the stairs.

By now, everyone in the hall had their eyes on Grant and his interest in John.

A voice called out, "Come find me, Grant."

Grant kicked again, nearly jumping out of Maitland's arms. So they headed for the staircase. "Stay hidden, John," Emmalin called out.

Maitland went up and headed in the wrong direction.

Grant squealed.

Maitland turned around.

Grant giggled.

Maitland went in the wrong chamber.

Grant screamed, crying this time.

Maitland came out of the chamber.

Grant smiled.

Then Maitland stopped to test him. "Which way, Grant?"

Grant's arm shot out as if he were reaching for something, so Maitland went that way.

Maeve said, "Oh my word. He is special. Dyna? Avelina? What is this? I don't understand. He knows where John is. How could he possibly know that?"

Avelina came up behind Maeve and squeezed her shoulders. "I don't know either, but he definitely has a special skill for finding someone."

Dyna tipped her head, pacing as she watched.

"Or is it a special tie to John? I think it's just John."

Grant found John, so the lad took the bairn into his arms and carried him down the stairs. Maitland leaned over the balcony railing and shrugged his shoulders. "What do we do with this, Maeve?"

Avelina said, "You love him. That's all you need to do. Love him with all your soul."

CHAPTER THIRTY-ONE

Magni

〰️

"HOW ARE WE going to get away?" Magni asked, leaning against Kyla after they'd been deposited in a chamber in a castle.

Lia said, "Fear not. They will come for us."

"But they already did, and they left us behind."

Kyla said, "Broc and Merryn took the two bairns first. You know that was the right thing to do. Broc fought four men off. He couldn't handle eight."

Magni jumped up from the bed, grabbing his imaginary sword and swinging it wildly. "If I had one, I would have killed Kelvan first. Then I'd go for Samuel and the other two."

"And remember, Magni. Broc told you to run. You could have gone with them." Lia sat on the bed and straightened her green skirt out, fluffing it just so.

"I know, but I couldn't leave you, Lia."

"Magni, you will promise me that if it happens again, you will run and leave me behind. You know I can handle myself."

Magni slumped into a chair. "But you said you

will always protect me. And you are my sister, Lia. I don't have anyone except you. I lost Mama and Papa, so I'm all alone."

"Magni, you have a grandsire, do you not?"

"He's adopted." Then Magni burst into tears. "And what if Grandpapa Logan dies? He got stabbed." Then he picked up his imaginary sword again and said, "I'd like to see that bitch who stabbed my grandsire. Lia, we have to find him."

"And you have Thane and Tamsin. Mora and Brian love you. We'll make it through if we do as they say."

The door opened and in came a woman. She was ugly and mean-looking. Magni didn't like her one bit. And she wore a gown with gemstones dangling from it. It had long sleeves and she swung one at him.

"What do you think of this, laddie?"

She swung her arm until the sleeve fell back, revealing the stub she had from the injury Broc gave her, still scabbed over.

Magni screamed.

"Who did this to me?" she asked, sticking her face into his.

"I didn't!"

"I know you didn't. But you know his name. Tell me who did it." She leaned down closer, and he could see she was missing two teeth on one side when she smiled. Magni frowned because he didn't like her at all.

"I don't know."

She swung her arm again, and the stub landed on his shoulder.

Magni screamed again and ran into Kyla's arms. Glenna was about to follow him, but Lia stepped in front of the mean woman, nearly tripping her.

"Little girl, stay away."

"Leave him be."

"Get out of my way." Then she tried to toss her stub onto Lia's shoulder, but the lass sidestepped her, and Glenna almost toppled forward.

"Glenna, you should stop bothering him. Look what your mean streak gained you already. If you weren't riddled with vengeance, you wouldn't have lost your hand to a sword. You struck first, or have you forgotten?" Lia stood with her hands folded in front of her.

"Who are you? Who told you all that?"

Kyla yelled, "Leave the bairns alone, Glenna. You want me, do you not? Well, here I am."

Glenna whirled to face Kyla. "There she is. The queen of Clan Grant. The one who had to come and butt into my grandsire's affairs. All because of you, he died at the hand of your sire."

"Nay. If your father hadn't had me beaten, my sire wouldn't have killed him. It was the cruelty at the hands of your grandsire and his men that caused everything. Don't be like them." Kyla hugged Magni tight against her.

"I don't like you," Magni said to Glenna.

"I hate all of you. I'll see you all dead before this is over, but not until I find out who wounded me. Who was he? I want his name."

"I don't know," Magni cried. "I wasn't here."

"It was my son, Glenna. And I'm glad he hurt

you after you stabbed an old man from behind. Are you proud of that?"

Glenna threw her head back in gales of laughter. Then she stopped suddenly and stuck her face in front of Magni's. "Aye. I'm proud of it. And I'll be even prouder when I finish off your clan."

She whirled and left, slamming the door behind her. They heard her voice down the hall.

"Kelvan, get them out of here before their friends come. Hide them in the secret holding."

Magni said, "We're leaving again?"

Lia said, "Never fear. It's for the best. You'll see."

Kyla said, "What does that mean, Lia?"

"It means the end of this nightmare is almost here. Magni, soon you will go home, and you'll never feel like you don't have a family again."

Magni frowned, trying to understand what she meant, but he didn't get to ask. They were taken out and tossed into a large cart.

He looked at his sister and said, "Here we go again, Lia."

CHAPTER THIRTY-TWO

Broc

B ROC TOOK MERRYN'S hand as they strode outside the gates around the castle and down toward the sea. "There's a beautiful spot where you can see the water in three directions."

Merryn had gotten Shealee down for her nap and as soon as she entered the hall, Broc had been waiting for her. He'd hoped to get her alone for a wee bit.

He found a spot covered in leaves and motioned for Merryn to sit. Once she was settled, he sat down next to her, wrapping his arm around her to warm her. "The morrow could be a big day. It could be the end of our troubles."

"Or the beginning of more troubles. But I hope you are right."

"Alasdair and John's patrol leave for MacVey's and the mainland. Simone and Artan leave for Mingary Castle. I hope they can uncover exactly where my mother and the two bairns are located."

"I hope you're right."

"I hope so too. Do you know why?"

"Besides the obvious? Getting your mother and the bairns home?"

"Aye. I'd like to have some calm over Duart Castle so I can explore the lass who is sitting next to me." He lifted the back of her hand to his lips and kissed it. "I feel we rarely have any time alone."

"I know. But …"

"What?" He had no idea what she was about to say.

"I was alone for nearly the last year. I had my brother and Shealee, but it was me and the men. Euna and Olivia came along, but Euna is much older. Does it make me sound selfish if I say I enjoy being here and making new friends with lasses? I love watching Shealee make friends. She adores them all. And I've so enjoyed learning how to read with you, how to shoot arrows with Eli and Dyna, how to cook fruit tarts … I've learned so much watching all the people here in Clan Grantham. It's quite a mixture, and you've been here such a short time. You've all accomplished much together."

"We have. I do love my clan and our allies. And we have new ones here on Mull. MacVeys, Rankins, MacQuaries."

"Is it always like this?"

"Like what?"

"Is there always some battle going on? Is it ever quiet?"

He chuckled, squeezing her hand. "Quiet? Nay. There are many times when there is no battle to fight. But we train hard."

"I want this to end, but I don't want it to … I feel bad even speaking my mind. But the thought of returning to build our castle with a few men where we are open to attack doesn't suit me well either. It was too quiet and unsafe." Then she ran her finger down his jawline and across his lower lip. "And I'll miss you so much."

Broc could see the misting in her eyes. "We don't have to go our separate ways. What if …"

"What?" she asked.

"What if we married? We could be together forever." He noticed the shock in her face and nearly jumped up. "I'm sorry. That was the wrong thing to say. It's too soon, is it not?"

"Nay. Don't leave me now. I liked what you said." She pulled him close and lay back in the leaves. Broc lay carefully next to her, propping his weight on his elbows.

He cupped her face, his thumb brushing her lower lip. "Merryn, you are so beautiful. I shouldn't have said anything like that. It's not the proper way to propose to someone."

"What is the proper way?" she asked as she reached for him, pulling him closer.

He settled himself over her and whispered, "The proper way is to ask you. Will you marry me, Merryn MacClane? Make me the happiest man on Mull?" His heartbeat sped up, but only because he had the sudden fear that she would turn him down. He loved her for seeing him for who he was, faults and all. But lasses wanted heroes, and he had no idea how to become one.

"Aye, Broc MacNicol. I would love to be your

wife. Spend our lives together building a new one. Having bairns and getting to know your clan."

Broc was so pleased with her answer that he thought his heart would pound through his chest. He leaned down, his lips descending on hers, and he lost all sense of restraint. He kissed her hard, his tongue teasing hers as he angled his mouth, deepening the kiss. Her hands wrapped around his neck, caressing his skin in a slow tease that he found oddly tantalizing.

She wanted him, and she didn't care that he was scarred. But he had to know one more thing. He sat up and said, "Merryn, I have to show you something."

She pushed herself up on her elbows. "What?"

"I have to know your thoughts. It would not be fair if I did not … Well, I'll just show you."

He lifted his tunic enough to show her the angry welt he still carried on his torso. It sat on one side, but he couldn't bear to have her look at it in disgust on their wedding night. If she was going to be repulsed, he had to know now. He watched her expression as she looked at it, waiting for her face to change to revulsion.

Except she didn't.

Her fingers touched him, the tenderest touch he'd ever felt, and she stared up at him. "Broc, this doesn't bother me. In fact, it's part of what has made you who you are. And I love you just the way you are." Then she bent down and kissed the middle of the scar.

He'd finally found the one for him.

"I love you too, Merryn."

CHAPTER THIRTY-THREE

Simone

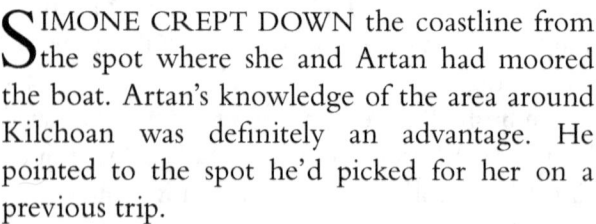

SIMONE CREPT DOWN the coastline from the spot where she and Artan had moored the boat. Artan's knowledge of the area around Kilchoan was definitely an advantage. He pointed to the spot he'd picked for her on a previous trip.

"Through there. They'll never see your approach. The wall crumbled a bit, and I found a hole large enough for you to climb through. I'm going inside to distract Glenna. See if I can calm her down or learn exactly where Kyla is. It will be a quick visit. I'll be waiting for you. In and out."

Simone arched a brow at her husband once they approached the opening. "Found a hole?"

Artan grinned. "I may have helped it along a wee bit."

"Well done. It's plenty large enough, and clearly, they haven't noticed it yet. If I have any luck, I'll be sending two bairns through. Keep your ears open." She arranged her bow and quiver the way she wished, checked for her dagger, then kissed Artan quickly before moving ahead.

Simone climbed inside the stone wall, tugging her accessories close, shocked at how narrow the curtain wall was. The walls at Duart were nearly twice as thick and protected the people she loved. This was another time in her life when she reveled in her good fortune to be adopted by Logan and Gwyneth Ramsay.

She'd been young when Maggie Ramsay had come along and saved her from the constant beatings she'd received at Wingate Castle as a kitchen servant. The woman she hated the most had ordered two men to drag her into the common courtyard to beat her in front of everyone. She'd dropped a bowl, an accident. One of the men had bumped into her in the hall and down it had gone, smashing into tiny pieces.

And she'd been dragged out quickly, a smile on the face of the sinister housekeeper who most enjoyed inflicting punishments. The evil woman had grabbed her favorite switch from the assortment on display and had the man bind Simone's hands on a tree, forcing her to bend over a big boulder. And the beating had begun.

Will loved to tell the story of how quickly Maggie had reacted. He said that the first sound of the switch on Simone's backside had set her face into a fury he'd never seen. Maggie had said, "I'm not leaving without that lass." Then she'd found her spot, fired one arrow into the monster's shoulder, aimed a second and hit one of the men in the side, then threw her dagger into a third man's leg. They didn't know what or who had hit them for several moments.

Plenty of time for Maggie to run over and grab Simone's hand to rescue her from her horrible life. Although Simone had been hesitant, not wishing to leave her sister Beatris inside, Maggie had promised to return for her, and she'd held true to her promise.

Maggie's adopted mother, Gwyneth Ramsay, had saved Maggie and Molly from the same cruelty many years ago when Sorcha had been a bairn tied to her father's chest. Molly had been tethered to a tree when Logan had found her. She was bruised from a beating she'd received from the lady of the manor for dropping a trencher on the floor. Her sister Maggie was inside so Logan and Gwyneth had taken Molly from the tree and gone back inside later to find Maggie. They'd promised never to beat them, and they never had. Their eldest daughter Sorcha had been a wee bairn at the time, but they still welcomed the two sisters into their family.

And when Simone and Beatris had come along, they'd welcomed them too. Her father had a gruff exterior to everyone else, but she knew him as the tender-hearted father that he was. She owed so much to the couple that she would see this through. And she did not approve of anyone mistreating wee ones.

It was time for Simone to save these two bairns inside. She'd wait no longer. And if she had to, she'd come back for the abusers later.

She held her breath as she climbed through the

stone, not wishing to jar anything in the tunnel. When she finally emerged from the wall, she peered out to check for guards in the area. Only one visible man appeared on the curtain wall, and he had his head propped on the parapets, dozing.

She made her way to a staircase that descended to a door a few steps below. It had to lead to the cellars and the dungeon.

That's where she headed. The wind blew enough to cover any slight sound her soft boots made on the dirt. Creeping down the steps, she jiggled the door handle, pleased to see it wasn't locked.

Not a soul to be seen down the stairs either.

The passageway held three doors on each side. If she had to wager, the captives would be at the far end. Several doors had windows above her line of sight, though she was able to hop up and peek inside each one.

No one in the first two, but as soon as she opened the third door, she heard movement. Peeking around the corner, her fingers tightly gripping the handle of her dagger, she shoved the door open and jumped to the side, just in case someone was waiting to attack her.

Magni ran straight at her. "It's Simmy! She'll save us. Is Artan with you?"

Simone smiled when she hugged Magni. She'd met the lad the last few times she'd visited MacQuarie Castle with her husband. The poor lad had such a difficult past that it was easy to love him. "Aye, he's outside, Magni. We must be quiet. Can you do that?"

"Aye, just take us away, please, Simmy. I don't like it here." He hugged her so tight that it brought tears to her eyes. She recalled feeling the exact same way when Maggie had cut her bindings and rescued her from her torture.

She knelt and set him a step away, keeping her hands on his arms so he wouldn't panic. "We'll leave in a few moments, Magni. Fear not, I'll not leave you behind, but where is Kyla?"

He shook his head and burst into tears. "They took her."

Lia approached, her hands demurely at her sides. "They have moved her to a place hidden in the forests on Morvern. They wished to be sure no one would get her. Glenna is better, but she struggles. The fever got her so she has been taken to a healer who will watch over her at a place on Ardnamurchan, though I don't know exactly where. I do not believe that it is a castle but a smaller manor home. We are ready to go home now, Simone. We are grateful you have come for us. Magni is quite hungry and misses his grandsire."

Magni threw his arms around her again and squeezed. "I want to go home. Back to Mull and I don't care where. Duart or Sloan's or Lennox's or Thane's. Somewhere where people love me."

Simone had to squeeze her eyes tight to stop the tears. "Listen to me, lad. We're going out the door and down the passageway. You are to stay behind me. There is one archer up on the wall, so we have to be as quiet as possible. Understand?"

"But how will we get out that way? I can't climb the curtain wall." His tear-stained cheeks set against her own before he pulled back to stare at her.

"There's a hole in the wall big enough for each of us. I'll show you. You will go first, and I promise you that Artan is waiting for you on the other side, so fear no more, Magni. You trust Artan, aye? We have a boat, and I vow you'll be home in no time. Or at least to Clan Rankin. Can you keep quiet for me?"

He nodded, so she opened the door and crept back down the passageway, making no sound at all, Magni and Lia behind her. When they opened the door to the outside, they made their way to the bottom of the steps, but Simone cursed. The man on the wall was now awake, but she knew better than to go back.

She whispered, "We're going up the stairs. The hole is over there. Run that way and you'll see it. If the guard sees us, I'll have to stay behind and shoot him. You keep going until you get to Artan. Lia will be directly behind you."

Magni nodded, squeezing Lia's hand. "I'll protect you, Lia. You must go ahead of me in the wall."

Lia smiled and nodded.

Simone took his hand and led him up to the top step and pointed to the crumbling spot in the wall. "See where the gravel is lying in a pile on the ground? It's just past there."

"Halt!" The bastard had seen them.

"Run, Magni. I'll take care of him."

Magni took off, hanging on to Lia's hand. Simone took out her bow, nocked her arrow, and fired. The quick wail told her she'd hit her target, but he wasn't dead yet.

He bellowed, and the door opened from another spot down the back of the castle, guards racing out from the main floor.

"Go, Magni!" Then she whistled for Artan, hoping he would hear her.

The lad made it inside the wall, pushing Lia ahead of him. The man on the wall continued to fire but shot wide. Simone nocked again and hit him in the neck this time, ending his assault.

That didn't stop the two men behind her, their swords at the ready. Simone raced to the wall, backing into the opening and as soon as the one man tried to enter, she threw her dagger and struck his knee. He fell back, blocking the opening for the next man, so she turned around and climbed out of the hole.

"Go, Artan. They're coming."

They made it to the boat, Artan shoving off with the two bairns inside, and Simone jumping in at the last moment. "Hurry, Artan. I've got them. Magni, help him row." She got the lad situated with the two oars, knowing they would be heavy for him, but prayed his fear and instinct would help him push along. She whipped back around and fired from the boat, catching the next assailant in the chest, but another slew of armed men came behind him.

The idiots made a sad attempt to use their bows, but Simone couldn't help but laugh.

She hollered to them. "Too bad, fools! You should have been taught by the master, a woman."

CHAPTER THIRTY-FOUR

Merryn

———

LATER IN THE day, Merryn and Broc were inside the castle walls practicing in the archery field. Astra and Sela had promised to watch the bairns so they could train. Merryn had just hit the target dead center when Broc's arms wrapped around her from behind and tossed her into the air, catching her before she hit the ground.

"Lass," he said. "I declare you must be the quickest learner I've ever seen." He set her down, kissed her neck, and peered back at the target. "An amazing shot. I can't beat that."

"Do you think I've improved?"

"I am amazed."

She glanced around, then whispered, "Then I wish to go when you search for your mother. I can help. I swear I can, Broc. You all have helped me so much that it's time for me to return the favor." After all Broc's clan had done for her, she needed to do what she could, and using her new skill was the best way to help them. "I hit Kelvan once."

"I will vouch for you, lass." He tugged her against him and kissed her with such a passion that she dropped her weapon and fell into his arms. How she loved his kisses, especially when his tongue sought hers, mating with hers until she was so heated that her breath would catch in her throat. When he ended the kiss, she whispered, "Oh, Broc." She tingled in places she'd never known existed until this man had come into her life.

He grinned. "I see I've kissed you senseless, lass. Always my intent." As soon as he stepped back, his head tipped toward the gates of the castle. She knew why. The wait for the return of Simone and Artan had gone on forever, even to her. Broc's mind was consumed with worry over his mother and the other bairns.

For him, it had to seem like an eternity. Would they be fortunate enough to see Kyla with Simone? Magni and Lia too? Or would they come home empty-handed?

She hated to ask her question, but she was compelled. "How long would you wait before someone will go after them? What if they were …" She couldn't even finish her sentence.

"You mean, what if they were captured too? I have to admit that I've wondered the same. I think since dark is nearly upon us that we would wait until the morrow to go after them. And I can promise you that if she does not return with all three, there will be another patrol leaving at dawn. Simone and Artan know the area. I trust them both."

A shout interrupted their conversation, and Broc reacted quickly, taking her hand and leading her to the curtain wall so they could climb up the steps to see who was approaching.

"I pray your mother is with them."

A young voice echoed over the wall. "I'm home! Tell Grandsire I'm here!"

It was Magni. Merryn smiled, saying a quick prayer of gratitude that he was freed. But who else was with him?

Broc leaned over the parapets, staring at the small line of horses. Magni rode with Artan, Lia with Simone, Sloan and Lennox behind them. "My mother?" Broc called out to Simone.

"She wasn't there. Lia will tell you where they moved her," Simone replied.

Merryn's heart sank, but not nearly as much as Broc's. He still had a tight grip on her hand, but the hope was vanquished so quickly that it pained her to watch him.

Once they came into the gates, the stable lads ran out to handle the horses. Artan jumped down, catching Magni as he leapt to the ground and ran toward the keep. "Grandsire! I'm here!" Then he spun around and said, "Lia, hurry!"

Lia waited for Artan to reach for her, calling ahead to her brother. "Go inside, Magni. I'll catch up with you soon enough."

Simone and Lia dismounted, Lennox and Sloan behind them.

Simone said, "I'm sorry, Broc. I searched each of the chambers in the cellars, but she was not there. Lia, tell everyone what you know."

"They took your mother to a manor home on Ardnamurchan. Glenna wished to be off the island. She told Kelvan they would have more men if they were on the mainland. But I also think they might move Kyla again. Come and check with me later," Lia said. "Oh, and Glenna does not like that home either. It's not plush enough for her, so she might move too."

Merryn took in the disappointment on Broc's face but squeezed his hand. "We'll go on the morrow."

Sloan said, "Inside. The bairns need to eat, and we need a brief respite and a meeting with the others. We will support whatever Connor and Maitland decide."

Lennox added, "Then I'll return home, but Meg and I will both go with you on the morrow. We can cross the sound from our land. We have some boats, Sloan has others. We'll get her, Broc. He doesn't have what he wants now."

"What the hell does he want with my mother?"

"You. He wants you, and he hopes to draw you out." Simone looked at him, but then added, "As you know, they are both mad for anything magical. Lia told us on the way back that they tried to make Lia cast a spell, but she was an expert at playing them. They asked her about the sapphire sword, so that is now their goal. Get Kyla's son or husband and find the sapphire sword. Glenna still wishes for revenge for losing her hand."

Artan said, "She'll want revenge for anything she can create in her mind. Mark my words, if she doesn't have a logical reason, she'll make one up."

Merryn's gut dropped to her toes, but she said nothing. After losing her parents and her sister, she couldn't bear the thought of losing Broc, Kyla, Shealee, or Tristan.

Artan approached Broc and said, "Inside. We need to make plans for the next patrol. And at this point, I would not work on patrols. I'd start planning a direct attack. We'll be on the mainland. Connor needs to use his men from Grant land, leave the others here to protect the wee ones."

They made their way inside, and Merryn had to smile at the greeting Lia received. Sylvi, Tora, and Sandor ran straight for her, wrapping her in a giant hug. Shealee tottered along behind them, giving Lia a sweet kiss. Lia giggled with delight, but then said, "I must find something to eat and make sure Magni is eating too."

Sylvi said, "Magni is already eating. He ran into the kitchens after he gave his grandsire a proper greeting."

Logan approached them slowly. "In the solar. Connor is waiting for you, Simone. Broc, Merryn, Artan, join us. Share what you've learned."

Connor and Finlay were already inside. Alasdair, Simone, and Artan followed them. Finlay clasped Broc's shoulder, shaking his head. His eyes misted, but he controlled himself and took a seat next to Broc, Merryn on Broc's other side.

Lia came in with Maitland, and Connor said, "Lia, we are so pleased you are back with us. If you would just tell us what you know of Lady Kyla, we will send you off and never bother you again."

Lia nodded and said, "My lady Kyla is hale. She has not been harmed. Glenna is interested in finding someone Kyla loves, whether it be her husband or son, so she can torture the person in front of her. She's angry with Kyla since her sire killed Glenna's grandsire." Then she glanced at Logan. "And of course she is angry with you, my lord, because she blames you for the loss of her hand."

Logan smirked. "Broc was so fast and powerful, she didn't have much of a chance."

"But you are hale now, my lord?"

"I'm fine. I'll be on the field when the battle time comes, though I'll not be swinging my weapon much."

"Lia, where is my sister exactly?" Connor asked.

"They moved her to Ardnamurchan. A manor home they have well hidden. One they are sure you will never find. But Kelvan's wish for the sapphire sword may make Glenna change her mind. She would give up all for Kelvan, and she is not well yet. She still suffers from the fever here and there." Lia waited to see if there were any other questions. "I will add they also have a verra well-hidden holding in Morvern. So if you find the place in Ardnamurchan and Kyla is not there, Morvern will be your next place to look. I have not been able to uncover the exact location yet, but I can if they move her."

"So, you think the priority is that weapon?" Connor asked. "Have they finally come to their senses and decided to stop attacking our bairns?"

"He wants the sapphire sword. He believes if

he can control that, he will be able to overtake all the Scots, even though I tried to explain to him that it didn't work that way."

"Our thanks to you, Lia. Please let us know if you think of anything else that could be important. Find your meal and then rest. You have been a blessing for all of us." Logan and Connor both nodded to her.

Lia moved to the door and opened it but then spun around. "Oh, and I will be going with you on the morrow."

Connor, Maitland, and Logan all turned to her, various expressions of fear and shock on their faces. "With whom?" Maitland called out, the higher tone of his voice indicative of where his mind had gone.

"Not Grant, my lord. He will be fine for many years. Do not worry overmuch."

"Then who?" Connor bellowed.

Lia smiled and took her leave without answering.

Broc was the first to speak. "I'm leaving at first light."

Merryn wasn't going to stay back. "I'll go with you." Everyone turned to face her. "I've been practicing my archery skills, and you need an archer. Eli is not feeling well, and Dyna needs to stay here."

Broc reached for her hand. "I will vouch that her skills are better than mine."

Simone said, "I will also vouch for her. I would like to have her along. She did well on Tiree."

"Fair enough," Connor said. "Alasdair?"

"John and I will both go."

The group fell silent, and it was Logan who spoke. "Alasdair, you're giving them what they want. I think it's a mistake."

"Not if he brings the sword."

Connor arched a brow but said nothing. Merryn had heard of the power the sword held, but John was young. Only four and ten summers, his height close to matching his sire's, but he didn't have the bulk of the others.

"I'm sending word for Alick to send two hundred warriors to Ardnamurchan. I will leave four score here to make sure the bairns are safe." Connor stroked his chin. "I don't like this. John is young, but …"

"But it's time to lead the bastards away from the bairns. If we take a score with us and meet your two hundred there, we should be safe. I believe in our warriors." Finlay stood up. "I'd like to go on this one. Please."

Connor said, "First light. Be ready. This will not be an easy one."

He glanced over at Logan, who gave him a subtle nod.

"This could be our biggest battle in a long time."

CHAPTER THIRTY-FIVE

Broc

BROC BRUSHED MIDNIGHT Majesty down, whispering sweet words in the animal's ear just the way he liked. The horse tipped his head back, then nuzzled Broc's hand, searching for its treat, so he moved to the apple barrel at the end of the passageway, bringing one for Midnight and one for himself.

After much discussion with Simone, they'd decided to take Merryn but only on the condition that she would ride with him. Simone was emphatic that if anything happened, he was to find a tree and get Merryn safely to a shooting spot. She'd vouched for the lass's ability and said they needed archers along, but she was not ready to battle from a horse.

She and Simone would be the only archers, so they needed a higher vantage point.

Merryn came out with her quiver and arrows, her bow over her shoulder, looking fine in her tight leggings.

"My, but you do look just like Simone and Eli in that outfit. I'm glad you found some to fit you.

Riding in one of your gowns would not have worked. How is Shealee?"

"She's awake and chattering with Tora and Grant. The three carry on a conversation as if they can understand every word that Grant says. And the lad sure does enjoy John, does he not? Whenever John is in his presence, his gaze never leaves him."

"True, but John enjoys him too. Grant is the little brother he never had. And Shealee loves them all."

Merryn said, "Dyna said she would watch over her while we are gone. Tristan is going home to work but will return in two days. He's still worried they'll not finish before first snowfall."

The stable lads ran back and forth, saddling the horses for Connor and Alasdair. John would ride his own horse. Simone and Artan joined them while Connor gave the lads instructions on which horses the guards would take.

The group readied themselves. Broc led his horse out, surprised to see his father was already near the gates waiting for the others. Once the group lined up, they numbered ten plus five guards. Their plan was to head to Craignure where Connor had obtained a large enough galley ship to take the horses across with them.

They were just about to leave when Lia approached.

They all froze.

Uncle Connor said, "Who are you looking for, Lia?"

"John, may I ride with you?" The wee lass had

on a green pair of leggings and a tunic with a green mantle.

Alasdair shouted, "Nay, nay … Lia, nay. Not John. You cannot choose him. Please."

They all knew at this point that Lia was the green faery who was here to protect someone.

"Then may I accompany you, please, Alasdair?"

"Me?" His eyes widened and he looked from one person to the other. "I don't need protecting, Lia. Go back and stay with the bairns."

She turned to Artan and said, "May I?"

Artan nodded. "I won't fight with you, lassie. If you feel the need to come along, then please join me."

No one said another word to Lia, and the group moved toward Craignure. Lennox accompanied them—Simone and Artan, Broc and Merryn, Alasdair and John, Uncle Connor, and Alaric.

And Lia.

They loaded the horses on the boat, the many stallions restless because they still hadn't adjusted to the ships yet, but they eventually settled. Lennox said, "I'll go as far as MacKinnis with you."

Broc stood next to Midnight Majesty and kept hold of his bridle. Midnight Moon stood next to him, the two nearly ready to go at it because a sweet mare stood on the other side of Moon, but with a firm command from Uncle Connor, Moon calmed immediately. He'd learned his horse skills well from Grandda Alex.

Broc had left Merryn on the upper deck with Simone because she still could be a bit unsettled around all the big warhorses, but Connor insisted on bringing the best of the beasts they had. Kelvan needed a reminder of who he was dealing with.

Broc had one goal—to find his mother. He had to. There was no option here. He would not go home without her.

Uncle Connor took one look at him and said, "If you feel that way, lad, you should have left the lass home."

"What?" Broc replied, shocked his uncle could interpret his expression so well. They were the only two on the lower deck with the animals, other than a few guards at the back.

"You have that look of determination I've seen on my sister's face before. The look that says she won't change her mind for any reason. You are committed to finding your mother, but do not forget you have Merryn's life in your hands too."

Broc had thought of that, so he nodded. "Understood, Uncle. I'll protect her with my life. You know that."

"I do. But I recall the day your mother vowed to protect another lass's life and thought it would be worth risking her own. Do what you must, but don't be foolish. You have not been in many battles, so keep your head where it needs to be."

The trip was a short voyage across the sound. They landed near Lochaline and Ardtornish Castle as Lennox had arranged with Angus MacKinnis. They didn't waste time visiting, instead heading straight up the path toward Aeoineadh Mor and the village. Lennox had suggested starting there because if there were any unknowns, the villagers would be aware of changes.

"Godspeed," Angus called out, Theebet next to him. "I'll have a few men at the ready should you need them. And we'll water your horses when you return."

They saw nothing for over an hour. Broc's gaze scanned everywhere and there was little to see along the way.

Halfway to the village, everything changed. The attack happened so quickly that no one was prepared. They headed down a wide pathway, forests on both sides, a fork in the path ahead of them.

Midnight Majesty let out a blow that told Broc something threatening was nearby. Alasdair was next to him and his stallion reacted the same.

"John, move closer to me," Alasdair instructed.

Artan moved toward John on the other side, and Lia hopped over onto the lad's horse, surprising him. The next moment, John was surrounded by three horsemen, yanked off by one, and tossed over the back of his mount. Lia followed, hopping onto another one's horse.

Broc had been searching for a tree to set Merryn in when the attack took place. He'd just gotten Merryn on a wide branch when the bellows happened.

Simone whistled and climbed up on an oak near Merryn. "Fire, Merryn!"

Broc unsheathed his weapon and attacked one of the group near John while Alaric sought another, giving Alasdair the chance to go after the horse John was on. Alasdair called out. "I have to follow him!"

Alaric and Broc fought hard, Broc's sword clashing with a masked man dressed in black, his grunts telling him the man wasn't going to give up easily. A score more men came out of the woods, some carrying small swords, some on foot, to join the assault. When Broc finally took one man down, two others came at him. An arrow flew from the trees, catching one man in the shoulder hard enough to knock him from his mount. The second man Broc went after with his sword over his head, bringing it down on his weapon arm and nearly amputating it. Then he followed the path that Alasdair had taken.

Alaric and his father followed him, his sire bellowing, "Don't be foolish, Broc. The bastards already have Mama. Do not give in to what they want!"

Alaric came abreast of Broc, his father behind him. They could see Alasdair a short distance ahead. "We're behind you, Alasdair. Don't slow!" Alaric yelled.

Alasdair glanced back but then was suddenly attacked by four men from the woods he'd passed. He bellowed and swung like a possessed man, taking one attacker out immediately. Broc went after one, using the Grant war whoop to give him the power he needed to knock that attacker off his horse. He swung hard enough to send another man's weapon into the forest and then plunged his sword into his chest, killing him instantly.

But five more came at them.

They were too far away for the archers to help them.

"Broc!" his sire called out when two men went at him. "Help me. I cannot take on both."

Alaric fought two of his own. Broc killed his attacker quickly, then went to help his father who was slowing. He couldn't lose his father.

Alasdair was nowhere to be seen.

Merryn was a distance away in the trees near Simone.

Uncle Connor hadn't approached yet and neither had any of their guards.

It was the three of them against this new onslaught that had burst forth from the trees.

His father swung but was losing strength. Broc could see it in the sweat on his brow and the slow arc of his weapon. Broc attacked one man from behind, striking his flank and sending him retreating into the woods where he lost his mount.

"Da, move back!"

Finlay pulled his mount out of the way and Broc maneuvered his black beast in front of his father. Midnight Majesty had seen enough and nearly tossed Broc by raising up on his hind legs, though it was too small an area for the attempt.

Broc had to finish quickly, or he'd be off. His horse landed and snorted, turning sideways, which gave Broc the perfect angle to thrust at the man's side, the life leaving his eyes as soon as the blade sunk into the soft flesh between his ribs.

Where the hell was Merryn? "Da, go back. Protect Merryn. I have to go after Alasdair and

Mama."

Alaric finished both of his attackers, and the two cousins stared at each other, heaving. Alaric said, "Alasdair's long gone. Out of sight. I'm not going alone. You want to go?"

Broc wished more than anything to find his mother. "Da, go after Merryn. I'm going for Mama." He turned his horse around and Uncle Connor galloped toward them. "Where is Alasdair?"

"Long gone," Finlay said. "You'll never catch him, and there were three men behind him. I can't do it anymore. The rest? Simone, Artan, Merryn?"

"We finally finished off the men who attacked back there, but there could be more coming out of the woods any moment. We have no idea how many they have. More than I expected," Connor said. "I don't have the strength to go after them. Where is Lia?"

"I'll go," Broc said. "Lia is with John."

Alaric said, "I'll go with Broc."

"Nay," his father said. "We don't know where your mother is. I cannot lose you, Broc. Don't go. It's too uncertain. And now they have John, Lia, and possibly Alasdair too."

Uncle Connor said, "I'm acting chieftain and I'm ordering both of you to stand down. We don't have enough men. How many were with Alasdair?"

Broc brushed the sweat from his brow. "He was after the one who had John, and four came out of the woods to follow him, keeping us back. I managed to take one and Alaric another, but then five more came at the three of us. I lost sight of him after that. At least two were behind him on horseback. Alaric and I can take them."

"You'll stand down. We'll return later with contingents. I need the men from Grant land. We return and regroup."

"Da?" He looked at his father, but then he thought of Merryn.

"Let Mama go for now. We'll get her."

"But it's my fault. I should go after her. I could have…"

"Nay, Broc. Stop," his father barked. "You've always been like this. You always want everything to end perfectly. It doesn't happen in life that way, son."

Broc, confused, wasn't sure what his father meant by that comment.

"When you were a lad, you were always competing with Alick and Paden. And all your cousins. Always wanting to be the best. You can't. You do the best you can and go from there."

"But I do the best I can." He believed he tried his hardest, but his hardest was always a failure. "And it's never enough."

"It is enough. You are part of a clan, Broc. Not fighting alone. Look how many men we fought off. You saved Logan, and Tora, and Shealee. You are only one person. You can't save everyone yourself. We have to be wise about our moves. Alasdair and John can handle themselves and

they will be there to help your mother. You're not

going after them. I agree with Connor."

Broc stared at the two men he admired more than any other, his gaze now taking in his surroundings. The injured and dead around them, some moaning, some not moving. The place wreaked of battle, of death, the smell of blood overwhelming. Every face he looked at appeared exhausted, making him wonder how he looked. His father was right. He'd always wished to fight on his own, always wished to be first.

Ahead of everyone.

Alaric moved closer and clasped his shoulder. "Your sire is right. We're fighting together now, and we just fought off double our numbers. Be proud, Broc, and stop torturing yourself. We'll get them. It's not your fault, it's the bastards who attacked us."

Uncle Connor said, "We're going back to reassess. You have a lass back there who has just experienced her first battle."

He nodded, knowing they were right. His father was right. He spent too much time thinking on his own efforts instead of the clan's efforts.

His father tipped his head toward the path back. "Get Merryn out of the tree."

He didn't wait, instead nodding to the two clan elders and retreating, though it went against his grain to do so. But he had to think of Merryn too, who had to be scared as hell over what had happened. He needed to go to her.

They left the dead, moving along to the clearing

where the attack had started, Simone and Merryn

still in the trees.

"Broc, you are hale?" The most beautiful lass in the world stared down at him, the fear and worry on her face so clear that it humbled him.

"I'm fine. You?"

Merryn nodded, but her eyes misted, and he fetched her down from the tree, tucking her in front of him on the horse. He kissed her briefly, then looked about to see what else, or who else, they'd lost. Simone and Artan were fine, but two of their guards were wounded.

"You can ride?" Uncle Connor asked each one. "Brenna and Eli will fix you both."

They headed back with heavy hearts because they were missing three, and Broc could feel the fine tremor in Merryn's body. This was her first true battle as an archer, but she'd seen death enough to know how disastrous it could have been.

He rubbed her arm and said, "You had fine aim, catching one in the shoulder and knocking him off his horse."

She whispered, "It was so odd. I didn't hesitate to fire for my sister and my parents. I shot and shot and never slowed, and now I'm shaking so badly that if I were on my own horse, I'd never make it."

"You were wonderful. What you're experiencing is common to some in battle. It happened to Alick many times, and Els too. It will pass."

But Broc thought about all that had just happened. He'd deserted one of his dearest cousins and lost the greatest chance he'd had yet to save his mother.

But he looked at it differently this time. It was the right thing to do. They were outnumbered.

They would regroup and, together, they would save his mother, Alasdair, John, and Lia.

CHAPTER THIRTY-SIX

Alasdair

A LASDAIR AWAKENED TO find himself chained to a wall in some unknown place. The cool, damp environment told him he was probably in a dungeon. He opened his eyes slowly so he could take in the situation without letting anyone know that he was awake.

It was dark. A torch set the only light they had through the small window in the top of the door. He studied the chamber he was in. He sat on a pallet, one foot chained to the wall, his bound hands in front of him allowing him little movement. Another bed held John, and the sight of him lying there looking so helpless nearly undid him. What the hell had happened out there? They'd never been overtaken by so many before, something they hadn't expected. It was as if they knew they would be coming.

John was asleep on the small cot, his hands and feet tethered by rope to the bed. Lia sat on a smaller bed near him, her hands tied and covered with some fabric.

She was awake, watching him.

"Lia?"

"Aye, my lord?"

"Alasdair. Is John all right?"

"Of course he is. His safety is the reason I'm here, my lord. I mean, Alasdair."

"Kelvan or Glenna?" he whispered, needing to assess the situation as quickly as he could. He may be chained to a wall, but he was far from helpless.

"Both are here somewhere."

"His sword?"

"I hid it under his tunic. Kelvan tried to touch it, but it burned his hand. It does not matter how much I warn him, he continues. Just like he did with Grant, and that wee lad burned his skin ferociously. Foolish K learned not to make that wee laddie angry. Now he needs to learn to leave John alone."

Alasdair had to smile at the lass who'd been along on the worst ordeals. "Will we ever stop needing you, Lia?"

"Jake says aye. He sent me to you."

"Jake? Jake who?"

"Your sire. John Alexander Grant. You look much like him."

Alasdair's eyes misted, though he had to wager that it was probably something in the chamber, not his emotions. Not the fact that he missed his mother and father every day of his life, or that it pained him to think that his parents had never met his wife or their bairns.

Neither he nor Aline had living parents, so their children hadn't had the luxury of grandparents to spoil them.

"But your grandfather spoiled them whenever he could," Lia whispered.

"I didn't say that. I was thinking it."

"I could hear it. Some thoughts are so important that they carry to me."

"What else can you do, Lia? Will you untie us so I can get us out of here?"

Lia sighed and untied the mitts on her hands, folding them in her lap. "Some things I am instructed to do, and others I'm not."

"So, you untied your hands? Release me, please."

"But I don't have the key."

"Find it? I'm guessing you can."

Lia chuckled. "I will when I'm told to find it."

"I don't understand. I want John to be safe."

"John will be safe. You will never have to worry about your son. He is a chosen one to bear the weight of the sapphire sword, and with Grant, they will have powers that even you won't understand. But there is time before that happens. For now, we must be patient."

"Why?"

"If I set you free and you untie your son and remove him from here, what would happen next?"

"I would find a way to walk away."

"And …"

"And what?"

"Kelvan and Glenna would still be free and alive to haunt and taunt you more. Steal more bairns. Stab more elders."

He was having a difficult time trying to reason

with a lass younger than John who had the power to do what she wished. Sitting there with her hands folded, Lia appeared to be in complete control of the situation. Why the hell wouldn't she set the two of them free and escort them out of this hellhole? "If you got us out of here, we would come back for them. And for Kyla. Where is she?"

"She is staying in a chamber in another area. You won't find her without help. And I don't know where she is yet."

Alasdair felt like he was talking in circles. If she would just unlock the chains, he would get John away. They could return for Kyla later.

"But they would move again."

He was beginning to understand. Something else needed to happen. Uncle Connor needed to bring the forces of Clan Grant down upon these evildoers, or the suffering would continue. "Can you read all my thoughts?"

"Nay, only the ones that are sent to me."

"Is my sire still here?"

"He is."

"Would you ask him why I am here? Why John?"

She paused for a moment and closed her eyes. "They will need someone on the inside to lead them to Kelvan and Glenna. Both must be destroyed, or Clan Grantham will never be free."

"So, we are here to help the others find us."

"Or Kyla would never be found. And she needs to be. They could take her and leave the area, never to return. But it's not her time yet."

"I still don't understand how we can help."

"It's simple, actually. No one can hurt John. Me, I'm a faery, so I am immune to their weaponry. And the two of us can protect ourselves and find our way out when the time comes."

"True. So I have no purpose?"

"Alasdair, there is another man standing next to your sire who looks like both of you, though he is taller."

Alasdair could barely contain himself, his thoughts going to the two men he adored and admired more than any other—his sire and grandsire. "Grandda?" His voice cracked, something he was powerless to stop.

"Aye. His name is Alexander. And he has a message for you."

Alasdair looked at every corner of the small chamber, wishing he could see any of the three— his father, his mother, or his grandfather. "I'm listening."

"Alex says, 'You have a verra important purpose and you must listen carefully.'"

Alasdair teared up. "I'm listening, Grandda."

"You were brought here for *my* daughter. Your grandmother and I pushed you to do all you did for this purpose. We will take care of your son, Alasdair. We cannot help Kyla. You must."

Alasdair covered his face with his bound hands, so humbled by the possibility that his grandfather was speaking to him. "I'm honored, Grandsire. I'll make you proud."

Then he swiped away the tear that had rolled down his cheek.

He had a job to do, and he would see it through.

On his honor as the grandson of Alexander and Madeline Grant.

CHAPTER THIRTY-SEVEN

Connor

———◦◦◦———

A S THEY APPROACHED the gates, Connor noticed several people on the parapets watching. The gates were opened, and they entered the courtyard, the wounded first.

Connor spoke to Dyna and Maitland both above them as they passed through. "Two wounded and in need of tending. Alasdair, John, and Lia taken. They had too many for us. We were outnumbered. Double what we had."

Maitland rubbed Grant's head as the lad kicked his legs in the strapping where he sat facing out. He whined, "Wia. Wia."

Maitland said, "I should have guessed. Grant's been unsettled for the past hour or so. Does that take on any meaning for you?"

Connor dismounted and said, "That's about when John was taken. They stole him away, came out of the forest and aimed straight for him. Lia jumped onto one of the horses to follow. Alasdair went after him while we fought off the other two score men who appeared all down the path. Alasdair never returned."

"Bloody hell," Dyna said, Tora next to her.

"Don't wowwy, Mama. Lia will save John."

They all gave Tora their attention. Dyna asked, "And who will save Alasdair, Tora?"

Tora shook her head. "I don't know."

Connor asked, "Who will save Aunt Kyla, lassie?"

"Alasdaiw."

Dyna smiled and hugged her daughter. "Does that make you feel any better, Da? John will be saved. And so will your sister. Just not yet."

Connor shook his head. "I'll not feel better until Glenna and Kelvan leave us alone. Tora, can you lead us to where John is? And Aunt Kyla? Are they together?"

Tora leaned against her mother. "I cannot, but he can. Lia will tell him."

Tora pointed to Grant.

Maitland, wide-eyed, said, "Nay, he's not going anywhere."

They both looked to Dyna, who barked, "Bloody hell, nay!" Dyna looked to her father and said, "My bairns are not going anywhere. They're staying inside these walls until those two bastards are gone. Do not ask me, Da."

Connor sighed and said, "I will not. We'll talk to her again, though. That I can promise. You and Avelina need to meet on the parapets shortly."

"Da," Dyna said. "You are all battle weary. Come inside. I'll start the evening meal a wee bit early. The fish pottage is ready and so is the bread. Then you can call a meeting. There's more wine, and Micheil brought amber brew too."

The others came through the gates, handling their mounts with care.

Maitland said, "She's right, Connor. Broc is the only reason Merryn hasn't fallen off their horse. Broc, his father, and Alaric are all covered in blood. We have the outdoor wash center all set up."

Broc dismounted and Maitland yelled to him, "Wash down all set behind the stables." Both Clan Ramsay and Clan Grant had outdoor spots near the stables where men could wash off the blood and muck from battle, something Aunt Brenna had started years ago.

Broc and Alaric headed straight for it, but Finlay came right over to Connor. "When do we go back, Connor?"

Dyna barked, "You'll go inside, eat, refresh, then meet after the meal, Uncle Finlay. And you're covered in blood. Go with Broc first."

Her uncle stared down at his plaid, then closed his eyes, but said nothing before following his son over to the wash-out area.

Connor dismounted, washed off what he could, then headed inside, greeted his wife, and went to their chamber to change his plaid and tunic. He couldn't imagine how badly Broc and Finlay both felt. They'd left hopeful and come back as failures, basically. That didn't happen often to Clan Grant.

Sela followed him to their chamber, hugging him from behind. "This is a new experience for you. We'll get your sister back, Connor. I think it's going to take a huge battle on the mainland,

Alick will come through with the warriors you need."

He wrapped his arms around his wife and inhaled her sweet scent. "My thanks to you, my ice queen. I needed your calm sense of reasoning. We'll be back on the morrow. Our men should arrive on Ardnamurchan then. It may take two hundred to comb the area to find the bastard's location."

Sela stood on her tiptoes and kissed him. "I have faith in the Grants. Always, Connor. Anyone who can find someone as evil as Hord and his spiders can handle Glenna of Buchan."

She helped him to dress, then led him out into the hall, the atmosphere a little more tense, but voices discussed and conjectured. Connor often thought it was what his clan did best.

Discuss, strategize, plan.

He took a seat next to Logan while Sela headed to the sideboard. Sloan joined them, bringing Connor a taste of his fine brew. "You know my sire thinks it is the best."

"My thanks to you, Sloan. It is a fine brew. I'll have to ask him for his secrets someday. What did you learn?"

"Mingary is deserted," Sloan replied. "No one there at all. The drawbridge is up. They've found a different spot."

Simone and Artan joined them. Artan said, "Glenna will be back. She will never sleep in some hovel. I would wager she'll be back at nightfall. She won't sleep in a small cottage or a hut in the forest." He glanced over at Simone who gave him a subtle nod. If Connor was to wager, he would bet they would be headed to Mingary after dark.

Magni came flying out of the kitchens and landed on Logan's lap with an oof from the injured man. "Are you going back to get Lia? Please, Grandsire?"

Logan cleared his throat. "Of course, we're going back for Lia. But we will also get Kyla, John, and Alasdair too."

"I know that. I just didn't want you to forget my sister."

"We won't forget to retrieve Lia. Tell me what else you recall about where you were held."

Magni scowled, then said, "She's mean, but she's sickly."

"And where did you live before, Magni?" Simone asked.

"We lived on an island."

"With your parents?"

"Aye."

"Which island did you live on?" Connor asked, changing the subject.

"I forget." He shrugged and hopped off his grandfather's lap. "When are you going?"

"Probably on the morrow."

"And you'll stay here, Grandsire? With me?"

"I thought you wished for me to go after Lia?"

"I do, but I need you to protect me."

"Dyna and Maitland will protect you. I may have to go find Lia. You know I'm one of the best trackers. Lia may need me."

"But you won't fight?"

"I won't be swinging any swords. Riding will be tough enough for me."

Magni hung his head but then picked it back up. "Promise to come back?"

"I promise," Logan said. "Are you sure you don't wish to go with me?"

Magni's face again lit up. "I'll wait for you, Grandda. Bring Lia home, please." And then he was gone.

Connor shook his head. "I wish I was as busy as that lad."

"He'll probably change his mind again," Logan said. "Your men be there on the morrow?"

"High sun at the latest," Connor said.

"What time are we leaving?"

Connor said, "First light or at the return of these two." He nodded toward Simone and Artan. "I want the information they get from Glenna, and I'd like them to come along."

Logan grinned. "How did you know?"

Connor scoffed. "She's your daughter, Ramsay." He got up and wandered across the hall toward the bairns. He then took a chair in front of the hearth, watching his grandbairns play. Nothing calmed him as much as that sight. They were all too young to be thinking of anything but what made them the happiest. He sat back and took a long draw of the fine Rankin brew, rolling the amber liquid over his tongue before swallowing it and sighing when it finally hit home.

He wasn't there long before wee Tora came over to set her hands on his knees, exactly the way she did when she needed his full attention.

"Grandda, dinnae wowwy. Alasdaiw will save Aunt Kyla. Alasdaiw and him." She pointed to a person seated at the table, whispering into Merryn's ear.

Connor glanced over his shoulder to make sure he knew who she pointed at.

Then Tora climbed onto his lap and cupped his face to turn him back, so he faced her directly, something she did whenever she was about to impart important information. How he adored her sweet face.

"Bwoc save his mama. Bwoc and Alasdaiw. Gwanda Alex said so."

Then she hopped down and returned to Sandor's side.

Connor could only pray she was right. His sister's life was at stake.

CHAPTER THIRTY-EIGHT

Merryn and Broc

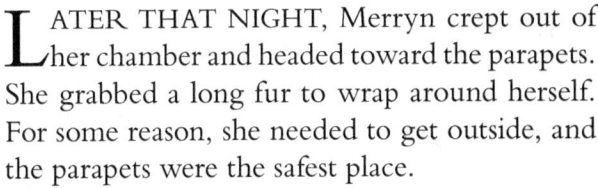

L ATER THAT NIGHT, Merryn crept out of
her chamber and headed toward the parapets.
She grabbed a long fur to wrap around herself.
For some reason, she needed to get outside, and
the parapets were the safest place.

She let the door close slowly so as not to
awaken anyone. Then she turned around, taking
in the gorgeous view of the sea in one direction
and the mountains in the opposite. She sighed,
tearing up at the beauty of the isle.

Only once had she been on the curtain wall
of her uncle's castle, and she'd been quite young,
only noticing trees that went on forever.

But here on Mull, it was different. The half-
moon lit up enough of the area for her to see
far across the water, the rhythmic lapping against
the rocks below calming her. She tipped her head
back in the breeze, the cool air refreshing.

What was to become of her? Of Shealee? Of
Tristan and Broc and Simone? All the people she
cared so much about, yet she feared something
awful was about to happen.

Had Kelvan built up enough of a force to take over the isle and send the Grant warriors back to the Highlands?

She jumped at the sound of boot heels, smiling when she caught sight of Broc coming toward her. "What are you doing here?"

He wrapped his arms around her and kissed her soundly. "I might ask you the same thing, lass."

"I couldn't sleep." She snuggled close to him, taking in his heat, the hardness of his body that made her feel safe and …

"You're blushing."

"I know."

"What are you thinking about?"

"You. Us. We. I don't know." She shrugged. "I like the feel of you against me."

He bent down and whispered in her ear, "I like the feel of your soft curves against me. You are the prettiest lass on all of Mull, Merryn MacClane."

"I think you are seeing things. There are many far prettier than I am."

"Nightmares?"

"Nay, I'm just worried."

Broc sighed and found a stool to sit on, settling her on his lap as he wrapped his arms around her. "You're cold."

"Not with you next to me," she whispered.

"What worries you?"

"Everything. Broc, what if we can't find them? What if Kelvan has more men than we do? What if Glenna sells John and Lia before we find them? What if he cuts Alasdair's hand off?" She couldn't stop the tears from misting her gaze. "What if you're hurt? Logan was stabbed, two guards were hurt. There could be many more injured the next time. And what if they come back for more bairns again?"

"Hush," he said, setting his fingers to her lips. "You're doing what I spent the last hour doing, and it gained me naught. We can't begin to guess what is about to happen. We have to trust in the elders of the group."

"But it didn't work before. More were taken. Are you not afraid, Broc?"

"I am. I hate to admit it, but I am scared. I thought I would come back with my mother, but we failed. So I understand your fear."

"Kelvan is so cruel. So evil."

"He is, but this was a patrol we were on. The next one will be a full battle with the Grant warriors called in from home. He'll not beat us. Trust me, lass."

"If you trust them, then I will too. I want so badly to have this all go away, so we can …"

"We can what?" He grinned, tipping his head.

How did she tell him what she wished? That she wished they could marry because she knew Broc would never hurt her like Kelvan had done to Nara. After watching her poor sister's relationship, she swore she'd never marry. She whispered, "So we can get closer."

Broc made her feel differently. She wished for them to explore each other's bodies, something she'd never thought to do before.

Never!

Now she wished to see what he looked like without his tunic on. With naught on.

Her dear mother was probably rolling in her grave at her thoughts.

He whispered, "I want the same. I wish you were mine. I wish we had the time to ride across the isle, to swim at the beaches, to hike over the mountain. Mayhap someday."

He didn't know how to tell her that, at the moment, he didn't deserve her. He'd failed his mother, failed his father, failed Logan. It was as if there were a wild boar standing outside the castle looking at him.

You'll never be rid of me, laddie.

Broc had the oddest wish to find a boar and stick his sword in its belly. But he'd yet to see a boar on Mull.

He held Merryn close. "Soon, lass. Soon."

"Good, because I'm falling more in love with you every time we are together, Broc MacNicol." His heart swelled at the words.

"I love you too, Merryn. Our time will come soon enough."

What he didn't say was that if he didn't save his mother, he'd never be able to marry. He wouldn't be worthy of Merryn's, or anyone's, love.

CHAPTER THIRTY-NINE

Simone

SIMONE AND ARTAN sluiced through the water in the small ship, one they'd borrowed from Sloan, and headed toward Mingary.

"She'll be there," Simone whispered.

They reached the beach in Bloody Bay, landed the boat, and hid it in the weeds. There were no lights on around the castle.

Luckily, the half-moon gave them enough light to find their way to the curtain wall opening they'd used previously. "You'd think they would have filled it in." Simone snorted.

"Never said she was smart," Artan joked. "Slimy, crafty, and a liar, but never smart."

Simone chortled. "I cannot wait to meet your dear sister."

"By marriage only. And she'll never admit it, but I know she had my brother killed. He was a fool. I cannot argue that."

They crept through the opening and through the unlocked cellar door.

Once inside, Artan reached back for Simone's

hand. "I don't wish to lose you. Have your bow ready?"

"Aye. Move along."

Artan crept up the stairs onto the main floor, surprised to hear no sounds at all. There was no one moving about the castle. Of that much Simone was certain.

"'Tan, there's no one here."

Artan turned back to her with a wide grin on his face. "Aye, there is. Listen carefully." He tugged her forward into the great hall—the empty great hall that showed no signs of an evening meal either.

But then she heard it.

The snore.

A loud snore came from a place above stairs. "Is that Glenna?" Simone asked.

"I'd recognize it anywhere, though it is a bit louder. Evidence of how sickly she is. There's probably one maid here with Glenna. No one else. Kelvan keeps her here out of his way, is my guess."

"Move along, then. I'll check the other chambers while you check hers for any guards by the door."

They separated, so Simone climbed the stairs and checked every single space, and all were empty but one, as Artan had thought. The servant was sound asleep in her chamber at the end of the passageway.

Simone met Artan back at the doorway and said, "It's time. Wake her up. She's put the people and friends of my clan through enough."

Artan said, "And mine. Tamsin is finally relaxing, but this is stirring her up again. Thane worries about her."

"Tamsin will be fine, but only if we get rid of the two blights on Mull—Glenna and Kelvan."

Artan nodded, then squeezed her hand. "Let's go inside. Ready your weapon and hide in a corner before I awaken her."

The chamber was dark, but with Glenna's snoring, it wasn't difficult to find an alcove opposite her bed in the huge chamber built for a king. Simone gave a short whistle to let Artan know she was settled. Artan stood at the end of the bed after he opened a shutter on the nearby window to light up the area a bit.

"Glenna, wake up."

Nothing.

"Glenna," Artan said a bit louder before he lifted the heather-stuffed mattress and dropped it again. "Wake up."

"What? Who? What is going on? Who are you?" The woman opened her eyes and looked about her, not settling on Artan for a few moments.

"Come now, Glenna. You must remember me. I was at your cottage often enough until you tired of my brother and killed him." Artan stood strong at the end of the bed, his shoulders back, his brown hair curling at the collar of his tunic. How Simone adored him, his power so subtle to most, but he was so intelligent that it amazed her. Smart and kind, something that was hard to find.

"I didn't kill him."

"Then you hired someone to kill him."

"You don't know anything. What the hell do you want, Artan? Your brother deserved to die. He kept everything from me—my jewels, the silks. He wouldn't allow me to shop either. He was a coldhearted bastard, and you know it. Get out of my castle." She sat up, her stump still wrapped in a bloody bandage, the green color telling Simone it had yet to heal. Glenna was not a beautiful woman, her hair a complete mess, her skin pale and sallow, something Simone could see in the light of the moon. The sickness in her gaze was also clear. This woman was cruel to the end of every one of her bones. Insufferable and vile, her insides rotting with hate. It oozed from her pores.

Simone had met women just like her before.

Artan said, "I'm not going anywhere until you tell me where the Grant woman is. Where are they keeping her?" He waited for another of her many lies, but Simone knew how to get her talking.

"She's not going anywhere. I owe her. It's her fault my grandfather died by her father's sword. And it's her fault I lost my hand. She owes me in so many ways."

"Och, the trials and tribulations of the world according to the twisted, maniacal beliefs of Glenna of Buchan. You tell so many lies that you believe them yourself. Where is Kelvan keeping her? You have no one here to help you but a tiny maid, so answer my question."

"She owes me." Glenna grabbed a pillow and nearly flung it at Artan but something stopped her. "Look what happened to my hand, and it keeps giving me the fever." She held up her bandaged stump, as if he would care.

"Kyla had naught to do with that."

"She did so. It's all her fault."

"You lie, Glenna. Tell me where she is."

"Never. I'll kill you first, Artan." She pulled a wee dagger from under her pillow and pointed it at him.

Simone didn't particularly like that move.

An arrow flew next to Glenna's head, landing in the wooden headboard behind her. Glenna screamed, hiding under the covers.

Simone had already had enough of the lying fool. Her husband was way too patient. She strode forward, her bow in her hand. She whipped the top coverlet back. "Get your bloody, lying arse out from under the covers. Look me in the eye if you want a chance at living long enough to see dawn."

Glenna dropped the covers and sat up. "Who the hell are you?"

"Logan Ramsay's daughter. I know the truth. I know that you jumped out of an alcove and struck my father from behind, and it was his guard's quick action that cut off your hand. If you hadn't tried to kill my father, you would still have ten fingers. Your fault. Not Kyla Grant's."

"It is her fault. She sent them to me."

"She did not. It isn't her fault. All. Your. Fault. You. Big. Lying. Bitch." She stretched the tone of the last word out long enough to make sure Glenna understood her well.

Glenna began to whine like a bairn. "It was Kyla's son who struck me, so it is her fault."

"You struck first, trying to kill my father."

"And I wish I had. Old bastard has caused Kelvan more trouble than anyone."

"For kidnapping bairns? Who kidnaps bairns but people who deserve torturous deaths? He'll get his just due soon enough. And as for your grandfather, if he hadn't tried to force his daughter onto my cousin Torrian, he wouldn't have become so cruel. He forced Davina to lie to our king. He had Kyla beaten so close to death that her father had to have her carried back home. I know all the history, Glenna, so don't think I'll fall for your lies. Now, where is Kyla?"

Glenna glared at Simone and crossed her arms, but then barked, "Ow!" when her stump hit the other arm straight on. "Hellfire. All Logan Ramsay's fault."

Simone took several steps back, nocking her next shot as she moved. "You forget who you're talking to, woman."

Glenna held up her arms. "I don't know where Kyla is."

The arrow hit just behind the other side of her face.

"Try again!" Simone yelled.

"She's not here."

Another arrow over her head.

"He has her hidden on the mainland."

"Not enough information. Where?"

"I don't know, I told you. I don't pay attention to that."

Three arrows flew around her and then a dagger
hit her shoulder. "Try again!" Simone whispered.
"This is your last warning. The next one will be
in your eye."

Glenna let out a scream that would surely draw
the dead from their graves. "Drimnin. She's in a
cottage underground in Drimnin. They took her
to Morvern where there's so few people. You'll
never find it because I can't. I honestly don't
know anything more than that. I've never been
in it. Kelvan had it made."

Simone said, "That's enough. If you're lying, I'll
be back."

They hurried out, down through the cellar
opening.

"I can't believe she is foolish enough to be here
without guards."

"There are probably a few at the drawbridge in
the front, and they're probably drunk and asleep."

"We'll row to Lochaline and find the man
awaiting our message."

Artan nodded and took Simone's hand, leading
her in the dark to the boat.

They rowed quietly, the half-moon-lit night
peaceful and beautiful as any she'd seen. Simone
paused once and reached for her husband. "Is it
possible it could be so quiet when the entire area
will be lit up with warriors on the morrow?" A
distant owl hooted, echoing in the silence, the
only other sound the quiet lapping of the waves
against the rocks on the shoreline.

Artan said, "I am worried when I think on
what she told us."

"Why?"

"If the entrance is buried and the building is underground, how will we discover it in a forest? It reminds me of the door hidden under the chest in the cottage on Ulva. Nearly impossible to locate."

"We'll find her."

They continued until Simone saw the messenger waiting by the water's edge, his horse and two mounted Grant guards behind him. She moved over to the man and said, "Drimnin on Morvern. Meet Connor at Drimnin."

The messenger nodded and mounted, the three animals galloping away from the shore.

Simone and Artan rowed back across to MacVey land, leaving the boat there for the morrow. As they climbed the hill to the main path, Simone said, "We'll save her."

"How?" Artan whispered. "Things built underground are impossible to detect."

"Lia and Tora and one more, I think. If his father can handle it."

"Who?"

"Grant."

"The bairn?"

"Aye. Grant is tied to John somehow. He'll help us. I would wager Grant knows exactly where John is."

Artan whispered, "Poor Maitland."

Simone squeezed Artan's hand. "Poor Maeve."

Chapter Forty

Alasdair

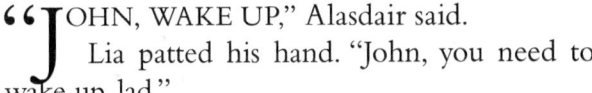

"JOHN, WAKE UP," Alasdair said.

Lia patted his hand. "John, you need to wake up, lad."

John opened his eyes and pulled on his bindings. "What the hell?"

Alasdair was glad it was a bit dark so his son wouldn't see the expression on his father's face after hearing him curse. His wee laddie was growing up. "John, don't pull, or you'll make the skin raw. We'll get out soon enough."

John wiggled around until he could set his eyes on his sire. "Da? You are here?"

"I am. You don't remember?"

He stared at the ceiling for a moment. "Aye, the attack. Lia was behind me on a different horse. They hit me over the head as soon as we stopped. Were others taken or just us?"

"The three of us. I'm sure the others will be here for us sometime today, but I need to let you know that I have a plan I must follow."

"What, Da? My sword will free us. It's under

my tunic but I'm not sure how it got there. I can feel the warmth of the hilt."

"Lia put it there."

John stared at Lia. "You truly have special powers too, I believe. What do you call yourself, Lia?"

"A faery. I can take different forms, but I'm here to help."

They could hear movement near them, so Alasdair said, "Lia, they're coming." He nodded at her freed hands folded in her lap that she so easily manipulated in and out of the restraints.

Lia put her hands back in the looped ties and Alasdair said, "Listen, John. I have to find Kyla. You and Lia will be fine together. I'm going to do something that will lead me to Kyla. You stay here with Lia. I doubt they'll take you with me. Remember that Uncle Alick will be along with two hundred Grant guards soon enough. They'll be along on the morrow or the next day. Stay safe until then. Just do as you're told and don't argue. I promise to be back."

"Da, don't leave me. Please."

There was the wee laddie he adored so much. "I have to. I'll explain later, but I believe you can handle yourself or I wouldn't go. Hush now, they're coming."

Two men came inside, broad-shouldered and carrying daggers. They stepped to the side of the door and a man entered behind them—Kelvan, if Alasdair were to guess.

"Greetings to you, Kelvan. How do you fare today?" Lia smiled at the evil man.

Kelvan reached for Lia and lifted her into the air. "How do you know my name?"

Lia giggled and said, "Because that brute next to you told me."

Alasdair nearly snorted at the lass's craftiness. Kelvan dropped her so quickly that she nearly fell, but she caught herself, hopping out of the way just before Kelvan swung a fist at the brute she accused of revealing the secret. She scurried back to John's side.

Kelvan turned his attention to Alasdair. "I need all the information you have on the Grants. Why are you here?"

"Looking for Kyla. Where is she?"

"Send me the lad with the sapphire sword and I'll release her."

Alasdair said, "You aren't highly intelligent, are you, K?"

Kelvan bent over to put a fist in his belly, but Alasdair quickly butted his head with his attacker's, knocking the fool backward. He repeated, "Where is Kyla?"

Kelvan reached for Alasdair, but a blue light stopped him, the glow coming from the blade of the sword, the hilt now in John's hand. "Leave him be."

"The sword!" Kelvan grinned widely. "Give it to me."

He reached for it, but Lia stopped him with the expression on her face. "Are you that foolish?"

"What the hell does that mean?"

"You burned your hand before. I wouldn't

touch that sword if I were you. Any number of things could happen."

Kelvan chuckled. "Well, as long as it doesn't have a hundred spiders crawling all over it, I'll be fine."

Lia shrugged and glanced over at John with a smile.

Kelvan picked up the hilt and a hundred spiders appeared from the tip and covered him. He screamed, dropping the weapon as he tried to kill the wee crawlies covering him. "Help me, fools!" He turned to his two guards, bellowing like a banshee in the woods.

The two men tried to squash as many as they could but as quickly as they arrived, the spiders disappeared. Kelvan glanced at his arms, shocked. "How? What?"

The sapphire sword lay on the floor, still glowing. Kelvan reached for it, but when Lia spoke, he froze.

"You really are that ignorant?"

He stood up and turned away from John and Lia, back toward Alasdair. "Tell me how to hold that sword."

"I have no idea. But I have a deal for you. Let those two go, and I can make your wife happy."

"They won't go anywhere unless he leaves the sapphire sword behind. And he has to teach me how to use it first."

"But I have something that will make your wife ecstatic."

"What?"

"Me."

"Who the hell are you?"

"Take me to Glenna and I promise you she will be pleased to see me."

Kelvan said, "Unless you are the one who cut off her hand, she won't be happy. And I know you aren't the one because I remember that face."

"But I promise you that she will be happy to see me. Take me to her and see for yourself."

Kelvan stared at him, but then said, "Take the chains off him, men. We have our entertainment for the morning. I'll come back for the sword later."

The men unchained him, and Alasdair stood, handing the sword back to his son before he faced Kelvan.

"Where did the spiders go?" Kelvan asked.

Alasdair retook the sword from John's hand and asked, "Want to try again?"

Kelvan stepped away. "Nay. Give it back to him."

Alasdair set it back in his son's hands, the glow again lighting up the cell.

Kelvan asked, "Who are you? Why does Glenna wish to see you?"

"Because I'm Broc, Kyla's son."

CHAPTER FORTY-ONE

Dyna

———ᴗᴗ———

THE NEXT MORNING, Dyna led the group down the staircase after spending some time on the parapets, not liking everything she had learned. Avelina and Sylvi had gone with her, and while she didn't think Sylvi had interpreted everything the same as she had seen it, she was quite certain that Avelina knew everything.

Everything.

Avelina had stopped her, conferring at the top before they went below stairs. "They aren't going to like this."

Dyna sighed. "Nay. But it makes perfect sense. They will have trouble accepting the truth of it, but everyone will understand. Grant has been unsettled ever since they were taken. Maeve said he hardly slept last night, and she's beside herself with worry over the sweet bairn." And she knew exactly how difficult it was to see your bairns be kidnapped and held away from you. There was no worse feeling in the world.

"My son will be wild and so will Drew at the mention of it."

"Lina, we are not here to force anything. Remember that we will tell what we learned. It is up to them to do what they wish with the information." Dyna took both of Lina's hands in hers and nodded. "We do what we must, and they'll decide. But I fear Kyla and Alasdair are depending on our help, however we do it."

Logan bellowed from the gathering around the hearth. "Stop your planning and get down here, Dyna. We need to know what you know."

Dyna said, "We're coming. I just wished to see if Avelina saw what I did." She approached the group around the hearth—her parents, Uncle Finlay, Broc, Drew, Merryn, Alaric, Emmalin, and Maitland. Maeve was feeding Grant in the tower.

Dyna moved over to join Derric, who came in the door. "Simone will be here shortly. I can see them on their way."

Her father said, "I wish to hear what you two learned before Simone arrives. Then we can compare it to what they discovered."

Avelina nodded to Dyna, giving her the opportunity to tell all. "They are all hale. Lina, if you saw anything different, please stop me. Kyla is kept in one spot while Alasdair is with Lia and John. At least for now."

"What the hell does that mean?" Logan asked.

"Are they in separate holdings?" Uncle Finlay asked.

Broc added, "I was hoping Alasdair would be with Mama so he could help free her. I considered him an asset."

Dyna glanced at Lina who nodded to her.

"Stop that, you two," Logan barked. "No secrets. Just tell us."

Lina said, "Alasdair is going to be moved to Kyla's chamber."

Connor thought for a moment, then said, "I don't understand. Why would they do that?"

Dyna looked to Lina again. She sighed and said, "I'll not hold any secrets. Alasdair told Kelvan he was Broc. He was taken away from John to go to Kyla's chamber."

Emmalin bolted out of her chair. "Please tell me they don't plan to cut off Alasdair's hand." She covered her mouth and then fell back in her seat.

"We saw no indication of that, Emmalin. Have faith in Alasdair. He had a reason to tell them he was Broc."

"What reason?" Broc asked. "That's a foolish move on his part."

Dyna and Avelina stared at each other, and Logan barked, "Hellfire, here we go again."

Tora ran over to her grandfather and climbed up on his lap. Everyone quieted to listen to the wee seer, her movements obvious now. She cupped her grandfather's face and said, "Gwandda Alex tole him to find his lassie." Then she hopped down and ran back to the other bairns playing.

Emmalin got up and paced. "Oh, this is too much for me. Ghosts, seers. Oh my. Alasdair, John, Lia, Kyla. We have to find them soon. I cannot bear this. What else do we know? Where exactly is Kyla? How far before Alasdair is with her? And is John still safe?"

"This is the problem. We couldn't determine

exactly where they were. There was no building, no cottage or castle. We have no hints as to where they are." Dyna looked at Lina who nodded her agreement.

"It was quite vague."

Connor cursed under his breath. "Hellfire. We don't know the area that well."

The door opened and Simone entered, Artan behind her.

Logan stood and said, "Tell us what you learned."

Brenna came out of the kitchens and handed goblets to both Artan and Simone. "Refresh yourselves first. The old goat can wait a few moments." Then she glanced over her shoulder at Logan and smiled.

Logan slapped his hand on his forehead. "Brenna, is it not time for you to go back to Ramsay land yet?"

Brenna leaned down and kissed Logan's cheek. "When I'm ready, I'll go and not before."

Simone took a few sips of the warm broth, then sat in the chair Broc offered her while he moved to stand behind Merryn. "I'll tell you all we learned, then see if it matches what Aunt Avelina discovered. They're all in the same place in Drimnin, but they're in an underground holding of some kind. The entrance is hidden and will be difficult to find. I gave this information to the messenger at Lochaline, and he left right away."

Connor said, "Perfect. Many thanks for that effort. So pleased to hear our men were waiting for you. Anything else?"

"Glenna slept in a large chamber in Mingary with only one maid. A few guards were at the drawbridge. No one at the water's edge."

"That's it?"

"Other than the fact that Glenna lies and twists everything to her benefit? It's your fault she lost her hand, Logan. Blames it all on you and blames her grandfather's death on Kyla. She didn't appreciate the truth as I told it, but she learned not to disagree with me."

Logan snorted. "Wish I'd been there to watch that. I'm betting she was convinced before you took your leave."

Artan only smiled.

Maeve came out of the tower chamber, Grant whining and wiggling in her arms, reaching for something. "Wia."

Maitland got up and took his son, kissing his head before finding the plaid to wrap him to the front of his chest.

Emmalin said, "He hasn't been happy since John was taken, has he?"

Maeve tugged on her hair, "He slept terribly and so did we."

Maitland paced with the lad; sometimes he would smile and then he would cry. "He's always been such a happy lad. Do you think he's teething or something, Aunt Brenna?"

"He's a bit young, but possibly. I showed Maeve how to feel his gums."

Maeve just shook her head.

Logan said, "Back to our problem. Does anyone have a suggestion on how we can find where the hidden holding is? Do we need to get Sloan and Lennox to help us?"

Artan said, "They are not going to know where something is if it was built into the ground near Drimnin. It's pretty isolated and there is lots of land—forests, hills, no inhabitants. It's lush with overgrowth and animals. It could be anywhere. Without landmarks, we'll never find them. Our only chance is to get the men at Mingary, if they are still there, and have them lead us to it."

"What about Glenna?"

Simone snorted. "Anyone ever met a wise Buchan? Because I surely did not. What a lying fool."

Logan snorted again.

No one answered.

Simone drawled, "And you never will see a wise Buchan. Glenna only knows her name and her enemies. Believe me, I tried my best tricks to get her to reveal all she knows, but she revealed naught. And I believe she knows naught."

Connor began to pace. "Did you see anything else, Dyna? Was there anything in your visions? Anything we could use to find this holding?"

Dyna stared at Avelina who shook her head so subtly that she hoped no one saw it. Fortunately, Tora interrupted everyone's thoughts, their gazes all following her path back to her grandfather. She tugged on his plaid and said, "Up, Gwandda."

Her father picked up her daughter, Dyna nearly in tears watching the two together. "Gwandda, Gwant knows." Then she slid down to the floor again and ran.

Maeve screamed, "Nay!"

They all stared at her.

"Nay, Grant is a wee bairn. He does not know where John and Kyla and Alasdair are. Lia will save them all. They do not need him." She teared up as she tugged on some loose strands of hair, wrapping them around her finger. "Nay, just nay," she whispered.

Broc strode over to Maitland and said, "Walk that way."

Maitland walked away from the door and Grant cried. The farther away he moved, the louder he cried. Maitland glanced back at Broc, who said, "Now, walk toward the door."

Grant stopped crying and kicked his legs, giggling. He pointed to the door.

"Nay!" Maeve moaned, her tears now flowing down her cheeks. "Maitland, please."

Broc went over to the door and said, "We have to test this out, Maitland."

Maeve yelled, "Do not leave here with our child, Maitland Menzie."

"Maeve, I promise we won't leave the gates, but I have to know. We'll be right back." Maitland adjusted his son before going outside, grabbing another plaid to cover him with. "Broc, open the door."

Dyna came up behind Maeve, hugged her, and took her by the hand. They followed Maitland and Broc along with Avelina, her father, and Uncle Finlay.

If Maitland moved toward the gate, Grant

squealed and kicked his legs, swinging his fists with joy. "Wia."

If Maitland turned back toward the keep, Grant screamed and cried and kicked furiously until his father turned back around. Maitland gave Maeve a look that said he was sorry. "I wish it weren't so, Maeve, but it is. I don't understand what their connection is, but it's there. You can't deny it."

They neared the closed gate just as a green light approached the castle. Everyone stopped as the gates opened, and Lia strode through. The fear coursed through Dyna as much as Maeve, if she were to guess.

"Nay, Lia. Nay. He's not going. He is too young to go to battle." Maeve walked backward as she spoke, her hands fisted. "I don't care if he does have Grant blood in him." Then she did the oddest thing. Maeve tipped her head back and screamed, "Da! Nay! Please. Mama, convince him it shouldn't happen." The tears covered her cheeks.

"I'm not here for Grant, Maeve." Lia strode over to her and took her hand.

"Then who?"

"Grant will not be hurt, but it will surely torture you when he goes. Maitland will handle him just fine. But I'm sure it will be difficult for you."

"Who are you here for then, Lia?" Maeve asked. Everyone held their breath.

"I'm here for you, Maeve. We're going too."

CHAPTER FORTY-TWO

Broc

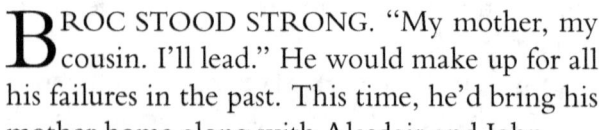

BROC STOOD STRONG. "My mother, my cousin. I'll lead." He would make up for all his failures in the past. This time, he'd bring his mother home along with Alasdair and John.

He didn't regret making that statement, but he had to admit, as they led the way from Lochaline to Drimnin, his belly was starting to flip-flop as if he were about to run into a thunderstorm with giant snakes falling from the sky.

He wouldn't allow his fear to slow him this time. Alaric had volunteered to head the group along with him, Maitland directly behind the pair, with the giggling Grant tied tightly to his chest, directing the group. Maeve had insisted the lad wear a hat, and he was as happy as he'd ever been. Merryn rode with Simone behind them. He wished to turn around and speak with her, but he vowed to keep his focus. This had to be the journey that would end this chapter of torture for his clan.

He hadn't slept well last night either. Awakened by boar tusks coming at him, he'd been in a heavy sweat, shouting enough to awaken Hagen in the bed next to him. "Sorry, Hagen."

"You all right?" his cousin had asked.

"Fine. Nightmare." One that made him think there was a boar in his chamber, a foolish thought, but it had seemed so real. The smell of the boar, the grunt as it reached him, the crush of its hooves on his leg. The searing pain as the tusk ripped into him. He'd escaped another goring. At least, that was what his mind kept telling him. *Breathe, breathe, Broc.*

"You gotta kill that boar sometime, cousin." Then Hagen had rolled back over, fast asleep a few moments later.

There were times he wished he'd find a boar on Mull, but he couldn't think on it now. He had to focus on saving Alasdair, John, and his mother.

Lennox pulled up next to Broc and said, "This spot up ahead is where I would leave some. There is a path that leads to a stream to water the horses. It's a lovely spot with a waterfall, yet isolated. Maeve, Lia, Logan, and Magni would be best staying here."

Connor said, "I'll stay back. I'm watching for our guards. I know the path they'll take, so I'll direct them."

Lennox and Meg led the group to the clearing near the waterfall. "If your men come down the path to Drimnin, that path we left is the only way. You'll hear them coming and see them as they pass by from here, Chief."

"My thanks, MacVey."

Maeve came over and gave Maitland and Grant each a kiss, her tears flooding her cheeks.

"Maeve, we'll protect him." Maitland kissed her on the lips. "Our son is special. We've known that. Look how happy he is."

"But he's just a baby, Maitland. Our beautiful baby." She lifted his wee hat and kissed the fine dark hairs on the lad's head, rubbing lightly. Grant tried to kiss her nose, making her laugh.

Broc said, "Alaric and I will not allow anyone near your husband or your son, Maeve."

She nodded, unable to speak. Lia said, "Grant will protect himself and his sire. Fear not, Maeve."

"I still don't understand why you can't take them there, Lia, and leave Grant here. He will be a hindrance if a battle starts."

Eli said, "You have three strong archers and two axe-throwers besides the many swordsmen. We can handle their two score men, Maeve. Trust us."

Grant began to whine, pushing against his mother's last hug. "Wia."

"We'll return soon, happy and whole. We need to put an end to this man's torturous reign of hell."

Maeve nodded and stepped back, Uncle Connor wrapping his arm around her shoulders. "I trust them, Maeve." She turned around and buried her face in her brother's chest.

Logan came over to Broc and whispered, "Make that bastard hurt, but keep him alive. I have questions for him before you finish him."

Alaric and Broc both nodded. Broc decided he'd save his questions for later.

The group headed out, everyone quiet as they approached Drimnin.

They came to a fork in the road, so Broc pulled his horse back. "Check for us, Maitland?"

Maitland led his horse down the choice he wouldn't have picked, and Grant let out a squeal and a cry. They took the other path and Grant reverted to his happy self, his fist now in his mouth, his legs kicking with excitement.

Broc looked back over his shoulder. "Do you wonder why he says Lia instead of John?"

Maitland said, "I've given it some thought, and I have concluded that Lia represents whatever special power my son has. The same type of magick or power that John holds with the sword. To me, I would bet *Wia* stands for John's sword. I think he's drawn to that. After all, we left Lia with Maeve, and he's still saying her name."

They reached Drimnin, the beach up ahead, so Lennox and Meg led the way. Lennox explained their goal. "We've discussed this with the local people. They directed us the last time to Egan's place. I'll see if they can help us."

He and Meg spoke with the villagers, then they returned, pointing back into the woods.

"Two of them said the men come and go from Egan's old place over there, but they don't go to Egan's hut, instead to a different spot back in the woods. In fact, they said they've tried to locate the exact spot, but they can't find anything."

Broc asked, "Which way?" While the coastline and the small village's well-kept huts were inviting, behind them sat nothing but thick woods with two paths, probably used by the locals for hunting.

"That way."

Broc and Alaric headed in that direction, following the indicated path. Wee Grant agreed.

But they didn't travel far down the path before it seemed to come to an end. "What the hell?" Alaric asked.

There was nothing but an endless forest in every direction.

"Maitland?"

He led his horse in three different directions, but only the fourth one pleased Grant. He pointed to a pile of brush that they hadn't noticed.

Maitland declared, "My son and I will not be the first ones. You and Alaric check. This is as far as my son goes."

Broc jumped down, glancing over at Merryn to make sure she was handling everything well. His hand checked for his dagger, pleased it was still attached to his belt. He wished this entire situation were over, that his mother was home with the others so he and Merryn could enjoy their new love.

Love it was, indeed. He adored Merryn.

Broc and Alaric approached, Lennox behind them. He said, "That pile is hiding something. Alaric, you grab that end. Broc, you over there." The three found branches to grab, lifting the brush, surprised to discover it was all tied together and lifted easily.

As soon as they tossed it aside, Grant giggled and pointed to the door in the ground. Maitland moved his horse back, but then said, "Wait. I wish to position the archers first."

Simone said, "I'll arrange us. We need to cover each angle for whoever comes flying out when you release the door. Open and stand back. I'll hit them."

The group situated themselves, archers in the trees, then Maitland stepped far enough away and said, "Unbolt it."

Broc pulled on the handle, lifting it easily, then dropped the door off to the side before jumping back.

Nothing there but a staircase.

"I'm going down," Broc said, Alaric following him, both with swords drawn. They weren't down long before they returned.

"What's wrong?" Maitland asked.

Grant began to wiggle and kick, whining and pointing at the staircase. "Wia, Wia."

"There's a point with three different tunnels off it. We don't know which way to go."

"Shite," Maitland said, closing his eyes to think. "I want Lennox, Finlay, and Artan to stay up here with the lasses." Grant continued to fuss, so he finally said, "We'll come, but one of you in front of us and one behind us. I can't hold my sword with him on my chest. I can only hold my dagger."

Broc said, "My mother. I'll lead." He would find his mother and bring her home, on his honor as a Grant Highlander.

They crept down the staircase, distant torches lighting up the tunnels. Once at the cross path, they stopped and waited for Grant to give them direction, and he did. They took the path to the right and passed two doors. On the third door, the bairn nearly jumped out of his restraints.

"Open this one," Maitland said to Broc, stepping past the door to protect his son.

Broc opened it, then stood back, his sword in front of him. No one came out.

"Wia."

Broc stuck his head in and noticed a pallet against one wall. "John?"

"Aye? Broc?"

"Aye, lad. We're here." Broc had a hard time holding back his excitement at finding the lad. Grant had done it, no one could deny it. He set his weapon down, nodding to Alaric to keep himself at the door. Maitland and Broc moved over to the lad, both using their daggers to set him free. Success at last! Now for his mother and Alasdair next.

"Wia! Wia!"

John said, "Greetings, Grant. Why is he here?"

"He led us to you. Where is your father? My mother?" Broc asked.

"I don't know."

Maitland asked, "Do you have your sword?"

"Aye." He held it up and Grant kicked and giggled.

"Wia, Wia." The blue glow filled the chamber. The wee lad reached over and grabbed the end of the sword, wiggling it without cutting his hands. Broc couldn't believe that not a speck of blood showed from the lad grabbing the blade of the weapon.

He was not about to try to touch it.

"They took my father because he told Kelvan he was you, Broc. Said he was Kyla's son."

"How long ago?"

"A quarter of the day?"

Maitland said, "Tell Grant to lead us to your sire, John. He listens to you."

John took Grant's hand and said, "Which way? Where's my father?"

He pointed back down the passageway to where they started, then led them down another hallway.

They followed the wee bairn's lead and found the door. Broc opened it, shocked to see his mother sitting on a stool, leaning against the wall. "Mama?" She looked so small, something he never would consider his mother to be. Kyla Grant MacNicol was always larger than life.

A man was chained to the stone edge. "Alasdair!" The man's head shot up.

"We've been waiting for you. Where's John?"

"Right here, Da." John came in and searched around for the key to his father's chains.

Broc moved to his mother and knelt beside her. "Mama?"

She had a black eye and a bruised cheek. Her lip was cut, but her eyes opened. "Broc?"

"Aye, Mama, I'm going to get you out of here. Da is waiting for us."

"I don't know if I can walk, Broc." Her eyes

teared up. "I haven't eaten much. I have no strength left. Been tied up too long."

Broc sheathed his sword, then lifted her while Alaric found the key and unlocked Alasdair's chains.

Alasdair said, "Hurry. They are returning. They went to get Glenna so she could return to cut off my hand. Says it was all Logan's fault that she lost her hand."

Maitland said, "Let's move quickly."

Broc carried his mother, and they headed back down the passageway. They nearly made it, but their escape was interrupted at the cross path.

Men came from four directions.

Broc shouted, "Maitland, get between us. Mama, you're going to have to stand next to him."

Alasdair took Maitland's sword and faced one direction while Broc pushed his mother behind him and faced two men coming at him.

Maitland, Grant, and Kyla were in the middle while Alasdair, Broc, Alaric, and John protected them.

Wee Grant giggled.

CHAPTER FORTY-THREE

Alasdair

"JOHN, GET BEHIND me when you need to!"

"I'm fine, Da."

Alasdair didn't like fighting like this because the small space restricted the arc of his weapon. It was a central area that had been there for a long time, if he were to guess, the different paths likely built at different times.

From what he could determine, there were eight men attacking the four of them, though the weapons were much smaller than the Grant swords.

He swung at one, a false swing, before he changed his drive and thrust into the man's belly, dropping him to the ground, though he had to fight to retrieve his weapon.

"Da!" John shouted, swinging his sword at the man who came at him while he readied himself.

"Behind you, John. I'm fine."

Broc let out a Grant war whoop just before he felled one of his attackers. Alaric followed his lead and whooped behind Broc, taking another one down.

But Alasdair struggled. He'd never had this much trouble fighting; he hadn't been fed much, and his thirst was overwhelming, so his strength waned because of it.

All he could think of was his father, how hard they'd always said Jake Grant fought. How he had the power of five men when he fought. Until the day he died.

Was he about to follow in his father's footsteps? Nay. His bairns were too young. He was *not* ready to leave his wife and bairns behind.

"Nay, Da. I'm too young. Not yet," he whispered to himself. "Help me. Da? Grandda? I'm fading."

The man he fought became more aggressive, making swings he wasn't anticipating. Then the bastard caught his thigh, almost dropping him, but he had a sudden surge of power that shocked him. He lifted his sword as if it were but a twig. What had happened?

The smell of mint leaves overpowered him. His sire was here, almost as if his arms were supporting Alasdair's. He deftly blocked three swings from his opponent. Then an unknown force overtook him, lifting his sword with a power he hadn't had a few moments ago.

Grant giggled loudly, and John's sword took on its blue glow.

The opponents dropped in such quick succession that it took Alasdair by surprise. He thought he was about to take a sword to his belly, but instead, his sire had somehow given him the strength and direction to end his fight, dropping his attacker easily. His leg bled from the one strike, but not too badly.

Spinning around, he watched a magical display as Broc finished his attacker, then Alaric ended his battle, and finally John struck the last man in the tunnels.

Maitland exclaimed, "What the hell was that? I've never seen anything like it. Well done."

Alasdair fought to regain his breath, heaving from the exertion of fighting in such a small space. Broc had turned back to his mother, checking on her, but all were hale.

"Mama, can you walk up the stairs? We're getting out of here. Da and Uncle Connor are waiting down the path."

"I can if you let me hold your arm, Broc. I'm just a bit weak."

"Then I'm carrying you out of here. When we're outside, you can stand."

Alaric led the way toward the stairs, Broc behind him carrying his mother, then Maitland, John, and Alasdair.

As soon as they all stepped out of the stairs, they froze at the sight in front of them.

Kelvan sat atop his horse, his arms crossed. "My thanks for bringing them up. This makes it easier for us now. Glenna?" he asked, looking over his shoulder at his wife on a horse behind him, a wide grin on her face. "Which one do you wish to start with?"

She pointed to Alasdair. "I want Kyla's son. Time to chop off a hand."

CHAPTER FORTY-FOUR

Broc and Merryn

BROC DECIDED IT was time to put an end to all this shite spit out by a man who was smaller than he was, and obviously, not as smart as anyone in all of Clan Grant. This time, with Kelvan and Glenna directly in front of him, he would not back down.

"I'm Kyla's son, and I'm the one who cut off Glenna's hand after she stabbed a friend of mine in the back. And I'd do it again." He set his mother down and moved her behind him. "You want me? Come and get me. I've had enough of the torture you've levied against the people of Mull. But you're not a big enough man to do that, are you, Kelvan? You let others fight your battles for you."

He scanned the area, noting the three archers in the trees, Meg and Eva innocently standing near the copse, their axes behind their backs. He checked for his dagger attached to his belt, just in case he needed it, but it was gone.

Hell.

He forced that into the back of his mind because he had to end this horrific threat now.

He also noticed that Uncle Connor and Logan had just come down the path behind Kelvan and Glenna, who both had three guards on either side of them. He prayed that meant the Grant guards were not far away.

Kelvan nodded to two of his men. "Get him and bring him to me."

The two dismounted but Logan called out from behind him. "If I were you two, I'd keep my eyes on the archers in the trees. One is a Ramsay who prefers to shoot men in their bollocks. Oh, and don't forget the two axe-throwers. One prefers to hit you right between your eyes."

The two men didn't move.

"You have no bollocks, Kelvan? You are the tough man who barks all your orders to steal bairns, hold old women and men captive. Come down from your tall horse and fight me. You and me," Broc said, moving closer.

"Broc, nay …" his mother whispered.

Kelvan laughed. "You think I'm going to fight you? That's what I pay these men for. And all the ones who are about to come over the hills and up the beach for you. They'll be here momentarily, and you are all dead men. But I did promise Glenna she could amputate your hand herself."

"Aye, it's my right. A hand for a hand," Glenna declared with a chuckle. "Get him."

One man moved and got an axe in the middle of his forehead from Meg.

Kelvan said to the other one, "If all four of you move at once, they can't get you all, fools!"

Broc caught something out of the corner of his eye, men coming from the beaches and through the forests, and they were not wearing red plaids. All on foot, but nonetheless, they would be outnumbered in no time. He had to move this along, but he wasn't quite sure how to do it.

Glenna said, "Go get him or I'll have you killed, Samuel. It's his fault I lost my hand."

Simone dropped out of her tree and said, "This is the last warning you will be getting from me, Glenna. Keep that dirty, lie-spieling tongue in your mouth, or I will end your life myself." She nocked an arrow and took aim, but didn't shoot. "Don't lie again or this is coming for you. Do you remember where I said I'd get you?"

Logan said, "I'd listen to her if I were you. And there are archers aiming for Kelvan right now."

"Get them, I told you," Kelvan said.

Another axe caught the next man who moved right in his chest.

"Get them!" Glenna yelled, standing up in her stirrups and pointing.

Merryn dropped out of her tree and marched forward. Broc had never been so proud of her. She strode toward Kelvan but stopped next to Simone. None of the men dared move because of the axes.

Even the ones coming from the beaches stopped to watch.

Eli dropped out and stood on the other side of Simone.

"Merryn? You think I'm afraid of you?" Kelvan began to laugh, but not for long.

"I'm glad you remember me. This is for my sister." She fired one arrow and hit him in the shoulder, and he screamed like a wee lass.

"You bitch!" Glenna shouted.

"You were warned," Simone said, setting her arrow free and catching Glenna in her eye. Glenna fell off her mount, her death quick. Kelvan took one look at her and headed into the trees, trying to yank out the arrow in his shoulder.

Suddenly, there were men everywhere.

The Grant warriors and archers made a line, protecting Kyla and Grant. Maitland handed his bairn to Kyla and grabbed a sword from one of the dead men, joining the fight.

Broc pulled Merryn in next to him. "Just fire, lass. We'll move toward my sire to get my mother to safety."

He fought each man as they came forward, but the melee was a battle like he'd never experienced. They were losing quickly because there were so many men coming at them from everywhere.

Simone grabbed Merryn, running toward the copse. "Back in the trees, Eli." The archers left while Meg and Eva stood behind their husbands.

Uncle Connor yelled to him, "Broc, we're fighting from here. Move in this direction and I'll get Kyla."

Broc swung and swung, the sound of metal clashing so loud it was something he'd never forget. Screams of pain, grunts, moans, bellows— the sounds of battle echoed through the air. Broc thought his shoulders were about to fall off, but he couldn't stop.

He could see his father's face on a horse not far from him, staring at him. "A little farther, son. I'll get her." His father and Uncle Connor struck down any man who came near them, all on foot.

Arrows took men out, axes sent men screaming, and swords cut paths of blood that dripped rivers in the dirt beneath their feet, but the battle continued. Then Alasdair let out a war whoop when John's sword lit up, the blue color bathing the entire area.

Broc heard a loud noise, a sound that made him fear more men were coming, but then he and his comrades all began to laugh at once. He'd never heard a sweeter sound in his life.

The Grant war whoop was so loud it was nearly deafening behind the rumble of the horses' hooves shaking the ground. Two hundred or more Grant guards covered the area, taking men down right and left. They battled on for only about half the hour before the rest of Kelvan's men retreated, running back on their ships and into the forest.

Uncle Connor came straight toward Kyla while Logan and Magni helped Simone onto his horse and headed into the woods, though Broc had no idea why. Broc turned around to find his mother with a wide smile on her face. He picked her up and carried her over to the two horses waiting for them, Uncle Connor on one side, his father on the other.

Uncle Connor tipped his head toward Finlay, so Broc handed his mother over to his father.

Uncle Connor said, "Well done, Broc. You fought like my sire did in battle. The same swing, the same gumption. I'm quite sure Logan and Simone went after Kelvan. And Glenna? She got what she deserved from Simone. As fine a shot as I've ever witnessed." Then his uncle grinned, something he hadn't seen much of lately. "Da would be proud."

Maeve and Lia galloped toward them, the other horses opening a path, Maeve sobbing while Maitland brought Grant back to his mother's arms. The lad fell asleep within moments. Maitland kissed her. "It's over, love. And Grant had a big part in finding Alasdair, John, and Kyla."

"Maitland, you're covered in blood. Are you hurt? Did Grant get …"

"He's fine. Neither of us were injured."

"Then how did you get… Never mind. I don't wish to know."

Broc cleaned his weapon on the grass, sheathed it, and went to find Merryn standing near a tree. "Sweeting, you are hale?"

Tears covered her face. "Aye, but he got away. Kelvan got away."

"Lass, you were amazing with your bow. You hit him perfectly. Enough to send him running, but not to kill him. Logan wished to deal with him."

Merryn fell into his arms and said, "But I wanted to kill him. Why couldn't I? He killed my sister and my parents. I don't understand."

"Because Logan wanted him. I don't know why, but we're about to find out."

Logan came out of the woods, still mounted with Magni in front of him. Lia came down from Maeve's horse and moved over toward the underground holding, but she stopped at the steps and folded her hands in front of her.

A circle surrounded Logan, and Alaric and Simone emerged from the forest with Kelvan now tied by a rope. Alaric led him over to Logan's horse and handed the rope to Logan.

"What the hell," Kelvan cried. "I'm hurt. I need a healer. I can't pull this arrow out of my shoulder."

"Oh, you'll get just what you need, K," Logan drawled. "And what you deserve. Connor, instruct your guards to protect the perimeter. We want no interruptions for this."

"You coldhearted bastards. You killed my wife in front of me." Kelvan wiped the sweat from his brow and tried to undo his bindings but was unsuccessful. "Where are my men? I order you to come and help me. Untie me and I'll give you ten gold coins." No rustling or movement answered his cry. The next came out in a bold shout, "Twenty! Twenty gold coins each. Forty if you cut my bindings to free me!"

Logan said, "I need everyone's attention. This is important. Alaric, I need you on one side and Connor on the other to hold this man in place."

Connor and Alaric did as they were told, Simone going to join Artan.

Logan said, "Now, if anyone has a gripe against this man and his actions, I'd like you to, in turn, step over in front of him, give your name, and stake your claim. That's all for now. We wish to hear who has a complaint against the man known as Kelvan, or K. If I tell you 'Just due,' I ask you to stay in your position. You'll get your chance, eventually. And let it be known to anyone listening that this is how Clans Ramsay, Grant, Menzie, and Grantham, along with all the clans of Mull, handle any assaults on their members."

Logan raised his voice. "It's time for just due for all who have claims."

CHAPTER FORTY-FIVE

Just Due

THE GROUP WHISPERED amongst themselves for a few moments while Logan waited. When he was ready, he asked, "Who's first?"

Kyla stepped up, her husband behind her. "He held me captive."

"Just due. Next?" Logan announced.

Meg stepped over, Lennox following her. "He had me held captive to take care of four bairns."

Logan nodded. "Just due. Next?"

And so it continued.

Sloan. "He stole my nephew away, wanted to sell him."

Thane. "He took my parents captive and tried to sell me and my siblings to another family in Europe."

Magni. "He kidnapped me." Then he looked at Thane who nodded to him. "He did it too many times. I don't like him."

Logan nodded to him and said, "Just due to my grandson." Then he tugged on the rope to pull him closer so he could slap Kelvan on the back of his head. "He's a lad, you cruel bastard."

Magni smirked.

"Next?"

Maitland. "Kidnapped my son and my wife."

Dyna. "He kidnapped my bairns. Multiple times, you bloody rotten bastard. Just due, Uncle."

Connor and Logan smirked and nodded in unison.

Logan leaned toward Kelvan and said, "Big mistake. Poor bastard when she comes at you."

Kelvan frowned but said nothing.

A woman arrived on her horse, coming in behind the others. Gwyneth. "Bastard dared to touch the bairns I adore. Let me at him, husband."

"Just due, Gwynie."

Logan asked, "Connor? You want just due?"

Connor declared, "Just due for kidnapping my grandbairns. However, I give my just due to my daughter."

"That's a powerful one. Dyna now has four counts against you, K. Did I mention that Dyna was trained by my wife? Know you my wife's reputation?"

Kelvan was now crying but shook his head.

"She likes to strike a man in his bollocks. Killed a couple of men that way."

Kelvan held his bound hands in front of his private parts.

"Anyone else want just due?" Logan asked.

Broc squeezed Merryn's hand and nodded to her. "I'll go with you."

Merryn strode over, her bow hooked on her

shoulder, and stood in front of Logan, Broc behind her with his hands on her shoulders for support. She needed this so much.

"State your case, lass," Logan said. "All of it." Then he nodded to Merryn.

"Merryn MacClane. He led the raid that butchered my village…"

Kelvan stopped crying to glare at her. "Aye, I did. Send me to my king, and I'll get my just due. I hated your sister."

"Hell, nay," Logan said. "If you survive our just due, I'll take you to our king, Robert. But chances are I'll send your dead body to Edward. Continue, lass. He interrupted you."

"I watched him kill my sister, his wife, from behind. Thrust his sword through her back while she tried to escape him." Merryn's tears started, but she wasn't going to stop without listing all his crimes. "I heard him kill both of my parents. He deserted his daughter and then went on to another village to kill more. Just due, if you please."

"You lying bitch!" K said. "I didn't kill your parents."

"I heard you from where I was hiding!"

Alaric's elbow came up and hit Kelvan so hard in the face that everyone heard the crack of the bone in his nose.

Logan said, "What, K? Did you have something else to say?"

The man cupped his face with his bound hands, blood covering his fingers.

"Anyone else just due?"

No one spoke. So, Logan said, "Here's how this will go. I'm going to ask you a few questions, K. After each, if you lie or refuse to answer, I will give just due to someone to strike you in whatever way they choose. They are not to use a killing blow until I give them the right to do so."

"What the hell does that mean? You're going to kill me? Just kill me now. Have some compassion."

Connor drawled. "Here's your compassion." Connor's elbow came up and smashed K's jaw. "Just due, Logan."

"Connor's is done. Now Kelvan, a while ago, you stole a lad's parents away and then sent him to Ulva. I want to know where his parents are."

"How the hell would I know?"

"Just due, Magni."

Magni ran over and kicked him in both shins, grinned, then ran back to his spot. Kelvan made the mistake of trying to touch the boy, but Connor grabbed him to hold him in place.

"I'll ask again. Where is that couple, K?"

"I don't know who you are talking about." The arrogance on his face was so glaring that he was making everything easy. Everyone hated the man who'd caused so much heartbreak on Mull.

"Sloan?"

"I give mine to Dyna."

"I do the same," Meg said.

Thane said, "I also give my just due to Dyna or Merryn."

An arrow flew out and caught Kelvan in his upper thigh. He screamed, hopping on his other foot.

"Gwynie, I didn't give you just due yet."

"I couldn't help myself, Logan. He's such a dark soul." Then she moved her horse back. "Dyna and Merryn."

"Maitland?"

"I give just due to Dyna."

"Magni," Logan said, waving to his grandson. "Please stand right over there. Do you see that boy in front of you? Where are his parents?"

"I don't know, I tell you!"

"Dyna?"

The arrow flew so fast, K never saw it coming, but it went over his head because he ducked. Then Dyna ran forward and knocked him down, yanking the other arrow out of his thigh, tossing it aside, and punching him with her fist until Connor lifted her. "Enough, lass."

Dyna burst into tears. "My bairns. You tried to hurt my bairns." She gave one last kick to his belly before she walked away.

Alaric and Connor lifted him to his feet, but he continued to complain. "I cannot walk!" He spit a tooth off to the side.

Logan asked again, "Where are they? The lad's parents."

Kelvan hung his head, his knees buckling while he struggled to stand. "In the tunnel to the left."

Logan pointed to the men closest. "Alaric and Broc, take Magni with you."

Lia said, "I'll go too!" Now they understood why Lia stood by the staircase. She'd been waiting patiently for this.

"Go with them, Lia."

Broc waited for Magni to join him, surprised when Magni reached up to take his hand. He whispered, "Promise not to leave me in there? It looks dark."

"I promise. Alaric and I will protect you."

"And I will always protect you, Magni," Lia added, taking his other hand.

The four headed into the tunnel, taking the passageway to the left, opening one door, then another, and finally the last one.

Magni said, "You go in. I'm scared, Broc."

"I'll go for you, lad." Broc opened the door and there, sitting on two stools, were a man with gray hair and a woman with her hair tied back in a loose plait. Their eyes lit up when they saw the door open, though they cringed at first. A boy of around ten lay on a pallet in front of them, asleep.

Broc said, "I'm not here to hurt you. Do you know a boy named Magni?"

The man nodded but said nothing, his eyes hopeful. Broc turned around, "Come on in, Magni."

Magni walked in, holding on to Lia's hand, and shouted, "Mama? Papa?" Then he ran to them, throwing himself at his mother, hugging her and burying his face in her lap. After a moment, he got up and hugged his father.

Broc moved over and knelt in front of the two. "Kelvan will no longer bother you. We've ended his entire operation. You are free to go. Who is the sleeping lad?"

Magni's mother said, "They stole him from a place in Aoineadh Mòr, tried to send him away, but he was violently ill on the ships, so they brought him back. He's to be sold in a sennight."

The man looked at his wife and said, "We'll not leave the poor lad here. He must go with us, but where will we go? They burned our village to the ground. Everything we had is gone."

Alaric came in behind Broc with Lia. Broc explained, "Magni has been living on the Isle of Mull with Clan MacQuarie. I'm sure you can join their clan. If not, you are welcome to join us at Clan Grantham."

Alaric motioned to them. "Can you both walk enough to follow us out? We have horses to take you back to Mull. There is no reason to stay here any longer."

"I'll help you, Mama," Magni said, reaching for his mother's hand.

The group headed down the passage, and all along the way, Magni babbled on, his joy contagious.

"You should see everything at Clan MacQuarie, Da. Thane is the chieftain, and he just got married. They're going to have a bairn, and his wife makes the best fruit tarts and meat pies, and I help Thane with the horses, and you can live there with us, Da. You can help with the horses too …"

They stopped at the end and Magni looked up at Broc and said, "Please don't tell anyone I cried."

"Promise."

They stepped outside, and Magni shouted for all to hear, "I found them!" Dyna and Eli came over to help the couple understand what was happening, getting them away from the main event in the center.

The boy who'd been sleeping trudged along behind them, confused by everything taking place. All three had been in the holding so long that they had trouble adjusting to the light of day.

Meg stared at the three strangers, then squeezed her husband's hand. "Lennox, look. Remember the cook at Aoineadh Mòr? Do you suppose that could be their son?"

Lennox said, "Heavens above us, I hope so." He approached the lad and asked, "Is your mother a cook in an inn at Aoineadh Mòr?"

"Aye," he nodded, rubbing his eyes as he tried to look up at Lennox. "My name is Errol. Can I go home now?"

Meg teared up and said, "Aye, we'll take you there." They ushered the lad off to the side and found him something to eat.

Logan still sat atop his horse in the center of the clearing, Kelvan barely able to stand on his own, but Connor insisted. Logan whistled for everyone's attention again. "The last just due goes to Merryn. Do as you wish, lass. I don't need him for anything."

Broc came over and nodded to her. She picked up her bow and nocked an arrow, then let it back down. "Broc, I want to, but I don't know if I can hold it tight any longer."

Broc said, "You aim, and I'll help you."

"I told you she was nothing but a liar and a weakling," Kelvan shouted, his voice sounding quite odd.

Another horse came close and someone hopped down. "My thanks to you, Broc, but I'm going to claim just due for my family. Merryn, nock your arrow, and we'll do it together."

Tristan came over to stand behind his sister, watched her set herself, then stood behind her and reached over her shoulders to steady her arm. "Kelvan Mortimer, this is for our parents and our dear sister Nara."

He pulled the bow with Merryn, and they let it go.

Kelvan would never steal another bairn.

CHAPTER FORTY-SIX

Everyone

L OGAN SCANNED THE area. It was finally
done.

Connor approached the head of his guards and
gave them instructions to bury the dead and then
head back.

"Where is he?" Logan asked Connor.

Connor smirked and said, "Just inside those
trees, waiting for you. I'll send a few more men
with you."

Logan sent his horse into the woods, smiling
when he came upon the man he'd been meeting
as an informant for so long. "Och, Samuel. Still
think I'm a daft old man?"

"How did you know my name?" Samuel
fidgeted with the ropes that bound his hands.

"I know more than you wish to give me credit
for. So, you operated as Kelvan's second, meeting
me secretly in the forest, took my information
directly to him, and have no guilt over hurting
bairns."

Samuel shrugged. "I did what I was told.

Naught more, naught less. I care not about bairns. They don't belong to me."

"You did all that just for the coin?"

"Aye. I wanted the coin so I could …"

Logan arched a brow. "And the truth comes out at the end. Because I wish to make sure you will not assume Kelvan's place and continue to bother the inhabitants of Mull, I've arranged for you and a few of your men to be taken into the Highlands."

"This is the Highlands."

Logan chuckled. "Clearly, you've not been deep in the Highlands, or you wouldn't make such a foolish mistake. I tire of you, Samuel. Connor Grant and his guardsmen will see you to the Highlands near Inverness. Leave my people alone."

Logan turned around and headed out.

"You're a mean son of a bitch, you are," Samuel called after him. "I'll work for you for less."

Logan laughed, a chilling sound that carried through the wind of the forest.

"Nay, you won't." He turned back to the area where everyone was taking their leave, finding Gwynie to ride back with him. As soon as she was settled in front of him, he whispered, "It's finally over, wife."

"Thank the Lord above, Logan. Enough is enough."

Maeve and Maitland mounted their horses, Maeve silently crying with Grant now tied to her chest, sound asleep.

Lennox and Meg mounted up on two horses,

the rescued lad seated behind Lennox, holding on tightly. They departed straight for Lochaline.

Alasdair approached Broc, Merryn, Alaric, and Eli, John behind him. "Many thanks for coming for us. It wasn't easy. John and I are grateful."

Alaric said, "You need to tie up that wound, cousin." He helped him get an extra plaid around the wound in his thigh. "You fought like a wild man. Great job."

Finlay approached, Kyla in front of him, exhausted but smiling. "Son, you were a sight to see fighting. You fight like your grandsire."

Kyla teared up and nodded. "My thanks to you and Alaric and Alasdair. It was a group effort, and we are finally done with the fools. But I don't think John was ever in trouble. Not with his sword and Lia nearby."

"I didn't like being tied up," John declared. "I wish to return to Duart, Da. I'm sure Mama is verra worried."

And another group departed.

Dyna rode next to them and said, "I'm going home to hug my bairns. Derric will be so pleased to hear they are done now. What a couple of fools. And one man caused so much trauma and devastation that it's nearly unbelievable. Good riddance to all of them." She rubbed her hand where she'd punched the fool.

Alasdair chuckled. "Derric will know exactly what that's from."

Dyna snorted. "He'd be disappointed if I didn't come back with ragged knuckles."

Broc and Merryn climbed on Midnight Majesty

and rode back together, following the long line of horses leading the way out of Drimnin and back to Lochaline where the ships awaited them. They'd borrowed many MacKinnis horses, but Majesty had been one that they insisted come along.

It was a quiet ride, so many exhausted yet grateful. When they reached Lochaline, Lennox and Meg headed toward Aoineadh Mòr.

Errol asked Lennox, "Do you think they'll take me back, Chief?"

Meg overheard his question and said, "We heard about you from your mother, Errol. She misses you verra much."

The lad began to cry and said, "Those men were so mean. I was just picking apples when they grabbed me."

"We're almost there, lad," Lennox said over his shoulder.

As soon as they headed down the path toward the inn, two others noticed Errol and took off toward the building. "Clara! Clara! It's Errol!" one shouted as they raced toward the tavern at the end of the street.

Clara came out the door at the same time they arrived. "Errol? Is it you? Oh, my wee bairn! Thank the Lord up above. Donnall! Donnall! He's home."

Lennox dismounted and helped Errol down. His mother rushed to his side and crushed the lad in a hug. "I thought we'd lost you forever, Errol."

A man came out of the inn and shouted so loud that everyone ran to see what it was about.

He strode slowly over to his son, stared into his eyes, and pulled his wife back so he could grasp the boy and hold him close. "Who do we thank for this?" Donnall asked.

Meg said, "Many people helped achieve this. We ended a big operation that has been selling bairns for a while. It took nearly all of us on Mull to discover who controlled it. The man in charge was buried in Drimnin along with many others. His name was Kelvan Mortimer, and he won't be stealing any more bairns."

Clara began to sob, her hand on her son's neck.

Meg took Clara's other hand and whispered, "We found him in an underground holding. A sweet couple who'd also been taken captive watched over him. The only information we had was that Errol became violently sick when they sailed away with the intent of selling him overseas, so he was brought back. We know little else other than he was poorly fed and sickly. Welcome him back with care. He's been confused but couldn't wait to get here."

"He's home. Come, lad. I'll take care of you. We'll fix you up." His mother led him to a cottage across from the inn. "Many thanks to you all. We are grateful."

His father barked at two of his workers who ran inside and came out with two wrapped parcels. "We're closing for the rest of the day. I give you what we have. A nicely smoked pheasant and a hunk of lamb. And a small barrel of our finest brew."

"Not necessary," Lennox said.

"Please," Donnall said. "The meat will be wasted because I'm closing to celebrate his return. Take the barrel to Duart Castle for those returning from battle. They probably could use it."

Lennox nodded. "Connor Grant and Logan Ramsay will appreciate it."

Lennox and Meg mounted and started back toward Lochaline. They hadn't gone far when she reached for Lennox. "Stop, please."

A sound caught her coming from the woods.

It was a horse, and it was running straight toward them.

"My mare!" Meg hadn't seen her beloved horse since she was locked up at the kirk not far from Oban. She'd been forced to leave her pet behind in order to save the bairns held captive. It had to be done, but her heart had missed the sweet girl so much.

She took off, but Lennox grabbed her. "Meg, she's been running wild for a bit. Let her come to you. I can't protect you if she's unhinged."

Tears ran down Meg's cheeks as she waited for the small horse to approach, but the familiar neigh greeted her. The horse approached and nuzzled her, putting her head next to Meg's.

Meg was so happy, she couldn't stop smiling.

***

Later that night, the group had gathered in the great hall, a celebratory evening meal behind them, including many draws from the brew brought from Errol's father. The younger ones had decided to take a late dip in the cool loch, but the elders remained, now gathered around the hearth, reminiscing, the wee ones playing nearby.

Connor and Sela, Logan and Gwyneth, Kyla and Finlay, Alasdair and Emmalin, Maitland and Maeve, Brenna, Avelina and Drew, and Dyna and Derric sat while the bairns played quietly. Thane, Simone, and Artan had returned to Clan MacQuarie with Magni and his parents going with them. Lennox and Meg had dropped off some gifts and were now in the loch with the other young ones.

It was a much calmer atmosphere than they'd seen as of late.

Grant was sound asleep on his sire's chest.

Maeve whispered, "Now that most are gone, I have a question for you, Alasdair. While you were held captive, did anything odd happen?"

Alasdair sat up, looking at his son. "What do you mean by odd?"

Maitland said, "Oh, I think there was verra much odd about that holding."

Alasdair peered over at Maitland. "Why do you say that?"

"Besides Grant knowing where you all were, I have to ask you about the strength that came out of nowhere. You were weakening, Alasdair, and for good reason. You probably were hardly fed. A sudden surge of strength sent you swinging like you were twenty summers again, taking down two men that I saw. Then, all of a sudden, the blue light appeared from the sword, and you all fought like you were possessed of some unknown power." Maitland paused for a moment, then squeezed Maeve's hand. "I felt it too. Maeve said Tora told her Alex warmed their cell on Ulva when they were taken. Did you see anything like that?"

Alasdair cleared his throat for a few moments. Then he said, "I know exactly what you are asking, and the answer is aye. Lia spoke to me." His gaze went to Uncle Connor and Aunt Kyla, knowing what it would mean to them. "She said my father was there and told me not to worry about John. She told me that another man named Alex was there with a message for me."

All had quieted to listen to his tale.

"And?" Kyla asked.

"I asked him why we were there. Grandda said I was there to save his daughter," Alasdair explained as his gaze locked on Kyla's. "I was there for you."

Kyla gasped. "Da said that?" Then she looked to her brother. "Didn't Tora tell you the same?"

Connor nodded.

"So Lia and Tora both said the same," Kyla whispered. "How can you not believe something like that?"

"I believe it. How would she know a man named Alex unless he was truly there?" Emmalin asked. "I think he was there to watch over you. I believe in angels." She squeezed Alasdair's hand. "I believe you."

Logan drawled, "I think we all do at this point after watching Lia."

Connor said, "I wish I could see them again."

Kyla added, "I miss them so much."

Alasdair sighed. "Maitland, you're right about

the surge of power too. I could feel my father with me when we were battling in the passageways. I thought I was about to drop when I could smell the mint leaves, and then a sudden surge of power came over me. It felt as though someone was using my arms. I know how daft that sounds, but it's how I felt."

Maeve asked, "Do you all think there's some special link between Grant and John?"

Four voices replied in unison, "Aye."

Avelina said, "I don't know what the connection is, Maeve, but there is definitely something there. They will be close all their lives, I think."

Maitland laughed. "Anyone who was there surely agrees. I don't understand it, but I accept it. I just pray that ..." He stopped and shook his head. "I can't even say the words."

"What?" Connor asked.

"I know what he's thinking," Maeve said.

"I do too," Dyna added. "Are they done? Is there another fool to take their place?"

Tora jumped up and ran over to her grandfather's lap, leaning into him. They all followed her every move. "Gwandda says no mowe bad men." Then she ran off.

Sandor jumped up with a squeal and ran in a circle, shoving at something as he giggled.

Alasdair immediately followed him. "Sandor, who is it?"

"Unca Shakie chaseen me aden."

"What does he say, Sandor?"

"He say no mowe bad men."

Sandor ran and giggled again. "'Top, Unca

Shakie. What?" Then he stopped to stare up at something. "He say Shon an Gwant awe safe."

The next morning, Broc and Merryn found Tristan in the stables, brushing down his horse. "Merryn, I assume you are staying a wee bit longer?"

"Aye, for now. Until I … I …"

Tristan came over and took Merryn's hand in his. "I understand. You've been through quite an ordeal. Take your time. I'm returning so we can finish the tower. The stable is done, and I'm hoping the men have most of the roof on the tower finished. As for the wall? Not yet, but we'll continue to work on it."

Broc glanced from Merryn to Tristan. "My lord, I wish to ask your permission to court your sister. And I have every intention of making her my wife when she's ready."

"Court?" Tristan grinned.

"I have asked Merryn to marry me, and she said aye, but she said she is not ready yet. We have agreed to wait until things settle down a bit."

Tristan looked at his sister, then clasped her shoulder. "It has been difficult for you both. Broc, what you went through was more difficult than anything I've ever done. Your relationship has grown, but in a chaotic time. I think it's wise to wait. But when the time comes, I welcome you to Clan MacLean. After speaking with my uncle, I've agreed to call the holding Clan MacLean. Our sire would accept that. I won't even discuss where you would like to live, but I pray that you will be willing to remain on Mull. I don't mind traveling to Duart to visit you and Shealee, Merryn, but across the water would not please me."

"I love Mull," Merryn said. "But everything has happened so quickly."

"Get to know each other. Broc, I thank you for guarding my sister so well. I think you will make a wonderful couple. I'm going home for a bit, but I'll be back in a few days to update you."

"And I'd be happy to come back and help wherever I can."

Tristan said, "I will accept any help you can give." Then he hugged Merryn. "I love you and Shealee, Merryn. Take care."

Merryn's tears ran down her cheeks, but they were finally the one thing she'd hoped for.

Happy tears.

CHAPTER FORTY-SEVEN

Simone

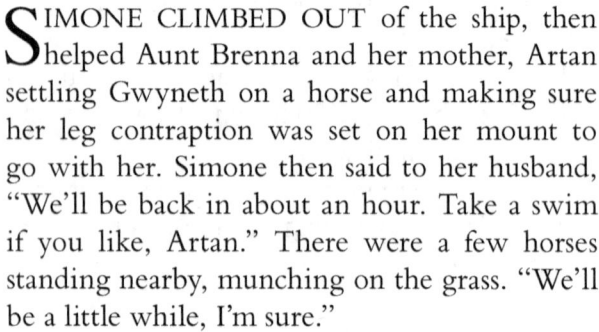

SIMONE CLIMBED OUT of the ship, then helped Aunt Brenna and her mother, Artan settling Gwyneth on a horse and making sure her leg contraption was set on her mount to go with her. Simone then said to her husband, "We'll be back in about an hour. Take a swim if you like, Artan." There were a few horses standing nearby, munching on the grass. "We'll be a little while, I'm sure."

"We will," he replied, pulling off his tunic while the other men did the same. "Take your time, Simone."

Magni rode with Simone while his parents rode together on another horse. "Lead the way," his father said.

Brenna pulled abreast of Simone. "This has to be the loveliest place I've ever seen, and you know how fond I am of Ramsay land, especially in the summer."

"You have a lovely loch, but we have the sea all the time. And the Iona chapel is peaceful and lovely."

"I see it," Aunt Brenna said. "I'm most anxious to see our girls again. How are they doing?"

"All are doing wonderfully."

They approached the row of small huts and Simone called out, "Beatris! I have a surprise!"

All of a sudden, the area was filled with bairns. The unwanted ones of the world, Simone thought of them. Most were lassies, but there were some laddies. Anytime someone in the church found themselves caretakers of bairns who'd lost their parents from sickness or other, the bairns were often sent to Ionaland, they called it.

Of course, her father had suggested calling it Loganland, but they all agreed on Ionaland.

Brenna helped Gwyneth down and assisted with attaching her contraption. Geva and Emma came out, calling to them. Geva said, "Mama, it is so good to see you again."

The four lasses—Simone and Beatris, Geva and Emma—had been adopted long ago. A group of evil men had built a chain nearly three decades ago to sell bairns they'd stolen. But the Grants and Ramsays had fallen upon their scheme and rescued as many as they could. Some were returned to their families, but others had no family to return to.

Simone and Beatris had been sold to a nobleman's family as servants, but they were beaten for any slight. After Maggie and Will had saved both of them, Logan and Gwyneth adopted the two into their family. Geva and Emma had been rescued and adopted into Quade and Brenna's family from a similar jaunt.

Brenna hugged both daughters, then her two nieces. "You all look wonderful. And how many bairns have you now?"

"Three and ten at last count. Three of Geva's and ten adopted."

Simone had married Artan, but they had no bairns. Geva had married, but Beatris and Emma hadn't found their persons yet.

Simone took Magni's mother's hand and brought her forward. "These two lovely people, Ella and Walter, had their hut burned with all their belongings by some cruel creatures, so they are looking for a safe, quiet place to live. The clans are too busy for them, and when they heard of the work you do here, they wondered if they could live here and help you. They have a son Magni who would love to help you too."

Walter said, "I'm verra good with gardens. I was able to feed most of our villagers with food from our land. I made a special mix using sheep … I made our garden flourish with a special recipe that I put on the plants to make them produce more. Beans and peas, oats, carrots. I even transplanted some berry bushes so we had more. And I'm handy at fixing things."

Beatris said, "Geva's husband is out hunting with a few others from the isle, so I would love to have you meet him. They'll be back soon."

Magni said, "I like it here. It's magical." He twirled in a circle, taking in the beauty and the wide expanse of the isle and the land the group lived on. "I can run everywhere, and no one would see me."

Ella's gaze scanned the large area, stopping on one lad, her finger pointing toward him. "Walter? Look at that wee laddie coming towards us. Is he not adorable?"

Magni took one look and raced over to the toddling lad. He said, "Greetings. I'm Magni. What's your name?"

As soon as the boy's gaze fell on Magni, he called out, "Manee, manee."

Beatris asked, "Do you know him? We call him Tenney. That was all we were told. They tried to sell him, but the ship overturned. The boy washed ashore here attached to the oddest-shaped floating object we've ever seen."

"Mama, can we adopt him?" Magni carried the lad over to his parents, grinning and kissing the boy's cheeks. As soon as he gave Tenney to his mother, Magni ran over to Lia and hugged her. "You saved him and sent him to me, did you not, sister?"

"I might have had something to do with it."

Geva said, "And the oddest thing was that the object he floated on disappeared when we turned our backs. It must have washed out into the sea."

Magni whispered, "It is magical here."

Beatris smiled and said, "We think it is, but tell me why you think it's magical, Magni."

"Look at my sister."

Lia stood a distance away near the abbey, her hands overhead pointing to the sky as she basked in a ray of sunshine, her green light brighter than they'd ever seen it.

Simone said, "Lia is a faery who adopted Magni as her brother."

"Wonderful. I would love to meet the faery when she arrives," Beatris said. "But who is the young lassie?"

Simone chuckled. "That's Lia. She talks like an adult, but she is six summers. She found Magni and stayed with him until his parents were rescued. And she obviously protected Tenney too. She was quite a help when it came to protecting all of our bairns from the kidnappers."

Magni proudly announced, "She'll never leave me. She said she could live here for a while. She's my protector."

His mother asked, "Magni, are you sure you like it here better than at Clan MacQuarie or Clan Grantham? They've all grown quite fond of you."

Magni smiled. "I know. I'm cute. But I can visit them anytime. I have a new brother, and he lives here."

And off he went, running toward Lia, his new brother in hand.

CHAPTER FORTY-EIGHT

Alasdair

A FORTNIGHT PASSED, AND Alasdair and his family sat around a fire under the stars near the beach south of Duart Castle. It was just the five of them, something they wished to do before they returned to the mainland.

"I know you think I'm daft, Emmalin, but this place was calling to me. I had to come. We will return in a few days, but I had to spend one more night on the coastline. No sandy beaches on Grant land."

"It is lovely here. I'll agree with you, though the nights are surely getting cooler." She tugged the plaid up over her lap, covering her hands.

Alasdair and Emmalin sat against a tree farthest from the water, Emmalin leaning against her husband so he could wrap his arms around her to keep her warm, the flames from the roaring fire not far away.

"But that chill is in the air to stay. We need to get back before the snow begins."

Their three bairns, John, Ailith, and Coira, spent their time combing the edge of the water for shells or anything else interesting, a pail set out to hold their best findings, the light from the fire helping them sort through their treasures.

"It's been a wonderful trip, but it's time to return," Alasdair said. "I thank you for your patience."

"Mama," Ailith called out. "May we return next summer? I wish to swim in the sea again. Mayhap when it's warmest."

Coira said, "I would like that too."

"Of course. I think this should become a yearly trip."

John added, "Good, because I would love to see Alaric and Eli's new bairn."

"Mayhap Merryn and Broc too. I wonder if they will stay," Emmalin said.

"I think they will because of Tristan. He adores Shealee. And after you lose that many of your family, you cling to the ones who remain." Alasdair stared up at the stars above. "The night is so clear. Mayhap we should stay."

"Da!" John stopped, spinning around to stare at them. "I smell mint leaves again. Just like before."

Alasdair stared out over the sea at a small light that appeared to be floating above the water. "Does anyone else see that? I'm not taking my eyes from it. Just tell me if you see it, Emm."

Emmalin stood up. "I see it. What is it?"

Ailith said, "It's getting brighter, and it's coming this way."

Alasdair got up, stepping in front of his wife to move closer as the light approached since he had no idea what it was. Sure enough, the strong aroma of mint leaves hit him as soon as he approached John and the sea.

John shouted, "Da! Grandda is here!" He pointed to a cloudy vision that floated over the water.

Ailith cried, "He is! There. And Grandmama!"

Coira murmured, "I feel his presence so strongly."

Two faces appeared in front of them, like apparitions, not as real as a person. The visions grew, then strode toward them, hand in hand, one woman and one man.

"Mama? Da?" Alasdair couldn't take his eyes from the visions, afraid that if he blinked, they would disappear.

"Grandda?" John asked.

"It's your grandparents," Alasdair whispered. "It's them. Jake and Aline, my parents. Mama, Da. I miss you so." His cheeks flooded with tears, and he only cared to keep them from blocking his vision.

His father's voice cut through the quiet, the only other sound the lapping of the waves. "Alasdair, we came to meet Emmalin. This will be brief, but we wished to meet your wife and our grandbairns."

Emmalin said, "Jake, Aline, I'm Emmalin, and these are our bairns, John and Ailith, and our adopted bairn Coira, who is loved as much as the other two. You raised a fine son. We all love him so much."

"We know who you all are," Aline said. "Alasdair, we're so sorry that we had to leave you at such a young age. We miss you terribly, but we are always watching. It was your father who gave you that surge when you needed it in battle. His arm supported yours. Know that you will always have us nearby when you need us."

Alasdair didn't know what to say. "Mama, you are as beautiful as ever."

Two other figures appeared.

"Grandda? Grandmama?" Alasdair couldn't believe his eyes. He wished to walk into the sea and hug them.

Emmalin whispered, "Alex? Maddie?"

Alasdair could only nod, the view of the four people he missed every day of his life so close that it overpowered him.

Grandda said, "We miss you, Alasdair, but you've done a fine job raising your family. Tell all we are proud of how you handled this chaos. The Isle of Mull will be a wonderful place for many of our clan, but it will eventually belong to the MacLeans."

"Should we stay?"

"Nay," his sire said. "We are here to tell you that you belong on the mainland. John and the sapphire sword belong on Grant land. It won't be needed for many years, but keep it hidden there. It was here when it was necessary, but it's time to take it back."

Alasdair still couldn't speak. All these years, so many questions to ask, but none came forth from his frozen tongue.

His grandmother said, "Ailith, you look exactly like your grandmama Aline."

Emmalin whispered, "She does."

Grandmama lifted her hand and waved. "We will always be in your heart, Alasdair. All of your hearts. We watch over each of you, whether you need us or not."

Grandda said, "It's our greatest pleasure."

And with a swirl of light, they were gone.

EPILOGUE

Broc and Merryn

A FEW DAYS AFTER Alasdair and his family
had returned to Grant land, Broc kissed the
beautiful lass next to him and climbed out of bed,
quietly making his way down to the kitchens to
grab two cups of warm broth, something he and
Merryn had liked doing every day now.

Dyna almost bumped into him as he exited the
kitchens. "Oops! Sorry, Broc." Then she stepped
back to take a full look at him. "Nice. I like it. I
know you're self-conscious about that scar, but
it's hardly visible, even with your beard gone. And
congratulations on your happiness with Merryn."

"My thanks, Dyna. I've never been happier.
And thanks for finding us a private chamber now
that we are married."

"There are no priests here, so what else could
you do? Handfasting started a long time ago on
Grant land. Who was the first?" She paused to tip
her head back. "Aunt Jennie, mayhap? I'm not
sure. Come join us for the midday meal." Then
she headed into the kitchens, calling out over her
shoulder. "And the girls are more than happy to

have Shealee with them for another night. She slept like a wolfhound in Torrian's pack."

Broc chuckled but left to go above stairs to their chamber, being careful with the broth. He managed to open their door without spilling anything, but he set them down on a chest immediately, his eyes wide.

"Merryn, what's wrong?" Merryn sat in a chair next to the bed sobbing her eyes out.

Did she regret their marriage? Had he done something wrong last night? He'd enjoyed every moment, but she had been quite reserved.

At first. She wasn't reserved in the middle of the night.

She continued to sob but handed him a piece of parchment, careful letters written. Even Broc had been surprised at how hard she worked to learn to read and write. He took the note and read it, Merryn's letters beautifully formed:

"I love you so much, Broc. Thank you for loving me because I love you more than I can express."

Broc set the parchment down and said, "I love you too. But why are you sobbing? You're making me feel badly. Was it something I did?"

Merryn climbed out of the chair and tugged him over, pushing him down before she settled herself onto his lap. She used a linen square to swipe at her tears, then managed to say between hitching breaths, "Tears of joy. I'm so happy."

He nuzzled her neck and whispered, "As am I. But why cry now?"

"Because." She stopped to wipe her tears again, hitched and gasped twice, then continued. "Nara had told me awful things about the marriage bed, and I was so afraid. Yet with you, it was wonderful."

"Nara married the wrong man, love."

"I know, but I feel so badly for her that she lived with him for so long. I hated him so. Did you find your dagger in the hall?"

"Nay, I don't need it. It can stay wherever I left it. You're sure you are happy, wife?"

She grinned at her new title. "I like that name. Broc's wife. I love it."

"Whew! I'm so glad. You nearly sent me into a panic when I heard you crying. I thought you wished to leave me."

"Never, Broc MacNicol. You are mine forever."

The End
www.keiramontclair.com

DEAR READER,

Thank you for continuing this new journey of mine through the Isle of Mull. I'm truly enjoying writing about new characters while also bringing back some of the old ones. I'm also loving the paranormal aspect—I hope you are too.

There are now over fifty books that connect with Clan Grant and Clan Ramsay in some way. If you don't recall or you haven't read it yet, Maggie and Simone were featured in *Highland Vengeance*, the first book in The Band of Cousins series.

There should be no strings untied at this point. I tried to tie up every last one, so I'm leaving no cliffhangers for Book 5.

I'm not sure where I'm going next, but I think it will be focused on the new clans. Sheona Rankin is one idea, but her hero could be many. Taskill? Tristan? Brian? I haven't decided yet.

As is my way, I love to leave things open for new series. I left two strong possibilities in this book.

First, I could return to visit Iona and the ladies there—Simone, Geva, Beatris, and Emma.

That made me think of all the characters' stories I've missed. Catriona and Alison could be a wonderful duology. So would Lise and Liliana.

I also could start a new series with the fourth generation. I see so many possibilities here that would allow me to continue the paranormal vein. What exactly is the tie between John and Grant? Is Lia part of that tie? Should she come back? And what of Sandor's and Tora's abilities? This could be a single book that sounds like fun.

I wish I could be the type of writer who plans their series out far ahead, but my mind jumps in too many directions.

I still have at least two books left to write in this series. The others will sit in the back of my mind and … mull.

Happy reading!

Keira Montclair

NOVELS BY
KEIRA MONTCLAIR

CLANS OF MULL
THE PLIGHT OF A SCOTTISH LASS
THE BURDEN OF A SCOTTISH
CHIEFTAIN
THE ANGUISH OF THE SCOTTISH
LAIRDS
THE TORMENT OF A SCOTTISH
WARRIOR

HIGHLAND HUNTERS
THE SCOT'S CONFLICT
THE SCOT'S TRAITOR
THE SCOT'S PROTECTOR
THE SCOT'S VOW
THE SCOT'S DESTINY
THE SCOT'S WARNING
THE SCOT'S RECKONING
THE SCOT'S LEGACY

HIGHLAND SWORDS
THE SCOT'S BETRAYAL
THE SCOT'S SPY
THE SCOT'S PURSUIT
THE SCOT'S QUEST
THE SCOT'S DECEPTION
THE SCOT'S ANGEL

THE CLAN GRANT SERIES
#1- RESCUED BY A HIGHLANDER-
Alex and Maddie
#2- HEALING A HIGHLANDER'S HEART-
Brenna and Quade
#3- LOVE LETTERS FROM LARGS-
Brodie and Celestina
#4-JOURNEY TO THE HIGHLANDS-
Robbie and Caralyn
#5-HIGHLAND SPARKS-
Logan and Gwyneth
#6-MY DESPERATE HIGHLANDER-
Micheil and Diana
#7-THE BRIGHTEST STAR IN THE
HIGHLANDS-
Jennie and Aedan
#8- HIGHLAND HARMONY-
Avelina and Drew
#9-YULETIDE ANGELS

THE SOULMATE CHRONICLES TRILOGY
#1 TRUSTING A HIGHLANDER
#2 TRUSTING A SCOT
#3 TRUSTING A CHIEFTAIN

STAND-ALONE BOOKS
ESCAPE TO THE HIGHLANDS
THE BANISHED HIGHLANDER
REFORMING THE DUKE-REGENCY
FALLING FOR THE CHIEFTAIN-3RD in a
collaborative trilogy

HIGHLAND SECRETS –3rd in a collaborative
trilogy

THE SUMMERHILL SERIES-
CONTEMPORARY ROMANCE
#1-ONE SUMMERHILL DAY
#2-A FRESH START FOR TWO
#3-THREE REASONS TO LOVE

ABOUT THE AUTHOR

KEIRA MONTCLAIR IS the pen name of an author who lives in South Carolina with her husband. She loves to write fast-paced, emotional romance, especially with children as secondary characters.

When she's not writing, she loves to spend time with her grandchildren. She's worked as a high school math teacher, a registered nurse, and an office manager. She loves ballet, mathematics, puzzles, learning anything new, and creating new characters for her readers to fall in love with.

She writes historical romantic suspense. Her best-selling series is a family saga that follows two medieval Scottish clans through four generations and now numbers over thirty books.

Contact her through her website:
www.keiramontclair.com